Changeling Press LLC

ChangelingPress.com

Hammer (Dixie Reapers MC 23)
A Dixie Reapers Bad Boys Romance
Harley Wylde

Hammer (Dixie Reapers MC 23)
A Dixie Reapers Bad Boys Romance
Harley Wylde

ISBN: 978-1-60521-960-8

Publisher:
Changeling Press LLC
315 N. Centre St.
Martinsburg, WV 25404
ChangelingPress.com

Printed in the U.S.A.

Editor: Crystal Esau
Cover Artist: Bryan Keller

The individual stories in this anthology have been previously released in E-Book format.

Table of Contents

Hammer (Dixie Reapers MC 23)
A Dixie Reapers Bad Boys Romance
Harley Wylde

Amelia: I know monsters. Hammer isn't one, regardless of what he says. He's a born protector with a big heart, and he's exactly what my family needs. Sure, there's a big age difference between us, but why should I care about other people's opinions? All that matters is that Hammer makes me happy. He's just what my sons need and he and the Dixie Reapers can protect me from my piece-of-s**t ex. Anything else is unimportant. Now I just have to convince him that we make a good team.

Hammer: I haven't walked the path of righteousness by any means, but it doesn't mean I'm a heartless bastard. Found out I had a kid who's now a Prospect. Discovered I had a granddaughter, and now I'm a great-grandfather. Adopted a kid who didn't have anyone. None of that makes up for the shit I've done in my past, or the fact I've been in and out of prison most of my life. So why does the sweetest woman I've ever met see me as her savior and not the monster I really am? Somehow she's become mine, along with her teen boys. If anyone ever said I'd be a family man, I'd have laughed in their faces. Guess the joke's on me.

Chapter One

Amelia

I sat on the deserted Florida beach as dusk painted the sky in shades of orange and pink, my boys flanking me like sentinels. The rhythmic crashing of waves against the shore masked our hushed voices, nature's white noise ensuring no one would overhear plans that could get us killed.

We'd chosen this spot carefully -- far enough from the tourist areas to avoid casual onlookers, but public enough that Piston wouldn't think to look for us here. My old man hated beaches, hated sand, hated anything that couldn't be controlled. The vastness of the ocean offended him somehow, as if the world had no right to be bigger than his ego.

The setting sun cast long shadows across the sand, stretching our silhouettes into distorted versions of ourselves. How fitting. We'd been living as warped reflections of a family for too long -- smiling in public while wearing concealer over bruises, making excuses for absences at school functions, practicing cover stories until they flowed from our lips more naturally than the truth.

"Do you think he knows we're gone yet?" I asked, my voice barely audible above the surf.

Neither of my sons answered immediately. They'd learned to measure their words, to calculate risks before speaking. Another gift from their father.

The breeze coming off the water carried a chill that had nothing to do with temperature. Until this week, I'd been biding my time and slowly preparing. I'd learned the hard way what happened when we ran. Then things changed and I knew I needed to get us out of there. Waiting wasn't a luxury we could afford.

Watching Piston, the boys' father, slam my youngest son's head against the kitchen counter had severed whatever twisted loyalty I still felt toward him. I'd been with the enforcer for the Devil's Minions for seventeen years. At least sixteen years too damn long.

I glanced at Chase's profile, so much like his father's it sometimes made my heart stutter with fear. But where Piston's features were permanently hardened by cruelty and excess, my sixteen-year-old son's face showed a different kind of hardness -- determination, protectiveness, the kind of strength that built rather than destroyed. He'd been taking the brunt of his father's rage for years, positioning himself between Piston and his younger brother whenever possible.

On my other side sat Levi, his slender shoulders hunched against the evening air. At fifteen, he should have been worrying about homework and video games, not researching safe houses and motorcycle club rivalries. The fading yellow-green bruise around his eye made my stomach knot with guilt. I should have left years ago.

"We've got about eighteen hours before he realizes this isn't a shopping trip," Chase said finally, scanning the beach for potential threats. Always vigilant, my oldest. "Maybe less if he checks the bank account. Especially since he thinks we're staying overnight somewhere. When we don't check into a motel, he'll come looking for us."

I nodded, feeling the weight of time pressing down. Piston hadn't wanted me to have access to money -- control was his favorite weapon -- but I'd been skimming cash from the household funds for months, hiding small bills in a tampon box he'd never deign to touch. It wasn't much but combined with the emergency credit card I'd applied for in secret, it might be enough to get us to safety.

"He'll come after us," I said, stating what we all knew. Piston, aka John Minsley, didn't lose possessions, and that's all we were to him -- things to own, to use, to break when the mood struck him.

Levi's fingers curled around mine, his palm clammy despite the cool evening air. "We planned for that, Mom. The Devil's Boneyard MC --"

"Keep your voice down," Chase hissed, though there was no one within a hundred yards of us.

The mention of another motorcycle club sent ice through my veins. Trading one MC for another seemed like jumping from the fire into a different kind of hell. But Levi had done his research, had shown me the forum posts from women who'd escaped abusive situations with their help.

"I know you're scared," I told them both, squeezing Levi's hand. "I am too. But we can't stay. Not anymore."

The evidence of that decision was written on my youngest son's face, in the shadows under his eyes that spoke of sleepless nights and the bruising from his father's temper. It was etched in the scars on Chase's back from that time Piston had caught him trying to call for help. It was branded into my own skin, hidden beneath long sleeves even in Florida's heat.

Behind us, beyond the dunes and the sparse vegetation, our packed car waited -- everything we could safely take without raising suspicion crammed into the trunk. Old clothes, important documents hidden in tampon boxes and hollowed-out books, the few mementos I couldn't bear to leave behind.

The sky deepened to purple as we sat there, three refugees planning a desperate escape from a man who would rather see us dead than free. But in that moment, with the endless ocean before us and my boys beside me, I felt something I hadn't experienced in years -- hope, fragile as sea foam but just as persistent.

Chase stood abruptly, his tall frame casting a long shadow across the sand as he paced a few steps away, never taking his eyes off our surroundings. At sixteen, he already carried himself like a man who'd seen too much, his shoulders set with a tension that no teenager should know. The ocean breeze ruffled his brown hair -- the same shade as mine -- but his green eyes, Piston's eyes, scanned the beach with a vigilance that broke my heart.

"Someone's coming," he muttered, nodding toward a couple walking their dog at the far end of the beach. "We should move."

I watched as he shifted his stance, angling his body to place himself between us and the distant strangers. The motion was so automatic, so ingrained, that I doubted he even realized he was doing it. Years of protecting his brother, of trying to shield me when he could -- it had become instinct. And it made me feel like a shit mother.

"They're just walking their dog, Chase," I said softly. "They're not his men."

His jaw tightened, the muscle jumping beneath his tanned skin. "You don't know that. Piston has eyes everywhere."

"We've been careful."

"Not careful enough." He glanced at his brother, his expression softening marginally before hardening again. "Levi's research is good, but Piston will call in every favor, track every account, hunt down every friend we've ever had." He knelt in front of me, his voice dropping to a whisper. "Mom, if we do this, there's no halfway. We either disappear completely or we don't bother running at all."

The fierce intensity in his eyes reminded me so much of his father that for a moment, fear flickered through me -- not of Chase, never of him, but of the genetic legacy he carried. Would my gentle boy who used to catch and release spiders from our bathroom eventually morph into the monster who'd sired him? Or was that intensity, channeled through love instead of hate, the very thing that might save us?

"I know what's at stake," I told him, reaching out to touch his cheek. He flinched slightly before allowing the contact. Another learned response that twisted my gut with guilt. "That's why we're here, making sure every detail is covered."

Chase pulled away, resuming his watchful stance. "I still think we should split up. I can lead him away, let you and Levi get clear --"

"No." The word came out sharper than I intended, drawing a curious look from Levi. "We stay together. That's non-negotiable."

My eldest son's face closed off, the way it always did when he disagreed but wouldn't argue. He'd been doing it since he was twelve, when he first stepped between his father's fist and his mother's face. The punishment he'd taken that day had taught him that open defiance had consequences, but it hadn't stopped him from protecting us -- he'd just learned to be smarter about it.

"I've got the burner phones," he said instead, changing tactics. "One for each of us. Untraceable. And I memorized the route to the meeting point. If anything happens, if we get separated" -- his eyes locked with Levi's --"we meet at the place we discussed."

Chase had always been the strategist, thinking

three moves ahead like a chess player. It was what had kept him alive in Piston's household -- anticipating rage, diverting attention, creating escape routes.

"What about school records?" Levi asked his brother, his voice cracking slightly. "What if they trace --"

"They won't," Chase cut him off, glancing at me apologetically. "Sorry, Mom. But I handled it. Don't ask me how. You don't want to know."

The grim set of his mouth told me I probably didn't want details. Despite his age, my son had already learned to navigate systems designed to track and trap. He'd had documents falsified, created distractions, probably broken laws I didn't want to contemplate. All to keep us safe.

"The Devil's Boneyard contact," he continued, addressing us both now. "I checked him out as best I could. Scratch has a reputation for helping women get clear of abusive situations. But reputation doesn't mean shit in the MC world." He dragged a hand through his hair, a rare gesture of uncertainty. "We're trusting our lives to a stranger who runs with a different pack of wolves than Dad. That's all."

His honesty was both terrifying and necessary. Chase never sugar-coated reality -- not since the day at fourteen he'd found me unconscious in our bathroom and had to decide whether to call an ambulance and risk his father's wrath or try to handle it himself. He'd chosen the former, and we'd all paid the price.

"I've been saving," he admitted quietly, pulling a worn envelope from his jacket. "Working at the garage, skimming from Dad's poker winnings when he was too drunk to count straight. It's not much, but it'll help."

He pressed the envelope into my hands, and I

felt the thickness of what had to be hundreds of dollars. Money earned from oil changes and tire rotations, stolen in increments small enough to avoid detection, saved for this exact moment.

"I should have gotten us out sooner," I whispered, the weight of the envelope nothing compared to the weight of my failure.

Chase's eyes met mine, and I saw reflected there not accusation but a bone-deep weariness. "We're getting out now," he said simply. "That's what matters." He straightened up, resuming his guard position as the couple with the dog disappeared around a curve in the shoreline. My son, the sentry, the protector, the strategist. My boy who'd never had the chance to be just a child.

Chase and Levi exchanged a look that spoke volumes, the silent communication of brothers who had weathered storms together. Despite their one-year age gap, they moved in tandem, anticipating each other's thoughts in a way that only came from shared trauma. I watched as Chase passed Levi a water bottle without being asked, and how Levi automatically shifted to make room when his brother finally sat back down beside us on the sand.

"We should head back to the car soon," Chase murmured, his voice low. "Being in one place too long isn't smart."

Levi nodded but made no move to get up. Instead, he pulled his knees to his chest and leaned almost imperceptibly against his brother's shoulder. For a brief moment, Chase's vigilant expression softened, and he allowed the contact.

These quiet moments of connection between them were rare and precious. Chase had learned to keep physical affection to a minimum -- displays of emotion had been dangerous in our household, seen as weakness by Piston and targeted accordingly. But with Levi, especially when we were alone and far from their father's watchful eye, he allowed these small gestures of brotherhood.

"The contact should respond by morning," Levi said, his eyes on the darkening horizon. "Scratch has a ninety-eight percent response rate according to the forums."

Chase snorted softly. "Forums can be faked, Lev. Especially when it comes to this sort of thing. I find it odd there's even a forum at all."

"Not these. I checked IP addresses, cross-referenced testimonials, verified identities through social media footprints." Levi pushed his glasses up with one finger, a gesture that made him look even younger than his fifteen years. "They're legitimate."

"Computer shit doesn't mean anything in the real world," Chase countered, though there was no heat in his words. "These are bikers, not tech support."

I watched the familiar dynamic unfold -- Chase, practical and street-smart, grounded in harsh realities; and Levi, analytical and tech-savvy, navigating the world through information and systems. Two sides of the same coin, both trying to survive in their own way.

"The Devil's Boneyard has successfully extracted eighty-three women and children from situations like ours in the past two years," Levi continued, unfazed by his brother's skepticism. "They have a network that spans --"

"I know what they have," Chase interrupted, his voice gentler than his words. "I'm just saying we need contingencies that don't rely on the goodwill of strangers."

Levi's shoulders tensed, and for a moment I

thought he might withdraw into himself, as he often did when stressed. Instead, he turned to face his brother directly. "Not everyone is like him, Chase."

The tension between them crackled in the salt-heavy air. This was an old argument -- Chase's deep-seated distrust of everyone versus Levi's desperate need to believe in something beyond our toxic family unit. Both perspectives shaped by the same abusive household but manifesting in opposite directions.

"I know that," Chase finally conceded, running a hand through his hair. "But until we're clear, we trust no one completely. Deal?"

Levi hesitated, then nodded. "Deal."

I watched my sons with a mixture of pride and heartache. They shouldn't have had to become this -- one a hyper-vigilant guardian, the other a strategic escape artist. They should have been arguing about video games or girls or whose turn it was to take out the trash. Normal teenage concerns, not survival strategies.

"Your brother has a point, Levi," I said gently. "The Devil's Boneyard might be our best shot, but Chase is right about having backups."

Levi glanced at me, then back at his brother. Something unspoken passed between them again, and Chase's posture relaxed slightly. The silent debate was over, at least for now.

"I already have three alternate routes programmed," Levi admitted, a small smile touching his lips. "And emergency contact protocols if we get separated."

Chase bumped his shoulder against his brother's. "And I already scouted two alternative meeting spots if the primary one is compromised."

I felt a swell of emotion watching them -- pride

tangled with sorrow, hope entwined with fear. My boys, so different in their approaches but united in their determination to get us to safety.

Levi hunched over his phone, his slender fingers flying across the screen as he checked his encrypted messages for the fifth time in twenty minutes. The blue light illuminated his face in the growing darkness, highlighting the fading bruise around his eye and the thoughtful furrow between his brows. My youngest son had always been my thinker, more comfortable with books and code than with the physical world that had brought him so much pain.

"Still nothing," he murmured, the disappointment evident in his voice. I took note of his nervous twitches and wished I could assure him everything would be fine. "They should have responded by now."

Unlike Chase's imposing build, Levi was slight, his frame still caught in that awkward transition between boyhood and adolescence. His blond hair -- Piston's color but softer, gentler somehow -- fell across his forehead in waves that no amount of combing could tame. But while he lacked his brother's physical presence, Levi's mind was a formidable weapon all its own.

"Give it time," I told him, reaching out to push that wayward hair from his eyes. "It's only been a few hours since you sent the message."

He nodded but didn't look convinced. "I included all the relevant data points -- Dad's MC connections, his typical surveillance patterns, our current status. I even encrypted everything using a protocol I modified myself." He glanced up at me, his brown eyes -- so like mine -- wide with a vulnerability that made my chest ache. "What if they don't want to help us?"

The question hung between us, heavy with fear. We'd pinned so much hope on this plan -- Levi's plan -- that the possibility of rejection threatened to unravel what little courage we'd managed to gather.

"Then we move to Plan B," Chase answered before I could, his voice firm. "Like we discussed."

Levi swallowed hard, the motion visible in his thin neck. "Plan B has a sixty-seven percent lower success probability."

Numbers and statistics -- they were Levi's security blanket, his way of making sense of a world that had never made sense to him. While other kids his age were memorizing football stats or video game cheat codes, my youngest had taught himself risk assessment and probability calculations as a survival mechanism. Although, there had been a few times his calculations had been a bit off, and his brother had teased him mercilessly for days. I smiled a little at the memories. Levi had narrowed his eyes at his brother and refused to believe he was wrong, until Chase had proven otherwise. The dumbfounded expression on Levi's face would probably stay with me forever.

"How did you find them?" I asked gently, wanting to redirect his spiraling thoughts. He'd mentioned a forum, but I had no idea what he was talking about. "The Devil's Boneyard. How did you know they could help?"

The question seemed to center him, pulling him back to firmer ground. He tucked the phone away and pulled out a small notebook instead, flipping to a page filled with his neat, precise handwriting.

"I started researching exit strategies six months ago, after the incident with Dad's gun." His voice was clinical, detached, as if he were presenting a school project rather than discussing the night his father had waved a loaded pistol at us during a drunken rage. "Most women's shelters don't have the security infrastructure to handle someone with Dad's connections. Police protection is statistically ineffective against organized MC retaliation."

He flipped to another page, this one containing what looked like a complex diagram. "I found references to the Devil's Boneyard on three different secure forums for abuse survivors. They specialize in extractions where conventional protection fails, particularly cases involving motorcycle clubs or organized crime."

"You've done amazing work, Levi," I told him, meaning every word. "None of this would be possible without you."

He ducked his head at the praise, but I caught the small flash of pride in his eyes. Approval had been rare in our household, compliments even rarer.

"I just don't want him to hurt you anymore," he said quietly, his voice suddenly that of a child again rather than the tactical analyst he'd been playing at. "Or Chase. Or me."

I gathered him close, feeling his thin shoulders under my arm. For all his intelligence and planning, he was still my baby, still the little boy who needed his mother's protection -- even as he was working so hard to protect her.

"He won't," I promised, hoping I could make that true. "Not ever again."

Levi leaned into me for a moment before straightening, some internal alarm seeming to remind him that vulnerability was dangerous. He adjusted his glasses again and pulled his phone back out, checking for messages that hadn't arrived.

"The statistical likelihood of successfully evading Dad decreases by twelve percent for every day we delay," he said, his voice steadier now. "If the Devil's Boneyard doesn't respond by morning, we should consider initiating contact with the secondary option I identified -- a women's advocacy group in Atlanta with connections to --"

A soft *ping* from his phone cut him off. We all froze, staring at the device in his hand as if it might explode. With trembling fingers, Levi opened the message, his face illuminated once more by the blue glow of the screen. I watched as his expression shifted from tension to cautious relief.

"They responded," he whispered, looking up at us with wide eyes. "Scratch wants to meet."

Chapter Two

Amelia

The crashing waves grew louder as high tide approached, the rhythmic pounding against the shore drowning out our whispered conversation. Darkness had settled fully around us now, the beach empty except for our huddled forms and the occasional ghost crab scuttling across the sand. I watched the white foam of the surf glowing faintly in the moonlight, grateful for the ocean's thunderous voice that made eavesdropping impossible.

"What exactly does he say?" I asked, leaning closer to see Levi's screen.

"He'll meet us tomorrow at ten o'clock," Levi read, his voice barely audible even though we were pressed shoulder to shoulder. "At the Coastal Coffee Shop on Palmetto Drive. Says to come alone but..." He paused, squinting at the message. "But he understands if that's not possible and suggests bringing only immediate family. No friends, no one who might report back to Dad."

Chase made a sound somewhere between a snort and a grunt. "At least he's smart enough to know we wouldn't let you go alone."

The waves crashed against the shore in a deafening rush before receding with a hiss across the sand. The water had crept closer to our position as we sat talking, forcing us to shuffle back a few feet. The constant motion of the ocean mirrored the restless energy running through all three of us -- the perpetual vigilance that had become our normal.

"I should respond," Levi said, his thumbs hovering over the phone.

"Tell him we'll be there," I confirmed after

exchanging a glance with Chase. "All three of us."

I watched as Levi typed the reply. For a moment, hope flickered in his expression -- a dangerous emotion in our situation, but one I couldn't bring myself to temper. We needed something to hold onto, some belief that tomorrow might be better than today.

A particularly large wave crashed against the shore, sending spray high enough that we felt a fine mist against our faces. The salt water mingled with the tears I hadn't realized were tracking down my cheeks.

"It's really happening," I whispered, more to myself than to my sons. "We're really leaving."

Chase's arm came around my shoulders, a rare gesture of comfort from my eldest. "About damn time," he said, no accusation in his voice, just grim satisfaction.

We sat in silence for several minutes, each lost in our own thoughts as the waves continued their relentless rhythm against the shore. Tomorrow would bring either the first step toward freedom or a devastating setback. There was no middle ground, no partial victory possible against a man like Piston.

"We should head to a motel," Chase finally said, glancing at his watch. "Make sure everything is ready for tomorrow, get some sleep." The way he said "sleep" made it clear he didn't expect any of us to actually rest.

I nodded, brushing sand from my jeans as I prepared to stand. The night air had grown chilly, and I shivered, though not entirely from the cold. The magnitude of what we were planning pressed down on me -- seventeen years of being Piston's old lady, of fear, of gradually shrinking myself to avoid his wrath, all coming to a head in a coffee shop meeting with a stranger.

"Mom?" Levi's voice pulled me from my thoughts. "Are you okay?"

I tried to smile, to project a confidence I didn't fully feel. "I'm fine, baby. Just thinking."

He didn't look convinced, his brow furrowing in that way that made him look so much older than fifteen. Without warning, his hand shot out to grip mine, his fingers interlacing with my own in a gesture that was both seeking and giving comfort.

The unexpected contact startled me. In our household, touch had become complicated -- sometimes a prelude to violence, sometimes a rare moment of affection, never predictable. We had all learned to minimize physical contact as a means of survival. But here, on this dark beach with the waves masking our presence, Levi held onto me as if I might disappear if he let go.

I looked down at our joined hands, noting how his fingers had grown longer over the past year, how the childish softness was giving way to adolescent angles. His grip was surprisingly strong, betraying the tension running through him despite the calm facade he tried to maintain.

Levi's hand gripped mine tightly, his knuckles white with tension. Despite his slim build and gentle nature, there was surprising strength in his grasp -- a physical manifestation of the determination that had driven him to research our escape routes, to reach out to strangers who might help us, to believe in a future without fear. I studied his profile in the dim light, taking in details I sometimes missed in our day-to-day survival.

The moonlight caught the discoloration around his left eye, highlighting the sickly green-yellow that had once been an angry purple. Six days. It had been six days since Piston had caught Levi using his laptop without permission, six days since my youngest son's head had been slammed against the kitchen counter when he'd tried to explain he was just working on a school project. The lie had been quick, intelligent -- Levi always thinking several steps ahead -- but not quick enough to avoid his father's rage.

I gently traced the edge of the bruise with my free hand, feeling Levi tense before deliberately relaxing under my touch. He'd learned to control his flinching response, understanding that visible fear only provoked Piston further. It was a skill no child should have to master, yet my fifteen-year-old had perfected it with the same methodical attention he gave to his coding projects.

"Does it still hurt?" I asked softly, though we both knew the question went deeper than physical pain.

Levi shook his head, the movement slight. "Barely notice it anymore."

The casual dismissal of his injuries -- that was new, a recent adaptation I'd observed with growing concern. Where once he would cry or seek comfort for his hurts, now he cataloged them with clinical detachment, assessing damage like a system diagnostic rather than a wounded child.

I remembered finding him in the bathroom that night, pressing a cold washcloth to his face, meticulously documenting the injury with his phone's camera. "Evidence," he'd explained when he saw me watching. "I'm creating a chronological record of escalation patterns." His voice had been steady, his hands shaking only slightly as he angled his face to capture the swelling around his eye.

That moment had crystallized something for me -

- the realization that my intelligent, sensitive son was being forced to mature in ways that would forever alter him. He was applying his analytical mind to our survival, transforming trauma into data points, fear into action items.

"You've been so brave," I told him now, squeezing his hand. "Braver than anyone should have to be at your age."

He looked at me then, his eyes -- so much like mine -- serious behind his glasses. "Bravery is just fear that's been properly analyzed and mitigated," he said, with the earnest wisdom that occasionally emerged from him like these startling gems. "I identified the threat, researched solutions, and formulated an exit strategy. It's just problem-solving, Mom."

But I knew better. I'd heard him at night, the muffled sounds of crying he tried to hide, the nightmares that left him gasping for air. Unlike Chase, who channeled his fear into hyper vigilance and physical protection, Levi processed his terror internally, transforming it through the alchemy of his brilliant mind into spreadsheets and contingency plans.

"It's more than that," I insisted. "You found a way out when I couldn't see one. You reached out when I was too scared to try."

He glanced away, uncomfortable with praise as always. The bruise on his cheekbone seemed to darken as he turned, a shadow within a shadow. "I just didn't want him to hurt us anymore." A simple statement that carried the weight of years of abuse, of watching his mother bleed, of feeling his own bones crack under his father's grip.

We stood together, brushing sand from our clothes as we prepared to leave the beach. Levi tucked his phone carefully into his pocket, the burner device that had become our lifeline to potential freedom. As he zipped up his hoodie against the night air, I noticed how the too-large garment hung from his slender frame, making him appear even younger and more vulnerable.

Yet there was nothing childlike in the way he surveyed our surroundings one last time, his eyes scanning for potential threats with a methodical thoroughness that mimicked his brother's. Or in the way he had meticulously planned our escape, calculating risks and probabilities with the precision of someone much older.

"Ready?" Chase asked, already a few steps ahead of us, impatient to get moving.

Levi nodded, giving my hand one final squeeze before releasing it. "Statistically speaking, nighttime departures reduce observation probability by forty-seven percent," he said, falling back on numbers for comfort as he often did when stressed. "We should be fine if we take the side path back to the car."

My heart ached for the childhood he'd never had, for the innocence stripped away too soon. But as we walked away from the crashing waves, following Chase's lead through the darkened beach access, I felt a fierce pride alongside the sorrow. My son carried the bruises of his past on his face, but also the determination for a better future in every careful step he took away from the life we were leaving behind.

We walked away from the ocean in silence, the sound of the waves growing fainter with each step. The sandy path through the dunes felt like a boundary between worlds -- behind us the vast, indifferent sea that had witnessed our planning, ahead the uncertain darkness that would either lead to freedom or danger.

This momentary passage, this comma in our journey, held us suspended between what was and what might be.

Our footprints trailed behind us, three sets of impressions in the sand that would be washed away with the tide, erasing all evidence of our presence. The metaphor wasn't lost on me -- we too were trying to disappear, to remove all traces that might lead Piston to our new life.

The narrow path forced us to walk single file, Chase leading, Levi in the middle, me taking up the rear. From this vantage point, I could see the similarities in their gaits despite their different builds -- the same cautious precision, the same awareness of their surroundings. My boys, shaped by the same cruel hand into complementary defenders.

At the end of the boardwalk, we paused together, a brief hesitation before stepping from the weathered wood onto the asphalt of the parking lot. None of us spoke, but I felt the weight of the moment, this small threshold crossing that represented so much more than a change in terrain.

Chase scanned the nearly empty lot, his posture alert despite his casual stance. Levi checked his phone one more time, before he tucked it away. I simply breathed, trying to capture this fragile instant of potential -- the three of us, together, poised on the edge of transformation.

"Car's clear," Chase murmured, breaking the silence. "No one's been near it."

I nodded, knowing he would have noticed if anything had been disturbed, if any unfamiliar vehicles had entered the lot during our absence. My oldest son paid attention to everything, his hyperawareness both blessing and curse.

Levi moved closer to me as we walked toward our nondescript sedan, his shoulder occasionally brushing against my arm. Not clinging, not exactly, but seeking proximity in his own subtle way. I matched his pace, offering the comfort of my presence without drawing attention to his need for it.

"Tomorrow," he said softly, the word carrying the weight of all our hopes and fears.

"Tomorrow," I echoed, neither confirmation nor promise, simply acknowledgment of the pivotal day ahead.

Chase reached the car first, circling it completely before unlocking the doors. I watched the practiced routine -- his eyes checking the undercarriage, scanning the interior, testing the door handle before actually opening it -- and wondered if he would ever be able to approach a vehicle without this ritual of verification. If any of us would ever live without looking over our shoulders.

As we settled into the car, I found myself studying my sons. This was a big change for all of us, and I worried what the future might hold for us. The car started with a quiet rumble, and Chase pulled carefully out of the parking lot, observing all traffic laws to avoid unwanted attention. As we left the beach behind, I felt the subtle shift in our reality -- the planning phase was over, the action phase beginning. That momentary pause, that breath between decisions, had passed.

We'd crossed a line, a point we'd never return to, and now came the harder part -- the follow-through, the meeting with Scratch, the leap into the unknown. I reached forward and placed my hand briefly on Chase's shoulder, feeling the coiled tension there, before turning to squeeze Levi's hand where it rested on his leg.

Tomorrow would be a new sentence in our story, one we would write ourselves.

* * *

Chase stood guard outside our motel room, his tall frame silhouetted against the flickering neon of the vacancy sign as his eyes methodically scanned the parking lot. Even in the dim light, I could see the tension in his shoulders, the way his gaze moved in a practiced pattern -- checking each parked car, noting the positions of the few people visible through lit windows, cataloging every potential threat. My oldest son never truly relaxed, his body a constant sentinel between us and the dangers of the world.

"Get inside," he said quietly when he noticed me watching him from the doorway. "I'll be in after I check the perimeter."

"Chase, it's nearly midnight. We're two counties away from home. He doesn't know we're gone yet." I tried to keep my voice gentle, not wanting to dismiss his concerns but aching at the burden he placed on himself.

His green eyes flashed to mine, briefly haunted before hardening again. "You don't know that. And it only takes one person recognizing the car, one call to one of his brothers, and he'll know exactly where we are. The motel clerk said they wouldn't run the card until tomorrow, so for right now, he can't track us through bank records."

I couldn't argue with that. Piston's reach extended far beyond our hometown, his motorcycle club connections spreading like a toxic web across the state. Chase was right to be cautious, even if the weight of that vigilance was crushing him.

"Ten minutes," I conceded. "Then you come

inside and get some rest."

He nodded but didn't promise. I knew he would take as long as he deemed necessary, regardless of my wishes. My son had long since stopped seeing my authority as absolute -- not out of teenage rebellion, but because he'd had to step into the protector role too many times when I couldn't.

Through the thin curtains, I watched as he moved methodically around the perimeter of the small motel. His movements were fluid but purposeful, nothing wasted, nothing showy. He checked the parking spots closest to our room, then the ice machine alcove, then the stairwell leading to the second floor. I saw him note the security camera positions, the blind spots in their coverage, the potential escape routes if we needed to flee quickly.

When he finally returned, he locked and chained the door behind him, then wedged a chair under the handle -- a habit he'd developed at thirteen after Piston had kicked in Chase's bedroom door during a rage.

"All clear?" Levi asked from where he sat cross-legged on one of the double beds, his laptop open before him.

Chase grunted an affirmation, moving to the window to adjust the curtains so they overlapped perfectly, eliminating even the thinnest sliver of visibility from outside. "For now."

I watched as he performed his nightly routine -- checking the bathroom, looking under the beds, testing the window locks, positioning our bags for grab-and-go access if needed. Every movement practiced, automatic, born from years of living on high alert.

"We're meeting at the Coastal Coffee Shop on Palmetto Drive," he said, finally sitting on the edge of the unoccupied bed. "I mapped three different routes.

We'll take a different one than we used coming in, just in case anyone's watching the main road."

Levi nodded without looking up from his screen. "I've been monitoring Dad's credit cards and phone. No unusual activity yet. He's still at The Rusted Chain, probably won't leave until after closing."

The Rusted Chain was Piston's favorite bar, the unofficial headquarters of his motorcycle club's local chapter.

"He'll notice we're gone in the morning," Chase said, his voice flat. "When Mom's not there to make his breakfast." The bitterness in his tone made me flinch. I wanted to defend myself, to explain again why we hadn't left sooner, but the yellowing bruise on Levi's face made any excuse hollow. I should have gotten my boys out years ago, before Chase learned to gauge a man's intoxication level from the sound of his footsteps, before Levi started keeping detailed records of abuse patterns and escape strategies. I'd been too scared. Still felt terrified. I knew if Piston caught us, we'd all be dead.

"We'll be meeting with Scratch by then," I said instead, trying to inject confidence into my voice. "He'll help us disappear before Piston even realizes we're gone."

Chase's eyes met mine, and I saw the doubt there, the hard-earned skepticism that prevented him from trusting anyone's promises of safety. "Maybe," was all he said.

He rose again, restless energy preventing him from staying still for long. From his duffel bag, he removed a hunting knife in a leather sheath -- a gift from his uncle before Piston had killed the man. He checked the blade before tucking it under his pillow, then positioned himself on the bed closest to the door.

"You should both try to sleep," he said, though he made no move to lie down himself. "I'll take first watch."

"Chase, you need rest too," I protested.

He shook his head. "I'll wake Levi in four hours. We've done this before, Mom."

"I can take a shift," I offered, though we all knew I wouldn't be much use as a guard. Maybe if I were stronger we wouldn't be in this situation.

Chase's expression softened slightly. "Get some sleep, Mom. Tomorrow's going to be rough enough without you being exhausted too."

As I prepared for bed, moving through my own abbreviated routine, I kept glancing at my oldest son. He sat with his back against the headboard, legs stretched out, looking for all the world like a typical teenager relaxing. But his eyes never stopped moving, his ears attuned to every sound outside our room, his body poised to react to any threat.

My son who had never been allowed to be a child. He'd grown up entirely too fast, and I felt wholly responsible, even though I knew his father shouldered a large chunk of the blame.

* * *

I lay in bed watching Chase through half-closed eyes, pretending to drift off while knowing sleep would evade me as it had most nights. The dim light from the bathroom -- left on at Chase's insistence for safety -- cast shadows across his vigilant form. He sat against the headboard, one leg bent, the other extended, his posture deceptively casual to anyone who didn't know better. But I knew. I recognized the alertness in his stillness, the way his head tilted slightly at each new sound from outside, the methodical pattern of his gaze as it swept the room every few minutes, checking on Levi and me before returning to the door.

Chase should have been worried about college applications, or a girlfriend, or whatever sport might have caught his interest if he'd been allowed to play one. Instead, my son had been molded into a sentinel by years of living with a predator.

The first time I'd seen this side of him -- this fierce, protective vigilance -- he'd been twelve. Piston had come home drunk and raging, dragging me from bed by my hair, shoving me against the wall hard enough to crack the plaster. And there, suddenly, was Chase, placing himself between us with a baseball bat clutched in white-knuckled hands.

"Leave her alone," he'd said, his voice breaking but his stance unwavering.

Piston had laughed, but something in his son's eyes -- something cold and determined and utterly unchildlike -- had given him pause. That night had changed everything between father and son. It had also changed Chase. He'd glimpsed his own power that night, discovered that his growing body could be a weapon, a shield. From that moment on, he'd dedicated himself to keeping our family safe.

I felt like the worst mother. It wasn't the first time I'd felt that way. I'd failed my boys up to this point. But I refused to do so any longer. I would get them to safety, no matter what it cost me.

Chapter Three

Amelia

I stood next to Scratch outside the diner at the edge of town, watching him inspect our car with methodical precision. The chill of the morning air seeped through my thin jacket, but it wasn't the cold making me shiver. Every second we remained in this town was another second Piston could find us, find my boys. I clutched my arms around myself, gaze darting to the trunk of the car, where Chase and Levi were retrieving our meager belongings, wondering if we were truly going to escape this time.

"Stand back," Scratch muttered, lifting the hood of our beat-up sedan. His weathered hands moved with practiced efficiency, checking something I couldn't understand. The leather of his cut creaked as he leaned forward, his shoulders blocking my view.

"Is something wrong with it?" I asked, my voice barely above a whisper. The parking lot was empty at this hour, but still, I couldn't shake the feeling of being watched.

Scratch straightened up and wiped his hands on a rag he pulled from his back pocket. "Car's fine. That's not the issue." His eyes, hard as steel, scanned the horizon before returning to me. "We need to ditch it."

My stomach dropped. "Ditch it? But that's all we have --"

"That's exactly why we gotta leave it behind." He crouched down, checking underneath the chassis now. What the heck was he looking for under there? "First thing Piston's gonna look is for this vehicle. Plates, VIN number, make, model... he's got people who can track this shit faster than you'd believe.

Especially if he's attached a GPS tracker to it."

I swallowed hard, knowing he was right. Piston had connections everywhere -- police, DMV, even some judges. That was how he'd found us the last time I tried to run. The memory of that night made my hands shake, and I shoved them into my pockets to hide my fear from Scratch. I'd found my courage once before, and after it ended so horribly, I'd vowed to never run again. Until now. "So what do we do? How do we get anywhere without a car?" The panic in my voice was rising, despite my efforts to stay calm.

Scratch straightened up and moved to check the license plate, giving it a tug to ensure it was secure. "Already taken care of." He reached inside his cut and pulled out three bus tickets, extending them toward me.

I stared at them, afraid to reach out, as if they might disappear. "Where do they go?"

"Alabama. Dixie Reapers will take care of you there." His voice softened just slightly, the closest thing to gentleness I'd heard from him. "You'll be far enough away that Piston won't think to look, and you'll have protection."

My fingers closed around the tickets, feeling the weight of what they represented -- freedom, safety, a chance for my boys to live without fear. "The Dixie Reapers... will they really help us? We're nothing to them."

"You're under their protection now. All of you." Scratch glanced at the boys. "Club takes that seriously. Their President, Savior, he's a good man. Better than most. He's arranged everything."

"What does that mean?" I asked, watching as Chase positioned himself slightly in front of Levi his gaze scanning everywhere for threats.

"Means you've got a job waiting. Place to live too." Scratch nodded toward my sons as they approached. "Boys will be able to go to school, have normal lives."

I clutched the tickets tighter, afraid to believe it could be that simple. "Why would they do all this for us?"

"Club has a code. Women and children don't deserve the shit men like Piston dish out." His expression darkened. "Besides, Piston's made enemies with more clubs than just ours. Dixie Reapers have connections to some of those clubs, including ours, so they have their own score to settle."

Chase reached us first, dropping the bags at his feet and eyeing Scratch with open suspicion. He already carried himself like a man, shoulders squared against whatever the world threw at us. Like he was ready to fight everything and everyone.

"We ready to go?" he asked me, not Scratch. Always protective, my Chase.

Levi hung back slightly, his slim frame nearly hidden behind his brother, but his eyes were alert, taking in everything.

I nodded, showing them the tickets. "We're taking a bus." I tried to sound confident, for their sake. "To Alabama."

Chase's eyes narrowed. "What about the car?"

"Can't take it," Scratch answered before I could. "Too easy to track."

I watched as understanding passed between them. Chase's jaw tightened, but Levi nodded.

"Dixie Reapers," Levi said quietly. "That's the MC outside Mobile, right? I read about them when I was looking for places we could go."

Scratch raised an eyebrow, clearly surprised by

Levi's knowledge. "That's right, kid. You did your homework."

A hint of pride crossed Levi's face, quickly replaced by his usual serious expression. "They have a reputation for protecting women and children," he added, looking at me. "It's a good choice, Mom."

I felt tears threatening and blinked them back. My boys -- one so physically strong, the other so mentally sharp -- both trying to be men before their time because they'd never had the luxury of being children.

"Bus leaves in an hour," Scratch said, checking his watch. "We need to move. Someone from the club will take care of this car, make it disappear."

I nodded, gripping the tickets like a lifeline. Hope mixed with terror in my chest -- terror that Piston would find us again, hope that this time, we might truly escape.

Chase picked up our bags, his uncertain gaze meeting mine for just a moment before his expression hardened into determination. Levi stood at his side, brown eyes resolute behind his glasses. They were ready. We all were.

It was time to leave the nightmare behind.

The walk to the bus station felt like running a gauntlet. Scratch led the way, his broad shoulders creating a shield between us and whatever dangers might lurk in the quiet streets. I kept Chase and Levi close, one on either side of me, my gaze constantly scanning our surroundings. Every car that passed made my heart stutter, every shadow seemed to hide one of Piston's men waiting to drag us back to that hell. The few blocks might as well have been miles.

"Keep your head down," Scratch instructed, his voice low enough that only we could hear. "Don't make eye contact with anyone."

Chase walked stiffly beside me, his body coiled tight like a spring ready to release. His hand kept brushing against mine, a silent reassurance that he was ready to protect us if needed. Levi stayed on my other side, his steps quick to keep up, taking in everything around us with those observant eyes.

"Are we being followed?" I whispered to Scratch when he glanced back for the third time in as many minutes.

"No," he answered, but his eyes never stopped moving, sweeping across rooftops, alleyways, parked cars. "Just being careful. Piston's got eyes everywhere in this town."

A chill ran down my spine at the mention of his name. For seventeen years I'd lived in fear of that man, walking on eggshells, protecting my boys from his rages. The bruises had faded, but the terror remained, embedded in my bones like a disease.

The bus station came into view -- a small, dingy building with a few benches out front. At this early hour, it was nearly deserted, just a couple of tired-looking travelers clutching coffee cups and an elderly security guard who barely glanced our way. The emptiness should have been comforting, but it only made us more visible, more exposed.

Scratch guided us to a corner away from the other passengers, positioning himself so he could see every entrance. "Bus will be here in twenty minutes," he said, checking his watch. "Once you're on it, don't get off until Alabama. Not for anything."

I nodded, clutching our meager belongings -- one duffel bag with clothes, a backpack with our important documents, and the small amount of cash I'd managed to hide from Piston over the years, as well as what

Chase had given me. Everything we owned, reduced to what we could carry.

Scratch reached inside his cut and pulled out a cheap flip phone. "Burner," he explained, pressing it into my palm. "There's only one number programmed in it. Call when you reach the station in Alabama. Someone will be waiting."

I stared at the small black phone, my lifeline to safety. "Who?"

"Don't know yet. Whoever Savior sends." He glanced at Chase, who was watching our exchange with distrustful eyes. "Could be a guy called Venom. Or Bull. Doesn't matter who -- they'll all be wearing cuts with Dixie Reapers patches. You'll know them when you see them."

I slipped the phone into my pocket, its weight both reassuring and terrifying. So much depended on this fragile connection. "Thank you," I said, my voice cracking slightly. "For everything. I know we're strangers to you --"

"Don't," Scratch cut me off, uncomfortable with gratitude. "Just doing what's right. What should've been done years ago."

Levi moved closer to me, his slim fingers wrapping around my arm. "What about our car? You said it would be taken care of, but how exactly?" he asked Scratch directly, his voice steadier than I expected.

Scratch gave him an appraising look. "Smart to ask. Someone from the club will pick it up from the motel. We'll strip it down, get rid of any evidence you were ever there. By tomorrow, that car won't exist anymore. Still run a chop shop on the side. A holdover from our more lawless days. Not that we're walking the straight and narrow exactly."

Levi nodded, seemingly satisfied with the answer. Chase remained silent, but I could feel the tension radiating from him, the distrust. He'd heard too many promises from his father before -- promises that broke like glass when tested.

"Bus is coming," Scratch said, nodding toward the road where I could see the vehicle approaching in the distance. He reached into his pocket and pulled out a small wad of cash. "Take this. Emergency money."

I started to protest, but he pushed it into my hand. "Take it. You'll need it."

The bus pulled into the station with a hiss of brakes, its doors opening like the gates to another world. The driver stepped out, calling for passengers to Alabama.

"That's you," Scratch said, stepping back to give us space. "Remember -- call as soon as you arrive."

I clutched the tickets in one hand, the emergency money in the other. "I will."

Chase picked up our bags, still eyeing Scratch warily. "Come on, Mom," he said, moving toward the bus with purpose.

Levi took my elbow gently. "It's going to be okay," he whispered, with a certainty I wished I could feel.

We boarded the bus, finding seats near the middle -- not too far back to be trapped, not too close to the front to be noticed. Chase took the aisle seat, his body positioned like a barrier between us and anyone who might come down the narrow passageway. Levi sat by the window, peering out as the other passengers slowly filed aboard.

I settled between my sons, clutching my purse. Through the window, I could see Scratch still standing there, watching us, a solitary figure in his leather cut.

He raised his hand in a brief salute as the bus engine rumbled to life.

The vehicle pulled away from the curb, and I watched out the window as we began our journey away from Piston and the state of Florida.

Chase stared straight ahead, his jaw set in determination, but his eyes flicked back once, briefly, toward the life we were leaving. Levi pressed his face to the glass, looking forward to what lay ahead, his expression a mixture of fear and hope.

I closed my eyes, feeling the vibration of the bus beneath me, carrying us away from danger and toward an uncertain future, the distance between us and Piston growing with each turn of the wheels. For the first time in years, I allowed myself to breathe without calculating the consequences.

Whether the Dixie Reapers would truly protect us or not, I couldn't know. But for now, we were moving, we were free, and my boys were safe beside me. It would have to be enough.

The bus rumbled along the highway. Each mile should have been a comfort, but I couldn't relax, not fully. My body remained tense, shoulders tight, gaze constantly scanning for threats. Every time the bus slowed, my heart nearly stopped.

"Mom," Levi whispered, his voice pulling me from my spiral of worry. "You should try to sleep. It's going to be a few hours."

I forced a smile for him, reaching over to smooth his hair. "I'm fine, baby."

"You're not," he said, voice low enough that only I could hear. "You haven't slept properly in days."

Chase shifted beside me, his arm pressing against mine in silent support. He hadn't said much since we boarded.

"I'll sleep when we're safe," I murmured, squeezing Levi's hand.

The truth was, I was afraid to close my eyes. Afraid I'd wake up to find this escape had been nothing but a dream, that we were still trapped in Piston's world of violence and control. Or worse, that I'd open my eyes to see him standing over me, those cold green eyes burning with the rage that had been my constant companion for seventeen years.

The landscape outside changed as we crossed state lines, the familiar giving way to the unknown. Small towns blurred past the windows. The bus stopped twice, passengers getting off, new ones climbing aboard. Each time, I held my breath until we were moving again.

"We should have a plan," Chase said suddenly, breaking his silence. His voice had deepened over the past year, sounding more like a man's than the boy I still saw when I looked at him. "For when we get there."

"We do have a plan," I reminded him gently. "We call the number Scratch gave us, and --"

"No," Chase cut me off, keeping his voice low but intense. "Our own plan. In case these Dixie Reapers aren't what they claim to be."

Levi leaned forward to look past me at his brother. "They'll help us. I researched them."

Chase's jaw tightened. "You researched what they want people to know. That doesn't mean shit, Levi."

"Language," I admonished automatically, though it seemed ridiculous to worry about curse words when we were running for our lives.

"Sorry," Chase muttered, not sounding sorry at all. "But we need a backup plan. Always."

I couldn't argue with him. After all, he'd learned that lesson the hard way -- we all had. The last time we tried to run, we'd trusted someone who betrayed us to Piston for a few hundred dollars. The consequences had been... I swallowed hard, pushing away the memories of that night.

"You're right," I admitted.

Chase's eyebrows shot up. He hadn't expected me to agree so easily. "We should scope the place out first, see what we're walking into. If anything feels off, we don't make the call."

"And go where instead?" Levi asked, practical as always.

Chase shrugged, his broad shoulders tense. "Somewhere else. Anywhere. We've got some cash now."

I nodded, feeling the weight of the emergency money in my purse. It wasn't much, but it might get us a motel room for a few nights, as well as some meals, while we figured out our next move.

"Alabama's a big state," I said quietly. "If these Dixie Reapers aren't what they seem, we'll just... disappear again."

Chase seemed satisfied with that, settling back into his seat. The muscles in his jaw relaxed slightly, though his eyes remained alert, scanning every passenger who walked past us to the bathroom.

Levi pulled his backpack onto his lap, unzipping it just enough to reach inside. He withdrew a folded piece of paper, carefully opening it between us.

"What's that?" I asked.

"Map of Mobile and the surrounding area," he explained. "I printed it at the library last week, just in case. The Dixie Reapers' compound is somewhere around here." He pointed to a small town that looked to be about thirty minutes from the city.

"Smart thinking," Chase acknowledged, leaning over to study the map.

For a moment, we were just a family on a trip, huddled together looking at directions. The normalcy of it made my throat tight with emotion.

"There are motels here and here," Levi continued, pointing to locations he'd marked with small x's. "And a bus station outside of town. If we need to leave quickly."

I wrapped my arm around his shoulders, pulling him close. "When did you get so grown up?" I whispered against his hair.

He pushed his glasses up, a small smile playing at his lips. "Someone had to make contingency plans."

The bus hit a pothole, jostling us. Chase's hand immediately went to my arm, steadying me.

"Try to get some sleep," I told them both. "I'll keep watch."

Chase shook his head stubbornly. "I'm not tired."

"Liar," Levi muttered, but there was affection in his voice.

I settled back in my seat, my sons on either side of me. We were together. We were moving forward. It was at least a step in the right direction.

The miles rolled on beneath us, the steady thrum of the engine lulling Levi to sleep against my shoulder. His glasses had slipped down his nose, and I gently removed them, folding them into my hand. He looked so young in sleep, the worry lines that had no business on a fifteen-year-old's face finally smoothed away.

Chase fought it longer, his eyelids growing heavy even as he continued to scan the bus for threats. When his head finally drooped against my other shoulder, I felt tears prick my eyes. My boys deserved so much better than this life on the run, this constant fear. They deserved stability, safety -- all the things I'd failed to provide them.

"I'm sorry," I whispered to their sleeping forms. "I'm going to make this right."

I'd let guilt weigh me down for so long it had become an ingrained reaction to our situation by this point. But when we'd set off to leave Piston and start over, I'd made the decision I'd jump in with both feet. I was tired of feeling guilty. It was time to start a new chapter, one where I became stronger and more reliable for my children, as well as for myself. We all deserved to be happy. But turning my guilt off wouldn't be an easy, nor a quick, process.

Outside the window, Alabama welcomed us with greenery and the occasional flash of water. Nothing like the Florida we'd left behind. Maybe that was good. Maybe here, we could truly disappear.

It wasn't much later when the bus driver's voice crackled over the intercom, announcing our approach to Mobile. Chase jerked awake instantly, his body tensing before he remembered where we were.

"We're almost there," I told him softly, watching as he blinked away sleep and immediately resumed his protective posture.

Levi stirred more slowly, reaching instinctively for his glasses. I handed them to him, and he slipped them on, peering out the window at our new surroundings.

"Looks different," he murmured. "Greener."

I nodded, gathering our few belongings as the bus slowed. My fingers found the burner phone in my pocket, tracing its edges. One call away from safety -- or possibly another trap.

The bus terminal was larger than I expected, bustling with activity even in the late afternoon. We disembarked cautiously, Chase insisting on exiting first, scanning the area before allowing Levi and me to follow. I clutched both their hands as we made our way through the crowd, my heart hammering with each step.

"We should find a bathroom first," I said, spotting the signs. "Then decide what to do."

Chase nodded, his eyes never stopping their constant surveillance. "I'll wait here with the bags. You and Levi go."

"I can stay --" Levi began, but Chase cut him off.

"Go with Mom."

There was no arguing with that tone. Levi and I made our way to the restrooms, which were mercifully empty. I splashed cold water on my face, trying to wash away the exhaustion of the journey and the fear that still clung to me like a second skin. After relieving my bladder, I washed my hands and went outside to wait on Levi. Except he'd beat me.

"Are you going to call them?" Levi asked.

"Yeah, I think I should."

He nodded and we went to join Chase. Something told me he was going to argue with my decision.

Chapter Four

Hammer

I leaned against the black SUV, squinting through my sunglasses at the bus terminal entrance. The Alabama heat pressed down like a weighted blanket, making my leather cut stick to my sweat-dampened shirt. It had been nice and cool this morning. Now the sun was trying to fucking kill me.

Saint stood beside me, his posture relaxed but gaze alert, scanning faces in the crowd. We'd been waiting twenty minutes already for this woman and her kids to arrive. Scratch had called ahead, given us the rundown on their situation. Another club wife on the run, another piece-of-shit husband who thought women were punching bags. Some things never changed, no matter how many years I'd been riding.

"Bus is pulling in," Saint muttered, nodding toward the far end of the terminal where a Greyhound was rolling to a stop.

I grunted acknowledgment, pushing away from the vehicle. My knees protested the movement, a reminder of sixty-plus years of hard living. "We got a photo?"

"Nah," Saint said. "Scratch said she's mid-thirties, brown hair, two teenage boys. One's around sixteen, built like a fighter. The other's a bit younger, wears glasses."

"Not exactly narrowing it down," I grumbled, but kept my eyes trained on the bus doors as they opened and passengers began to file out.

They weren't hard to spot once they appeared. Two teens and a woman who looked both worn out and terrified. The older boy, tall and muscular for his age, exited first, positioning himself to scan the terminal before allowing his mother and brother to step down. Smart kid. The younger one stayed close to his mother, his glasses magnifying wary eyes that took in everything.

"That's them," I said, recognizing the fear and vigilance that radiated from the trio like heat waves off asphalt.

Saint nodded and started forward, then stopped. We watched as the mom and youngest went to the restrooms. So far, the oldest hadn't spotted us, or he wasn't letting on if he had. We hung back to wait and see what happened.

After the others returned, they talked amongst themselves for a moment. Then Saint decided we'd waited long enough and headed off in their direction again. I followed a step behind, keeping my movements deliberate, non-threatening. Too many years dealing with frightened women and children had taught me how easily a man my size could intimidate without meaning to.

The older boy spotted us immediately, his body tensing as he registered our cuts. His hand moved slightly to his waistband, and I noted the motion with approval. Kid was ready to defend his family, even if he didn't actually have a weapon.

"Ms. Decker?" Saint called softly as we approached, keeping a respectful distance. "I'm Saint, Vice President of the Dixie Reapers. This is Hammer. Scratch sent us to meet you."

The woman -- Amelia -- tightened her grip on her duffel bag, nodding slightly. "Yes, I'm Amelia Decker. These are my sons, Chase and Levi."

Up close, I could see the toll that running had taken on her. Shadows hung beneath her eyes, and tension lined her mouth. Still pretty, though, in a worn-down kind of way. Brown hair pulled back in a ponytail, a few strands of silver catching the light. She couldn't have been more than thirty-six, thirty-seven, but fear had aged her.

Over the loudspeaker, someone announced the next bus leaving the station and a group of people rushed by us. I gave them a quick glance, making sure none of them were a threat. A few feet away, someone dropped a bag, the loud *bang* making a few people jump, then laugh nervously.

I went back to observing the little family, once I knew they weren't in danger from the people here. The older boy -- Chase -- stepped slightly forward, angling his body between us and his mother. "You got ID?" he demanded, his voice deeper than I expected.

Saint's lips twitched, not quite a smile. "Smart question." He reached slowly into his cut, pulling out his wallet to show his driver's license. "Scratch said he gave your mother a phone. You call the number yet?"

"We were about to," Amelia said, her voice soft but steady.

I studied Chase while they talked, recognizing the hardness in his eyes. Kid had seen things no teenager should have to see, done things no kid should have to do. Reminded me of Prospects who'd grown up too fast, the ones who came to us already battle-scarred by life.

"We've arranged a place for you to stay," Saint was explaining. "Apartment above Jessie's Diner on Main Street. It's not fancy, but it's clean, furnished, and the rent's covered for the first three months."

"Covered by who?" Chase asked sharply.

"The club," Saint answered easily. "Consider it a loan if it makes you feel better. Your mother can start paying it back once she's on her feet."

I noticed the younger boy -- Levi -- watching us with calculated scrutiny. Unlike his brother's confrontational stance, this kid's observation was more analytical, measuring us against some internal scale.

Another announcement blasted through the place, making us pause our conversation. Otherwise, we'd have had to shout to be heard. "Bus 426 to Birmingham is now boarding!"

The announcement repeated twice. Once it was finished, the regular noise of the station filled the space again.

"I understand there's a job waiting for me?" Amelia asked, her fingers nervously plucking at the strap of her bag.

Saint nodded. "Waitressing at the diner. Owner's a friend of the club. Hours work with the boys' school schedule, tips are decent."

I shifted my weight, drawing Chase's attention. His gaze locked onto me, assessing the threat. I met his gaze steadily, seeing the fear beneath the bravado.

"How do we know we can trust you?" he asked bluntly.

"You don't," I said, speaking for the first time. My voice came out rougher than intended, gravel over steel. "But we ain't him."

Chase's jaw tightened at the reference to his father. Good. Kid understood what I meant.

"The Dixie Reapers have a reputation for protecting women and children," Levi said quietly, adjusting his glasses. "Especially from other MCs."

I raised an eyebrow at the kid. Hadn't expected that kind of research from someone his age.

"That's right," Saint confirmed, shooting me a glance. "Devil's Minions aren't welcome in our territory, and Piston knows it."

At the mention of her ex's name, Amelia flinched. Just slightly, but I caught it. Fucking bastard. Men who hit women deserved whatever hell came their way.

"Our SUV's right over there," Saint continued, gesturing to where we'd parked. "We can take you straight to the apartment, get you settled in."

I watched as Amelia and her sons exchanged glances, having one of those silent family conversations. After a moment, she nodded.

"Thank you," she said, the words sounding rusty, like she wasn't used to accepting help.

As we turned toward the parking lot, I noticed Chase quickly scan for exit routes, memorizing landmarks. Good instincts. Kid would make a decent Prospect someday, if that was a path he chose.

"Might not seem like it now," I said quietly as Chase passed me, "but you're safe here."

He glanced up, surprise flickering across his face before the mask of distrust slipped back into place. He didn't believe me. Didn't need to. Actions would prove our words true or false soon enough.

I followed behind as Saint led them to the SUV, watching their backs, scanning the terminal for threats. Old habits. Necessary ones when dealing with a situation like this. Piston might be in Florida, but men like him had connections, and a wounded ego made for dangerous desperation.

The family's possessions amounted to a single duffel bag and two backpacks. Everything they owned in the world. I'd seen it before, too many times. Women and children running with nothing but the clothes on their backs and whatever they could grab in the minutes between violence and escape.

As Saint helped them load their meager

belongings into the back of the SUV, I caught Amelia looking at me, a question in her eyes.

"We'll keep you safe," I said simply. No promises beyond that. No bullshit. Just the truth.

She nodded once, then climbed into the back seat with her boys, Chase taking the spot behind the driver, Levi in the middle beside his mother. Strategic positioning. These three had done this before.

I got into the passenger seat as Saint started the engine. In the rearview mirror, I could see the wariness in their faces. It would take more than words to earn their trust.

But that was all right. We had time.

The SUV's air conditioning fought a losing battle against the Alabama heat as we pulled away from the bus terminal. Saint drove with one hand draped over the wheel, casual as always, while I kept my attention divided between the road ahead and the rearview mirror. Chase had positioned himself directly behind Saint, where he could watch both of us and still keep an eye on his mother and brother. Smart kid. Tactical thinking. In the mirror, I caught him studying me. Been a long time since I'd seen a teenager with the hardened gaze of a soldier, but I recognized it all the same.

"Town's not much to look at," Saint said, breaking the silence as we merged onto the main road, "but it's quiet. Good place to disappear."

Amelia nodded stiffly, her hands clasped tight in her lap. She sat ramrod straight, like relaxing might be dangerous. Beside her, Levi fidgeted, his fingers moving in rhythmic, nervous patterns.

I shifted slightly in my seat, angling the side mirror to check behind us. No tail. Force of habit more than immediate concern.

"That's the high school there," Saint continued,

nodding toward a brick building as we passed. "Both boys can enroll next week. Principal's wife is friends with some of our old ladies. She'll help smooth things over with paperwork and such."

In the mirror, I saw Chase's eyes narrow at the mention of school. Kid probably hadn't had much stability, at least from what we'd heard from Scratch. Living with an abusive asshole wouldn't have been easy on any of them. He had to know enrolling in a school could make it easier for his dad to find them.

"How far is it from the apartment?" Amelia asked, her voice soft but steady.

"About a mile," Saint answered. "Walkable, but the club can arrange transportation if needed."

I grunted in agreement, earning a quick glance from Chase. His wariness was like a physical thing, filling the car with invisible barbed wire. Couldn't blame him. Trust was a luxury they couldn't afford.

We drove through the center of town, past the courthouse with its white columns and the row of storefronts that hadn't changed much since I'd first ridden into this town decades ago. Small-town Alabama, frozen in time in some ways, changing in others. The hardware store where Pop Jenkins had sold nails by the pound was now some kind of artsy coffee shop, but the barber pole still spun outside Floyd's, where three generations of men had gotten the same crew cut.

"Grocery store's there," Saint pointed out. "Pharmacy's next door. Doc Miller's office is around the corner if you need medical attention."

I watched Amelia taking mental notes of each location, mapping out their new territory. Survival skills. Woman had learned to be prepared.

The younger boy, Levi, leaned forward slightly.

"Is there a library?"

"Two blocks past the courthouse," I answered, surprising myself by speaking. "Open till eight on weekdays."

Levi nodded, a flicker of something like hope crossing his face. Books were safe havens for kids like him.

"The diner where you'll be working gets busy for breakfast and lunch," Saint continued, addressing Amelia. "Dinner crowd's smaller, mostly regulars. Owner's name is Jessie. She's good people. Lost her husband in Afghanistan about ten years back. When the diner went up for sale last year, she bought it."

I noted the slight relaxation in Amelia's shoulders at this information. A widow rather than a man running the place. One less thing to worry about.

Chase hadn't taken his gaze off me, watching my every move. Testing me, maybe. Waiting for the mask to slip, for the monster to emerge. I met his gaze steadily, neither challenging nor backing down.

"Club's on the outskirts of town," Saint said, turning onto Main Street. "But there's usually at least a couple members around town at any given time. Any problems, day or night, you call the number Scratch gave you."

I shifted my attention back to the road as we passed the police department. Officer out front raised a hand in greeting, which Saint returned with a nod. Good to have law enforcement who understood the arrangement. Didn't always happen that way.

"Local cops know about us?" Chase asked sharply, catching the exchange.

Smart question. Again.

"Chief Anderson and the club have an understanding," Saint explained. "We keep the peace;

he doesn't hassle us. He knows you're under our protection."

"And if my ex comes looking?" Amelia's voice was barely audible, fear threading through the words.

Saint's hands tightened on the wheel. "Then he'll have a problem bigger than the law. Devil's Minions aren't welcome in our town."

I nodded in silent agreement. Piece of shit like Piston would find himself surrounded by men who specialized in solving problems permanently if he showed his face here. At least, as long as the Pres let us handle it. We might be lending a hand right now, but truth was, this little family wasn't ours. If Savior thought the club would be in danger, he'd take a step back and reassess.

The SUV slowed as we approached a two-story building with weather-beaten clapboard siding freshly painted a pale blue. The sign over the door read *Jessie's Diner* in cursive neon that would light up after dark.

"Here we are," Saint announced, pulling into a parking space at the side of the building. "Diner's downstairs, your apartment's upstairs. There's a private entrance around back."

I watched the family's reaction, noting the way Chase's body tensed further while Levi's eyes widened with cautious hope. Amelia stared at the building like she couldn't quite believe it was real.

"It's not much," I said gruffly, "but it's clean. Safe."

Amelia's eyes met mine in the mirror. "Thank you," she said simply.

I nodded once, then opened my door and stepped out into the heat. I scanned the street out of habit, checking for unfamiliar vehicles or faces. Nothing seemed out of place.

The back door of the SUV opened, and Chase emerged first, standing protectively as his mother and brother got out. I noted again the way his gaze never stopped moving, cataloging every detail of their surroundings. Kid would make a good soldier. Or a good outlaw. Paths weren't so different when it came to the skills that kept you alive.

Saint led the way toward the stairs at the back of the building, keys jingling in his hand. I brought up the rear, giving the family space while keeping an eye on our six.

As we approached the stairs, I noticed Chase glance back at me, measuring the distance between us and his family. Preparing for a potential threat. I deliberately slowed my pace, letting him see I understood his concern.

The kid's shoulders relaxed a fraction. Not trust, not yet. But maybe a beginning.

The wooden stairs creaked under our weight as we climbed to the second floor. The stairwell was narrow, the walls freshly painted a neutral cream that couldn't quite hide decades of lives lived and left behind… a few dings here and there no one had bothered to patch, and a deep scratch in another spot. At the top landing, a single door stood closed, a new deadbolt gleaming in the afternoon sun that slanted through a small window. Saint unlocked it, pushing it open with a slight flourish that didn't match the wariness in the family's posture as they hesitated on the threshold of their new beginning.

"Here we are," Saint said, stepping aside to let them enter first. "It's not the Ritz, but it's yours for as long as you need it."

I remained by the top of the stairs, giving them space. Crowding frightened people into new territory was never smart. Besides, from here I could watch their reactions, gauge their comfort level without looming over them.

Amelia stepped inside first, her movements tentative, like she expected a trap. Chase followed right behind, gaze sweeping the room for threats or hidden dangers. Levi entered last, his gaze more curious than fearful as he took in their new surroundings.

The apartment wasn't much, but the club had made sure it was decent. Living room with a worn but clean sofa and armchair. Small TV mounted on the wall. Kitchenette with appliances older than the boys but scrubbed spotless. Down a short hallway, two bedrooms and a bathroom. Windows overlooking Main Street, with new blinds for privacy. Everything basic but functional.

The place smelled of fresh paint and pine cleaner, with undertones of the diner below -- coffee and grilled onions and something sweet. Not unpleasant. Lived-in smell.

"Bedrooms are through there," Saint explained, pointing down the hall. "Bathroom's been updated, got a new water heater last month."

Chase moved into the center of the living room, positioning himself where he could see both the entrance and his family. Kid moved like someone who'd learned to fight from necessity, not training. Stance slightly off-balance but ready, weight on the balls of his feet.

"Who lived here before?" he asked, suspicion still edging his voice.

"Waitress named Darla," I answered from my position by the door. "Moved to Birmingham last month to be near her daughter. Place has been empty since, except for the cleaning crew the club sent in."

Levi had wandered toward the kitchenette, opening a cabinet cautiously. "There's food," he said, surprise evident in his tone.

"Basic supplies," Saint confirmed. "Enough to get you through a few days. Club took care of it."

Amelia stood in the middle of the living room, looking lost and overwhelmed. Her fingers twisted the strap of her purse, knuckles white with tension. "I don't know how to thank you," she began, voice unsteady.

"Don't need thanks," I cut in, not unkindly. "Just doing what's right."

Saint moved to the refrigerator, tacking a piece of paper to it with a magnet shaped like a coffee cup. "Emergency numbers," he explained. "Club, police, fire department. Jessie's direct line downstairs. My cell and Hammer's are at the top."

Chase moved closer to read the list, and I wondered if he was memorizing the numbers. He glanced back at me, then at Saint. "Scratch said Piston won't find us here."

"Not if we can help it," Saint assured him. "Devil's Minions know better than to ride into Dixie Reapers' territory without invitation. And Piston specifically has been warned to stay out of Alabama altogether."

Of course, neither of us said that while they *shouldn't* enter our territory, it didn't mean they wouldn't. If Piston discovered they were here, I wasn't sure he'd care about any warnings he'd received. He'd likely come for them, and I couldn't be entirely sure what Savior would do. Reaper families came first.

"Warned by who?" Amelia asked, a tremor in her voice.

"By men who don't make idle threats," I said

simply.

The family exchanged glances, a silent conversation passing between them. Levi had moved to the window, peering out at the street below through the slats of the blinds. "There's a bookstore across the street," he noted, a hint of excitement breaking through his caution.

"Owner's daughter is a friend of the club," I told him. "She'll give you a decent discount if you mention you're under our protection."

Levi's eyes widened slightly behind his glasses. Good to know. Kid liked books.

Saint set the keys on the counter. "Two sets of keys. Figured you'd want a set and leave one for the boys. Deadbolt was changed yesterday."

Chase picked up one set, testing their weight in his palm like he was weighing a weapon. "And the job?" he asked, looking at his mother.

"Jessie's expecting you tomorrow morning at seven," Saint explained to Amelia. "She'll train you on the breakfast shift. The apartment comes with the job, for a discounted rate. Like I said, club paid the first three months. You want to stay after that, you'll have to pay Jessie." A weight seemed to lift from her shoulders at those words. Financial independence -- the first step toward real freedom.

"Boys can start school Monday," I added. "Principal's been notified to expect you. No questions asked about transcripts or previous schools."

Chase's jaw tightened at that, but he nodded once.

"The club will check in regularly," Saint said, moving toward the door where I still stood. "Not to intrude, just to make sure you're settling in, have what you need. Piston finds you, or contacts you in some way, tell us."

I noticed Amelia's hand trembling slightly as she reached out to touch the back of the sofa, as if confirming it was real. Too many promises had been broken for them before. Words meant little without actions to back them up. "Things get rough," I said quietly, meeting her eyes directly, "day or night, you call. We come. That's how it works here."

Something flickered in her expression -- not quite trust, but the shadow of relief. She nodded. "Thank you, Hammer."

Hearing my name from her lips startled me slightly. Most people outside the club used it reluctantly, intimidated by what it represented. She'd said it simply, with dignity.

"We'll leave you to get settled," Saint said, sensing the family needed space more than company now. "Jessie will probably pop up to introduce herself later, but otherwise, you've got privacy."

I stepped back into the hallway, giving them room. Chase followed us to the door, still on guard. As Saint headed down the stairs, I paused, turning back to the boy. "You did good," I told him quietly. "Got your family here safe. Not many could've managed that."

Surprise flickered across his face, followed by the faintest hint of pride before suspicion closed over it again. "We're not safe yet," he countered.

"Safer than yesterday," I replied. "Trust comes with time."

He didn't answer, but he didn't need to. I understood his wariness better than he knew. I'd been around long enough to recognize the look of someone who'd been betrayed by everyone who should have protected them.

I descended the stairs, hearing the *click* of the

deadbolt behind me. Good. Kid was taking security seriously.

Outside, the heat hit me like a physical blow after the air-conditioned apartment. Saint was already in the SUV, engine running. I climbed into the passenger side, settling my bulk against the leather seat with a grunt.

"Think they'll stay?" Saint asked as we pulled away.

I watched the apartment window in the side mirror, caught a glimpse of the younger boy peering out through the blinds. "Depends if they learn to trust."

"That boy -- Chase -- he's wound tight as a spring."

I nodded. "Got reason to be. Protecting his family from a monster ain't easy at any age."

The SUV turned onto Main Street, the diner fading into the background. The club would keep its word, keep the family safe. Whether they'd ever believe that, whether they'd ever stop looking over their shoulders -- that was harder to guarantee.

"Some people never learn to trust men in cuts," I said after a moment. "Can't blame them, given what they've seen."

Saint shrugged, philosophical as always. "We're not all Piston."

"No," I agreed quietly. "But to them, we all look the same at first. Takes time to see the difference."

As we drove away, I couldn't help wondering if that family would find peace here, or if the shadows of their past would keep them running forever. Some ghosts weren't so easy to outrun.

But at least for tonight, they were safe. Sometimes, that had to be enough.

Chapter Five

Hammer
Two Weeks Later

I stabbed at a chunk of pot roast with my fork, savoring the way it fell apart without much effort. There was something to be said for a home-cooked meal, even if neither Aura nor I were winning any culinary awards. The kitchen light buzzed overhead, casting shadows across our modest table. Through the doorway to the garage, I could see the disassembled parts of my project Harley spread across a tarp. Some men my age took up golf. I preferred keeping my hands dirty with things I understood.

"This turned out better than last time," Aura said, gesturing to her plate with her fork. "Remember when I forgot to add liquid to the crockpot and nearly burned down the kitchen?"

I grunted in acknowledgment, the corner of my mouth lifting despite my best efforts. "Hard to forget the smoke alarm screaming for twenty minutes."

My adopted daughter smiled, the ink on her arm shifting as she reached for her glass of water. Eight years she'd been with me now, ever since I'd found her in that hellhole in Georgia. The memory still made my blood boil. She'd been just sixteen then, terrified and broken. Now at twenty-four, she was strong, capable, and wore a smaller version of our club's colors mixed in with her sleeve tattoo -- a privilege the Dixie Reapers rarely granted to anyone outside full members.

"So," she said, dragging out the word in a way that immediately put me on alert. When Aura used that tone, she was working her way up to something. "Everyone at the compound's talking about the new arrivals."

I focused on scooping up some mashed potatoes. "That right?"

"Mmm-hmm." Her brown eyes, so different from my own yet somehow carrying the same stubborn glint, studied my face. "The mother and her two kids. They've got that little apartment over the diner. Atlas mentioned something about it."

I grunted, refusing to comment, even though I knew damn well every detail about the situation. The woman's name, her children's ages, the clothes she'd been wearing when she arrived -- all filed away in my mind despite my best attempts to appear uninterested. I'd done my best to convince myself and everyone around me I had no interest in her. Hell, I was probably old enough to be her dad. She had to be younger than my son, Sam.

Aura wasn't buying it. "Dad, come on. Everyone knows you went with Saint to meet them. You know exactly who they are and why they're here."

I set down my fork with a sigh. My fingers, calloused from decades of wrenching on bikes and throwing punches when necessary, not to mention my time behind bars, drummed once on the wooden tabletop. "What exactly are you fishing for, darlin'?"

"I want to know their story. People don't just get help from the Reapers unless there's a reason."

She had me there. I took a long drink of my beer, giving myself a moment before answering. "Her ex belongs to the Devil's Minions MC down in Florida. One percent club with a reputation that makes even hardened bastards like me think twice."

Aura's expression shifted to concern. "She's running from him?"

I nodded, feeling the weight of my silver beard

move with the motion. "Scratch over at the Devil's Boneyard helped them get on a bus and sent them here."

"And Savior offered to help her." It wasn't a question.

"Yeah," I said. "Yeah, he did."

I shifted in my seat, my lower back protesting after a long day in the garage. At sixty-one, I wasn't as resilient as I'd once been, though I'd sooner take another stint in prison than admit it to anyone.

"That's not all of it though, is it?" Aura pressed, setting her silverware down and folding her arms. "I heard the club pitched in to cover her rent for three months, found that job for her, and Saint even gave her a list of contacts."

I sighed. No point hiding it from her -- she'd find out eventually anyway. "Her ex is an officer with the Devil's Minions, and she's worried he'll kill them if he finds them. Probably has a good reason for that. I could see the signs of abuse on her and the kids."

Aura nodded, a small smile playing at her lips as she watched me intently. I realized I'd been sitting up straighter while talking about the woman, my voice taking on a harder edge at the mention of her ex. I deliberately slumped back in my chair, focusing on my nearly empty plate.

"We protect those who need it," I said gruffly, knowing I sounded defensive and was only digging my hole deeper. "Always have."

"And it has nothing to do with the fact that you keep looking toward the diner every time you ride through town for the past two weeks?"

I glared at her, but there was no heat behind it. "You got too observant for your own good, girl."

She laughed, the sound brightening our worn

kitchen. "And you're too stubborn for yours."

I shrugged and stuffed the last bite of pot roast into my mouth, chewing slowly to avoid further conversation. But even as I tried to appear indifferent, my mind wandered to the slight woman with haunted eyes who'd arrived with two children and three bags to her name. The way she'd stood tall despite her circumstances spoke of a strength I couldn't help but admire.

Not that I'd been paying special attention or anything.

Aura set her fork down with a deliberate *clink* against her plate, leaning forward with that look in her eyes that told me I was about to be interrogated. "So what was she like? What did you talk about?"

I grunted noncommittally, staring at my empty plate.

"That's not an answer," she pressed, the smile in her voice evident even without looking up.

"I helped bring her to the apartment, said a few words to her oldest," I muttered, trying to sound disinterested. "Nothing more to it than that."

The truth was, the second we'd gotten the call a woman needed our help and Savior had set up the job and apartment for her, I'd spent nearly two hours there the day before they'd arrived, fixing a leaky faucet in the bathroom and making sure the ancient HVAC unit would survive the coming fall weather. I'd even planned to come back to repair the wobbly steps -- a task any Prospect could have handled, but somehow I'd volunteered before I could stop myself. And that had been before I met her. Now I found myself wanting a reason to ride past the diner and check on her.

I was desperately trying to avoid this

conversation but was running out of ways to do it without getting up and leaving. The kitchen smelled of rosemary and meat, comfortable and homey in a way my life hadn't been for a long time before Aura came along.

"Is she pretty?" The question landed like a grenade, and I nearly choked on my swallow of beer.

"Jesus Christ, girl."

"That's not an answer either," she said, grinning now. "Your ears are turning red."

I drained the last of my beer to buy myself some time. At my age, I thought I'd be past this kind of adolescent bullshit. The woman was in her thirties -- younger than my son, for fuck's sake. The thought alone should have been enough to kill any inappropriate interest. Not to mention, I hadn't exactly been father of the year, and Amelia had two boys. I'd pushed Sam away, tried to keep him from this way of life. Instead, he'd ended up being a Reaper anyway. There were times we still butted heads, but for the most part, we'd made our peace. Hadn't had much choice when my granddaughter had shown up with a heap of trouble on her heels. She'd needed us to be united, not snapping and snarling at each other over old wounds.

"I'm too old for those kinds of thoughts," I grumbled, setting the empty bottle down with a hollow *thunk*.

Aura laughed, the sound filling our small kitchen. "Dad, you're not dead yet. Last I checked, if you're alive and have working eyes, you can still tell when someone's attractive."

I rolled my eyes and shook my head, though the gesture felt painfully transparent even to me. "You've been hanging around the club too long. Starting to sound like Sticks with all his dirty talk."

"Don't change the subject." She reached across the table to collect my empty plate, stacking it on hers. The ceramic clinked together as she stood. "Besides, I've seen the way some of those club groupies look at you. The whole silver fox thing works for some women."

"Christ almighty," I muttered, dragging a hand down my face, feeling the coarse hair of my beard against my palm. "We are not having this conversation."

But as Aura turned to place our dishes in the sink, I allowed myself a moment of honesty in the privacy of my own thoughts. The woman -- Amelia, though I hadn't let on to Aura that I knew her name -- was quite possibly the most beautiful woman I'd ever seen. Not in the polished, artificial way of the club women who hung around the compound, but in a way that seemed to radiate from somewhere deeper.

Her eyes had caught me first -- wary but determined, the eyes of someone who'd seen too much but refused to be broken by it. Then there was the gentle curve of her mouth when she'd thanked us for helping her, a genuine smile that had reached those guarded eyes for just a moment. Her hair had been pulled back in a simple ponytail, dark strands escaping to frame her face, and I'd had to fight the absurd urge to brush them back.

"You know," Aura said, returning to the table with a dish towel in hand, "there's nothing wrong with being interested in someone."

I scoffed, the sound harsh in the quiet kitchen. "She's got enough problems without adding a worn-out old biker to the mix."

"You're not that old," she argued, but I waved

her off.

"I'm old enough to be her father," I said, though I wasn't entirely sure that was true. I was assuming she was in her thirties. Didn't know for sure. Wasn't like I'd asked. "And she's got two young kids and an ex who'd like nothing better than to put her in the ground. Last thing she needs is complications."

Aura's expression softened. "Maybe what she needs is someone who understands that kind of life. Someone who can help protect her."

"That's what the club's for," I countered, pushing back my chair. The legs scraped against the linoleum, the sound cutting through our conversation. "Savior's got Prospects taking turns watching over the apartment and diner. She's safe."

"Safe isn't the same as happy," Aura said quietly.

I stood, my knees cracking in protest. "Happy's a luxury some people don't get to worry about." The words came out harsher than I'd intended, and I saw Aura flinch slightly. I sighed, softening my tone. "I'm gonna head out to the garage, finish putting that carburetor back together."

Aura nodded, knowing me well enough to recognize when I needed space. "I'll clean up here."

As I turned toward the garage, my sanctuary of tools and motorcycle parts, I couldn't help but think about Amelia again. The gentle sway of her hips as she'd moved around the small apartment, the strength in her slim arms as she'd carried her bags into the apartment. She couldn't be much over thirty-five, and here I was almost old enough for social security.

No, I decided firmly as I flipped on the garage light. Some lines weren't meant to be crossed, no matter how pretty the view on the other side. But even as I settled onto my stool, the familiar comfort of tools and grease couldn't quiet my mind. I reached for a wrench, the weight of it solid and real in my hand as I leaned over the disassembled parts of my Harley. The carburetor needed to be put back together -- a simple job that should have kept my attention, but my thoughts kept drifting back to those haunted brown eyes.

The scent of motor oil and metal filled my nostrils as I worked, the rhythmic sound of metal against metal usually soothing my nerves. Not tonight. Tonight, I kept seeing the way Amelia had flinched when Saint moved too quickly near her. The way her hands had trembled slightly the entire time we were there. The protective way she'd gathered her boys close, like she was expecting someone to try and snatch them away.

I knew those signs better than most. Had seen them before in women who'd escaped bad situations. Hell, I'd helped more than a few over the years get new IDs, new lives far away from the men who'd hurt them. The club had connections for that sort of thing. But something about this woman's circumstances had gotten under my skin in a way the others hadn't.

Maybe it was the quiet dignity she projected, despite everything. Or the way she'd looked me straight in the eye when she thanked me -- no artifice or flirtation, just genuine gratitude.

I sat staring at the disassembled carburetor, not really seeing it. Instead, I was remembering Amelia's oldest boy -- Chase, if I recalled correctly.

My phone buzzed in my pocket, interrupting my thoughts. I wiped my hands on a shop rag before pulling it out. Saint's name flashed on the screen.

"Yeah?" I answered, wedging the phone between my ear and shoulder as I picked up my wrench again.

"Need you at the clubhouse tomorrow morning," Saint said without preamble. "Eight sharp."

I frowned. Early morning meetings usually meant trouble. "Something wrong?"

There was a pause on the other end. "Got word from Scratch down in Florida. Seems our new friend's ex is making noise about his missing family. Putting out feelers. Nothing concrete yet, but we need to be prepared."

My grip tightened on the wrench. Which meant, it might not be long before he realized they were here. The calm I'd been cultivating all evening evaporated. "How solid is the intel?"

"Solid enough that I'm calling everyone in," Saint replied, his voice grim. "He hasn't connected Alabama to their disappearance yet, but he's asking questions in Georgia, Tennessee. Working his way north. When those states run out, he'll head this direction."

I set the wrench down, no longer interested in the carburetor. "Does she know?"

"Not yet. Thought we'd discuss how to approach it tomorrow."

I grunted, already calculating what needed to be done. The apartment above the diner had decent security -- Saint had made sure of that -- but it wouldn't stop a determined one-percenter with resources. "I'll be there."

After hanging up, I sat motionless on my stool, staring at the concrete floor without seeing it. The peaceful evening had turned sour in my mouth. I'd seen enough club wars play out to know how ugly they could get, especially when women and children were involved. And from what little Amelia had shared about her ex, the man was a special kind of monster.

The thought of her facing that bastard again made my blood run cold, then hot with a fury I hadn't felt in years.

I stood abruptly, my back protesting the sudden movement. The half-built bike could wait. I strode into the house, finding Aura curled up on the couch with a book.

"Saint called," I said without preamble. "Her ex is looking for her."

Aura's eyes widened. "Shit. Is he coming here?"

"Not yet. But he probably will eventually." I grabbed my cut from where it hung by the door, the leather well-worn and familiar as I slipped it on. The weight of it settled on my shoulders like armor.

"Where are you going?" she asked, setting her book aside.

"Need to clear my head." It wasn't entirely a lie. The vibration of my Softail between my legs and the wind against my face had always been the best way to sort through my thoughts.

But we both knew there was only one place I'd be heading tonight.

The night air was cool against my face as I rolled my 2010 Softail Custom out of the garage. Late September in Alabama meant the days were still warm, but the evenings carried a hint of the coming fall. I fired up the engine, the familiar rumble settling something in my chest that had been restless since Saint's call.

The streets were quiet as I made my way toward town, the headlight cutting through the darkness ahead of me. Muscle memory guided me through the familiar turns while my mind churned over what Saint had said. If Amelia's ex was looking for her, it was only a matter of time before he found her. The Dixie Reapers could offer protection, but we couldn't keep her locked away forever.

Chapter Six

Amelia

The lunch rush hit like clockwork at Jessie's Diner. I balanced three plates along my left arm while my right hand gripped a fresh pot of coffee. I'd been here a few weeks now, and I still hadn't gotten used to how these folks took their coffee -- strong enough to strip paint and dark as midnight. Nothing like the sugary Cuban blends back in Florida. I weaved between the red vinyl booths, dropping off burgers and fries with practiced efficiency, my ponytail swinging as I pivoted between tables.

"Need a refill, hon?" I asked the trucker in booth three, already tipping the pot toward his cup before he nodded.

The bell above the door jingled, and a gust of hot air followed a group of men inside. One of them wore a leather vest over a faded T-shirt, the scent of motorcycle exhaust clinging to him like cologne. My hand trembled slightly, coffee sloshing dangerously close to the rim of the cup.

"Careful there," the trucker said, steadying my wrist with calloused fingers.

I muttered an apology and moved on, but my mind had already slipped backward through time, the diner's chatter fading to the pulsing bass from a Florida dive bar seventeen years earlier.

The first time I saw Piston, he'd been leaning against his Harley outside The Rusty Nail, a cigarette dangling from lips that curved into a smile when I walked past. The moon hung low and yellow, casting him in dangerous shadows that should have been a warning, not an invitation.

"Where you headed, sweetheart?" he'd called

out, his voice rough like gravel under tires.

I should have kept walking. Instead, I'd stopped. "Nowhere special."

"That's a damn shame." He'd pushed off his bike, stepping into the light. The Devil's Minions patch on his leather cut gleamed against the black leather. His fingers had been warm when they brushed mine, offering me a cigarette I didn't want but took anyway.

The memory of his bike's engine still vibrated through me -- the way it had rumbled between my thighs that first night, his broad back solid against my chest as we tore down A1A with the ocean a dark blur beside us. The wind had whipped my hair into knots, but I hadn't cared. I remembered pressing my face between his shoulder blades, breathing in leather and sweat and something dangerous that made my heart skip.

"Order up, Amelia!"

I blinked back to the diner, taking the plates of meatloaf and mashed potatoes from Ronnie's weathered hands. He raised an eyebrow at me. "You with us today, girl?"

"Sorry," I mumbled, loading up my tray. "Just thinking."

Thinking about how Piston's kisses had tasted like whiskey and promises -- promises that had started to crack the moment Chase was born. How quickly his charm had curdled into control, his smile into a sneer.

I delivered the meatloaf special to the elderly couple by the window, refilled three more coffee cups, and wiped down a vacated table. My reflection caught in the chrome napkin dispenser -- brown eyes that had seen too much, the tiny scar near my hairline that the makeup couldn't quite cover. I still vividly remembered when I'd gotten it.

Three days. He'd been gone three days without a word, and I'd had the audacity to ask where he'd been when he finally stumbled home reeking of cheap perfume and cheaper booze. Chase had barely been crawling then, asleep in the next room, and I was already pregnant with Levi.

"You questioning me?" Piston had growled, grabbing my upper arm so hard I felt the bruise forming instantly.

"I was worried," I'd whispered, already knowing it was the wrong thing to say. Worry implied he couldn't take care of himself. Worry implied ownership.

The wall had come up fast against my back, his forearm across my throat. "You don't worry about me. You don't ask about me. You take care of my kids and keep your fucking mouth shut."

Later, I'd stood in our bathroom, examining the purple fingerprints blooming on my arm, the angry red mark across my throat. I'd pulled out my concealer, expertly dabbing it over the evidence before my shift at the diner back then. Different diner, same skills -- balance plates, smile through pain, hide the bruises. Any cuts or open wounds had been harder to deal with. They probably thought I was a klutz as many times as I tripped and fell. Well, if I'd actually done that. I couldn't very well have said my husband beat the hell out of me.

I'd gotten good at turtlenecks in Florida's heat, and at making excuses. "Walked into a door." "Fell down the stairs." "Just clumsy. You know me."

The coffeepot was empty. I headed back to the kitchen, passing a booth where a young mother struggled to keep her toddler entertained. She looked tired but happy, her husband's arm draped protectively around her shoulders. Nothing like Piston's arm across my throat.

"You need a top-off of your sweet tea, sweetie?" I asked her, and she nodded gratefully. I went to swap out the empty coffeepot for a pitcher of sweet tea.

As I poured, I watched her child scribble with crayons, his little face scrunched in concentration. Just like Chase at that age. Just like Levi. My boys, the only good things to come from those years of hell.

I straightened my apron and grabbed a fresh pot of coffee. It had only been a few weeks since I'd found the courage to come here. The boys were settling in nicely, or so I thought. As for me... I still felt the need to constantly look over my shoulder. Especially after I got word a few days ago that Piston was searching for us.

I pasted on my best waitress smile and moved on to the next table. One foot in front of the other. One day at a time. That's how we survived.

The lunch rush trickled to a halt around two-thirty, leaving me with a moment to breathe. I leaned against the counter, massaging my lower back where an ache had settled after hours on my feet. The diner hummed with the quieter sounds of afternoon -- forks scraping plates, ice clinking in glasses, the muffled conversation of the few remaining customers. I grabbed a rag and started wiping down the counter, my mind drifting back to the night that had changed everything, the night I'd decided I'd waited long enough and we were leaving. I'd found myself reflecting on the past rather frequently of late. Mostly wishing I'd done something sooner. Maybe if I'd known about the Devil's Boneyard or the Dixie Reapers months, or even years ago, we could have escaped Piston before now.

When we'd decided to let the Devil's Boneyard help us, I'd thought we were crazy to trust someone in an MC. But after meeting Scratch, I'd decided he'd seemed kind, and genuinely wanted to help us get away. It didn't mean we'd relaxed our guard. We'd lived through too much pain and fear to do such a thing.

The clatter of dishes brought me back to the present. I blinked, realizing I'd been wiping the same spot on the counter for God knows how long. I dropped the rag and grabbed my order pad, moving to check on the few remaining tables.

That's when I saw him.

He sat in the corner booth, angled to see both the door and the windows -- a habit I recognized from years with Piston. His silver beard contrasted starkly with the black leather cut he wore, and I knew the Dixie Reapers patch would be prominent on his back. Even seated, I could tell he was tall, his broad shoulders taking up most of the booth's width. But it was his eyes that caught me -- deep brown and watchful, focused on me with an intensity that made me freeze, coffeepot suspended mid-pour over a customer's cup. Hammer. He'd been one of the men to pick us up at the bus station.

"Uh, ma'am?" The customer tapped the table, snapping me back to attention.

"Sorry," I murmured, finishing the pour and moving quickly to the next table, acutely aware of the biker's gaze following me.

My body tensed automatically, muscles remembering years of survival instincts around men in leather cuts. But something else stirred too -- the knowledge that this man represented safety now, not danger. The Dixie Reapers had given us a fresh start.

They stood between us and Piston.

Still, old fears died hard. I wiped my suddenly damp palms on my apron, deliberately avoiding his table until I'd served everyone else. Finally, with no more excuses, I approached him, coffeepot held like a shield.

"More coffee?" I asked, proud that my voice didn't shake.

He nodded, pushing his cup forward, his weathered hands covered in faded tattoos. I poured carefully, feeling the weight of his assessment.

My world had changed so completely. Not even a month ago, a biker watching me would have meant danger -- Piston sending one of his brothers to keep tabs on me. Now, it might mean protection. The problem was, my body couldn't tell the difference. It just knew to be afraid.

My shift continued, and I kept an eye on the biker. Even though he'd finished eating long ago, he remained, ever vigilant. At some point, I'd stopped being quite as hyper-aware of him. Now, hours later, the late afternoon sun slanted through the blinds, casting golden stripes across the diner's worn linoleum floor. My shift would end in twenty minutes, but Hammer showed no signs of leaving.

I'd deliberately saved his section for last as I wiped down tables and refilled salt shakers, postponing the inevitable. My uniform stuck to my back in the Alabama heat, and I could feel a headache building at my temples -- from stress or exhaustion, I couldn't tell anymore.

"Amelia, honey, you can head out early if you want," Jessie, the owner, called from behind the counter. "We're dead as a doornail anyway."

"Just need to settle up with the gentleman in the

corner first." I glanced at Hammer, who raised his empty cup. I stopped at his table, forcing a smile as I pulled his check from my apron pocket. "Anything else I can get you?" I asked, my practiced waitress voice betraying none of the anxiety churning beneath my ribs.

Hammer looked up, his eyes the color of strong coffee, deep and surprisingly warm in his weathered face. Up close, I could see the lines etched around them -- laugh lines, not the hard creases of perpetual anger I'd grown accustomed to with Piston.

"No, darlin', I'm good." His voice rumbled like distant thunder, low and graveled from years of cigarettes or shouting over motorcycle engines.

I turned to leave when his hand moved, not grabbing me -- thank God -- but reaching for the check. I'd forgotten I was holding it. His fingers brushed mine, calloused skin against my knuckles, and something electric jolted through me. I hadn't felt that kind of spark in years, had trained myself not to feel it, not to want it.

"Everything good with you and the boys?" he asked, those coffee-dark eyes studying me with an intensity that made me feel simultaneously exposed and sheltered.

The question caught me off guard. Not "How are you settling in?" or "Need anything?" -- the usual questions from the MC members assigned to check on us. This felt personal. Like he actually wanted to know.

"We're settling in," I replied, my gaze darting to his cut, to the Dixie Reapers patch that represented my salvation and my deepest fears all at once. "The boys like the school."

Hammer nodded, his silver beard catching the sunlight. "Chase came by the garage yesterday. Kid's got a knack for engines."

My stomach tightened. "He was at the garage?"

"Just lookin'. Nothing wrong with that." Hammer's expression softened slightly. "He wants to protect you. Reminds me of my boy."

I didn't know what to say to that. The thought of Chase anywhere near the club both terrified and exhausted me. We'd fled one MC only to land in the shadows of another. Different, yes, but still men who lived by their own rules, who carried guns beneath their cuts, and settled scores in ways the law wouldn't sanction.

My body tensed as Hammer shifted in his seat, but he only reached into his pocket. He pulled out a worn leather wallet, extracting several bills that he placed on top of the check.

"Your boys are safe here, Amelia," he said, his voice dropping lower. "And so are you."

I nodded, not trusting myself to speak. I picked up the money -- far more than his coffee and pie had cost -- and turned away before he could see the tears threatening to spill. It wasn't his kindness that undid me. It was the possibility that I might actually believe him.

From behind the counter, I watched as Hammer stood, his height impressive even from a distance. He nodded to Jessie, who waved back with the easy familiarity of someone who'd known him for years. These men were part of the community here, not outlaws passing through. The realization felt strange, like trying on shoes that might fit but weren't yet comfortable.

I moved to the window as Hammer pushed through the door, watching as he crossed the street to where his motorcycle waited. Unlike Piston's flashy custom Harley with its chrome skulls and flame paint job, Hammer's bike was understated -- solid, practical, much like the man himself. He swung his leg over the seat with a grace that belied his age and size, then paused, looking back toward the diner. Toward me.

I stepped back from the window, but not before our gazes met. He nodded once, a gesture both reassuring and respectful, before starting his engine and pulling away.

I felt something twist inside me -- relief that we'd escaped Piston's brutality, fear that he'd find us anyway, and something unexpected: a flutter of interest in the gruff older biker who represented both my past trauma and current hope for safety.

"He's a good one," Jessie said, suddenly beside me. "Comes in every Thursday, same time."

I didn't always work this shift, or that section. Even still, I didn't remember seeing him on a Thursday until now.

"You know him well?" I asked, trying to sound casual as I counted out Hammer's change for the register.

"Sure. His son used to work over at Camelot's Garage & Towing." She patted my arm. "The Reapers take care of their own, honey. And right now, that includes you and those boys of yours."

I nodded, sliding the generous tip into my pocket. The money would help with Chase's growing appetite and Levi's need for new glasses. But it was Hammer's words that I carried with me as I clocked out and headed for the small apartment upstairs -- *"Your boys are safe here, Amelia. And so are you."*

My years with Piston had taught me not to trust promises from men in leather cuts. A few weeks with the Dixie Reapers hadn't been nearly enough to unlearn that lesson. Yet something about Hammer's steady gaze and the gentle brush of his fingers against mine had cracked the wall I'd built around myself.

As I walked to the rear stairs behind the building, I glanced over my shoulder, half-expecting to see someone in a Devil's Minions cut lurking in the shadows. Instead, there were only the empty parking spaces, and the lingering rumble of Hammer's bike fading in the distance. For the first time since seeing Piston's true colors, the sound of a motorcycle engine didn't fill me with dread.

Maybe that was progress. Or maybe it was just the beginning of a whole new kind of danger.

I climbed the stairs to our apartment, each step a reminder of how far we'd come -- and how far we still had to go. The apartment above Jessie's Diner wasn't much, but it was clean and safe. Most importantly, it was ours.

"Mom!" Levi called as I pushed open the door. My younger son sat cross-legged on our secondhand couch, homework spread across the coffee table.

"Hey, baby." I dropped my purse on the counter that separated our tiny kitchen from the equally tiny living room. "Where's your brother?"

Levi's shoulders tensed slightly. "He went out with some friends."

The alarm bells in my head started ringing immediately. "What friends? From school?"

"No," Levi admitted, looking down at his math worksheet. "Some guys from the garage."

My stomach dropped. It was one thing for him to stop by there and maybe learn a thing or two, even though I wasn't thrilled about that either, and another for him to go off with those men. None of them had done anything to make me feel ill at ease, but it was still damn hard to trust people. "The Reapers' garage? Levi, you know I don't want --"

"They're just teaching him about motorcycles, Mom." Levi's voice held a defensive edge. "They're not like Dad and his friends. Chase says they're actually nice."

I pressed my fingers to my temples, trying to ward off the headache that had been threatening all day. "When did he leave?"

"About an hour ago. He said he'd be back for dinner."

I took a deep breath, battling the urge to call someone. No, I had to let him spread his wings a bit. Although, we'd be having a conversation when he came home.

"Finish your homework," I said, moving to the refrigerator to figure out dinner. "I'll talk to Chase when he gets home."

The refrigerator's contents were sparse -- some eggs, half a gallon of milk, leftover spaghetti from last night. My tip money would help, but not until I hit the grocery store tomorrow. I pulled out the spaghetti container, resigning myself to reheated pasta.

"Mom?" Levi's voice was quieter now. "Are you mad?"

I turned to find him watching me, worry etched across his young face. He'd always been sensitive to moods, could read tension in a room before it erupted. A survival skill I wished he'd never had to develop.

"Not at you, baby." I managed a smile. "Just worried."

"Chase is okay. He texted me twenty minutes ago. Said he was having fun."

Fun. When was the last time either of my boys had described anything as fun? I nodded, swallowing the lump in my throat.

"That biker was at the diner again, wasn't he?" Levi asked, his perceptiveness catching me off guard. "The older one with the silver beard."

"Hammer," I said.

"Yeah, Hammer," Levi confirmed. "Chase says he's got a granddaughter, and even a great-grandkid."

I busied myself with the microwave, not wanting Levi to see my expression. The thought of Hammer as someone's grandfather, much less a great-grandfather, didn't fit with the imposing figure who'd watched me while I worked today. But then again, nothing about the Dixie Reapers matched what I'd expected.

"Did he talk to you?" Levi asked, his voice casual in that deliberate way that told me he was fishing for information.

"Just asked how we were settling in," I replied, keeping my tone neutral. "Nothing special."

The microwave beeped. I stirred the pasta, added more sauce from the fridge, and put it back in for another minute. My mind kept circling back to Chase at the garage, surrounded by bikers. The rational part of me knew these men weren't Piston, but the mother in me couldn't stop the parade of worst-case scenarios.

"He was in prison for a while," Levi continued, eyes back on his homework. "I looked him up."

I froze with the refrigerator door half-open. "You did what?"

Levi shrugged, not looking up. "Just wanted to know who was watching our backs. Scratch told me to always verify information."

The microwave beeped again, but I ignored it. "Levi, I thought we agreed -- no more online digging. No more contact with Scratch or anyone from the clubs."

"Mom, information is safety." His voice took on that older-than-his-years quality that broke my heart. "And anyway, the Dixie Reapers aren't our enemy. They're the only reason Dad hasn't found us yet. Even though some of them have spent time in prison, they're nothing like Dad and his club. These are good people."

The truth of his words hit me like a physical blow. I leaned against the counter, suddenly exhausted. "I know, baby. I just... I don't want you or Chase getting pulled into that life."

"We're already in it," he said quietly. "We were born into it."

The front door opened before I could respond, and Chase strode in. His dark hair was windblown, and there was a smudge of grease on his cheek. But what caught my attention was the light in his eyes -- a spark of excitement I hadn't seen in years.

"You will not believe what I learned today," he announced, tossing his backpack onto the floor. "Tank showed me how to rebuild a carburetor, and --" He stopped abruptly, noticing my expression. "What's wrong?"

"You went to the garage without telling me," I said, trying to keep my voice steady.

Chase's shoulders stiffened. "I'm sixteen, Mom. I can hang out with friends after school."

"They're not friends, Chase. They're --"

"They're what?" His voice hardened.

"They're bikers," I finished, hating how my voice shook.

Chase's face darkened in a way that reminded me too much of his father. "So what if they are? These guys actually give a damn about us, which is more than Dad ever did."

"Language," I said automatically, then

immediately regretted it. My son towered over me now, nearly a man, with shoulders broadening every day. Correcting his language felt ridiculous when we were discussing motorcycle clubs and violence.

"You don't get it," Chase continued, running a hand through his hair in frustration. "These guys aren't like Dad. They don't hit their women or terrorize their kids. They've got actual jobs and families they take care of."

"And prison records," I said. "These men may be helping us, but they aren't fluffy bunnies, Chase. They can be dangerous. I just worry and want you to be careful."

He sighed and nodded, but I knew he'd be back at the garage first chance he had. But that was a battle for another day.

Chapter Seven

Amelia

The Wednesday lunch rush had just begun to taper off when I spotted him through the front window. Black leather cut with the Devil's Minions patch, a Prospect rocker where a full member would have his road name. My coffeepot tilted mid-pour, scorching liquid splashing across the table and onto my customer's lap as recognition hit me like a physical blow. The Devil's Minions. Piston's club. They'd found us.

"Jesus Christ, lady!" The trucker jumped up, napkins clutched to his soaked jeans.

"I'm so sorry," I stammered, my voice sounding distant to my own ears. My hands shook so badly I couldn't even set the pot down properly. It clattered against the table edge, more coffee sloshing over the rim.

The Prospect lounged against a streetlight, pretending to check his phone, but he kept slightly turning his head and glancing toward the diner. He was young -- maybe early twenties -- with the hungry look of someone eager to prove himself. Those were the worst kind. The ones who'd do anything for their patch. Anything Piston asked.

"Hey, you okay?" The trucker's irritation had shifted to concern.

I couldn't answer. My chest had constricted, each breath shallow and insufficient. Black spots danced at the edges of my vision as sweat beaded along my hairline despite the air conditioning. I gripped the edge of the table, the room spinning slightly as blood rushed in my ears.

"Amelia?" Jessie called from behind the counter.

"Everything all right over there?"

My mind flashed to a night three years ago -- Piston dragging me by my hair through our kitchen after I'd answered a text from my cousin. "Who the fuck is Michael?" he'd demanded, my scalp burning as he twisted his fist tighter. "You fucking some guy behind my back?" The memory of my head slamming against the refrigerator door made my temple throb in phantom pain.

"Amelia!" Jessie's voice was closer now, her hand on my arm. "Honey, you're white as a sheet."

I tore my eyes from the window, struggling to focus on her concerned face. "I... I need to go. Family emergency."

"What happened?" Her eyes darted to the mess on the table, then back to me.

"The boys," I managed. "School called. Chase is... sick." The lie tasted bitter on my tongue, but Jessie was already nodding.

"Of course, honey. Go take care of your boy." She squeezed my arm. "Don't worry about this. I've got it covered."

I mumbled thanks, my eyes drawn back to the window like a magnet. The Prospect had moved, stepping into the shadow of the building across the street. But he was still watching. Still waiting.

My fingers fumbled with my apron ties, the simple knot suddenly as complex as a puzzle box. After three failed attempts, I yanked it over my head instead, nearly taking my ponytail with it. I hung it on the hook by the kitchen door, missing twice before it caught.

"Here." Jessie handed me my purse from beneath the counter. "You sure you're okay to drive? You don't look so good."

"I'm fine," I lied, forcing a smile that felt more like a grimace. "Just worried about Chase."

Through the front windows, I could see the Prospect moving again -- this time toward a motorcycle parked across the street. My stomach lurched as he swung his leg over the seat, but he didn't start the engine. Just repositioned it for a better view of both the diner's front door and the side alley.

He knew. He knew we lived above the diner. Unless it was a coincidence, but my gut said Piston had sent him to find us.

My purse slipped from my shoulder, hitting the floor with a *thud*. Lipstick, keys, and loose change scattered across the linoleum. I dropped to my knees, scrambling to gather everything, aware of how exposed my back felt to the windows.

"Amelia, for God's sake, leave it," Jessie said, crouching beside me. "I'll get this. You go check on Chase."

I nodded, cramming items back into my purse with trembling fingers. As I stood, a wave of dizziness washed over me, and I had to grab the counter to steady myself.

"I'll use the back door," I said, not wanting the Prospect to see me leave.

Jessie's forehead creased with worry. "You sure you're all right? You look like you've seen a ghost."

Something close to it. The ghost of my past life. The ghost of the monster I'd thought we'd escaped.

"I'm fine," I repeated, edging toward the kitchen. "Just worried about Chase."

In the kitchen, the cook gave me a curious glance as I hurried past. The back door stuck as it always did, requiring a hard shove with my shoulder. Outside, my gaze swept the empty back lot, searching for any sign of another biker. Nothing. Just dumpsters and the old Honda parked in the corner. The club had given it to me last week so we'd no longer have to walk everywhere. Just as a loaner.

I looked over my shoulder every three steps, keys clutched between my fingers as a makeshift weapon the way women have taught each other. As I approached my car, I checked underneath it, behind it, even in the back seat before unlocking the door and sliding behind the wheel.

Only when I had the doors locked and engine running did I allow myself a full breath. It caught in my throat, morphing into a sob that I quickly swallowed. No time for that now. My hands shook so badly I had to try three times to shift into reverse.

In the rearview mirror, I watched the back door of the diner, half-expecting the Prospect to burst through it at any second. Nothing moved except a stray paper bag tumbling across the lot in the breeze.

I backed out too fast, tires squealing slightly. As I pulled onto the street, I kept my gaze locked on the mirrors, watching for the Prospect's bike. No sign of him following. Not yet. But they'd found us. Somehow, they'd found us.

My mind raced faster than my car as I sped toward the boys' school. We needed to move again. We needed help. We needed the Dixie Reapers.

* * *

I ran two stop signs and barely touched my brakes at a third, glanced at the rearview mirror every few seconds. The school was only ten minutes from the diner, but it felt like hours. My knuckles bleached white against the steering wheel as I took a corner too fast, the tires protesting with a squeal that made my already frayed nerves jangle. A Prospect. A fucking

Devil's Minions Prospect in our new town. It wasn't coincidence. They'd tracked us somehow.

A motorcycle appeared in my mirror, and my heart lodged in my throat before I realized it was just an old man on a Honda Gold Wing -- nothing like the Prospect's Harley. Still, my foot pressed harder on the accelerator, the Honda's engine whining in protest as I pushed it past sixty on a thirty-five mph road.

"Shit, shit, shit," I muttered under my breath, my mind racing through possibilities. Had I slipped up somewhere? Had one of the boys contacted someone back in Florida? Had someone in Florida seen us leaving? Or had Piston's reach always been longer than I'd estimated? Sure, they'd said he was trying to find us. But some part of me had hoped he'd never figure out where we were.

The high school came into view, its red-brick walls and American flag a picture of normalcy that felt obscene against my panic. I jerked the wheel, pulling into the first parking space I saw -- a loading zone clearly marked "NO PARKING." The car rocked as I slammed on the brakes, my seat belt catching painfully across my chest.

I checked all my mirrors one last time before killing the engine. Nothing. No motorcycles, no leather cuts, no hint of pursuit. But that didn't mean they weren't coming. Prospects never worked alone. They were always just the eyes and ears for someone higher up the food chain.

I made it to the front door and pressed the buzzer. A woman's voice came over the intercom. "May I help you?"

I cleared my throat. "Yes, I'm Amelia Decker. I need to pick up my sons Chase and Levi. Family emergency."

It was quiet for a moment before she responded.

"Hold your ID up to the camera, please." I did as she asked. "I'll buzz you through. When you come through the doors, take the door on the right."

I heard the buzzer and I popped the door open, then went through the entrance she'd told me about. The main office smelled of copier toner and stale coffee, an administrative blandness that clashed with the adrenaline coursing through my system. The secretary looked up from her computer, mild irritation crossing her face at the interruption.

"Can I help you?" Her drawled question carried just enough Southern politeness to mask her annoyance.

"I just spoke to you, or someone. I'm Amelia Decker. I need to pick up my sons," I said, the words tumbling out too fast. I forced myself to slow down. "Chase and Levi Decker."

She raised an eyebrow. "Both of them?"

I nodded, trying to look appropriately hassled rather than terrified. "Family emergency."

"I'll need to see your ID," she said, holding out her hand.

My fingers trembled as I fumbled with my wallet, nearly dropping it before extracting my driver's license. Why had they asked to see it before I entered the building if they were going to ask for it again? The secretary examined it longer than necessary, glancing between my face and the photo.

"I'll call them down," she finally said, reaching for the phone. "Have a seat."

I perched on the edge of a plastic chair, my back to the wall so I could watch both the office entrance and the windows overlooking the parking lot. Each second that ticked by on the wall clock felt like a minute, each minute an hour. My legs bounced with nervous energy, heel tapping against the industrial carpet.

The office door opened, and I leapt to my feet. A teenage girl entered, dropping a tardy slip on the counter before heading back out. I sank back down, my heart pounding so loudly I was sure everyone could hear it.

Reaching for my phone, I nearly called one of the Dixie Reapers but stopped myself. They'd said I could call if we were in trouble, but what if I was wrong and panicking over nothing? Or even worse, what if they didn't really want me to bother them about this stuff? It wasn't like they could do anything while I was at the school waiting on the boys. As far as I knew, I'd lost the Prospect. He could be anywhere by now.

After what felt like an eternity, the door opened once more, and Chase appeared with Levi trailing behind him. One look at my face, and Chase's expression hardened.

"What happened?" Chase asked, his voice pitched low as he moved immediately to stand between me and the office door.

"Aunt Betty is in the hospital," I said, the code we'd established years ago for emergencies. "We're running late."

Levi's eyes narrowed behind his glasses, his gaze sweeping over me with analytical precision.

"Both of you need to sign out," the secretary instructed, sliding a clipboard across the counter.

Chase kept his body angled so he could watch the door while signing his name. His shoulders had squared up, his stance widening slightly -- unconsciously preparing for confrontation. Levi signed after him, his signature as precise as always despite the tension crackling in the air.

"Hope your aunt feels better," the secretary called as we headed for the door, finally noticing the gravity in our postures.

Chase merely nodded, his hand on my elbow as he guided me out, his height making him seem older than sixteen as he scanned the area before letting us proceed. Levi fell into step on my other side, his smaller frame tense with unspoken questions.

Outside, the afternoon sun beat down on the empty parking lot. No motorcycles. No Prospects. Just the shimmer of heat rising from asphalt and my illegally parked Honda.

"Keys," Chase said, holding out his hand.

"I can drive," I protested.

"Your hands are shaking," he replied, not unkindly. "And you parked in a loading zone. Come on, Mom."

I surrendered the keys, allowing Chase to guide me to the passenger side while Levi climbed in the back. As soon as the doors closed, Chase turned to me.

"What's happening, Mom?" His knuckles were white on the steering wheel, just as mine had been. "Is it him? Did Dad find us?"

My throat constricted with the effort of holding back tears. Both my boys watched me -- Chase's green eyes sharp with worry, Levi's brown ones steady behind his glasses. They deserved the truth, but not here. Not in an exposed parking lot where anyone could drive past.

"Not yet," I managed, shaking my head. I wasn't going to panic them right his minute. "When we get home. Just… drive carefully. Watch for motorcycles."

Chase's jaw clenched as he started the car and pulled out of the parking space with precision I hadn't known he possessed. In the rearview mirror, I could see Levi's reflection, his face calm but alert, taking in everything.

"Did someone come to the diner?" Levi asked softly from the back seat.

"Later," I said, eyes scanning the road ahead and behind. "When we're home."

Chase took a route I didn't recognize, making several unexpected turns. I raised an eyebrow, and he shrugged.

"Just making sure we're not followed," he said. "Tank showed me how to spot a tail."

Tank. One of the Dixie Reapers. Under different circumstances, I might have been upset that he was learning such things from bikers. Now, I was pathetically grateful.

"Good thinking," I said, trying to keep my voice steady. "You're doing good, baby."

Chase's expression softened slightly at the endearment he usually protested. "We're okay, Mom. Whatever it is, we'll handle it."

The confidence in his voice nearly broke me. My son, trying to reassure me when it should have been the other way around. I nodded, not trusting myself to speak as we made our way home, each of us scanning the roads for signs of the men I'd spent years trying to escape.

* * *

I fumbled with the keys three times before successfully unlocking our apartment door. Chase gently took them from my still-trembling hands, opened the door, and ushered us inside. The moment we were in, I flipped the deadbolt, slid the chain into place, and secured the extra lock we'd installed our first week here. Still not enough. I moved to each window, checking the locks, drawing the blinds until the room dimmed to a muted gold, dust motes dancing in the narrow strips of sunlight that managed to break through.

"Mom," Levi said quietly, setting his backpack by the door. "You're scaring me."

I paused, trying to compose myself. My boys stood watching me -- Chase with his fists clenched at his sides, Levi with his arms wrapped around himself. I'd promised myself when we left Florida that I wouldn't let fear rule our lives anymore. Yet here I was, checking window locks for the third time.

"I'm sorry, baby." I forced my hands to still. "Let's sit down."

I moved to the refrigerator first, eyes finding the list of phone numbers stuck to the door. Emergency contacts. Men with road names instead of real ones. Tank. Saint. Hammer. Men who'd helped us escape Florida. Men I'd been both grateful for and wary of.

The boys settled at our small kitchen table, schoolbooks still in their backpacks, forgotten in the rush. Chase pulled out a chair for me, the scrape of its legs against linoleum abnormally loud in the tense silence.

I sat, hands flat on the table to steady them. "I saw a Devil's Minions Prospect at the diner today," I said, the words dropping like stones. "He was watching me."

The effect was immediate. Chase shot to his feet, the chair tipping backward and crashing to the floor. His face flushed with anger, green eyes flashing as his hands curled into fists.

"Fuck," he spat, the word explosive in our small kitchen.

Levi remained seated, but his face had drained of

color, making the light dusting of freckles across his nose stand out in stark relief. His expression remained composed, but I didn't miss how his fingers gripped the edge of the table, knuckles white with tension.

"Did he follow you?" Levi asked, his voice steady despite the fear I could see in his eyes.

I shook my head. "I don't think so. I was careful. Went out the back door and watched my mirrors the whole way to your school."

"Are you sure it was Devil's Minions?" Levi pressed. "Not just some other MC passing through?"

"I know what I saw." My voice came out sharper than intended. I softened it. "Black leather cut, red devil's head with horns, 'Devil's Minions' above it, Florida territory rocker at the bottom. Prospect patch on the front. I lived with those colors for nearly seventeen years, baby. I know them."

Chase paced our tiny kitchen, five steps one way, five steps back, like a caged animal. He'd grown so tall in the past year, his movements reminding me painfully of Piston when he'd been younger, before the drugs and alcohol had bloated him.

"We need to tell the Reapers," Chase said, stopping his pacing to look at me. "That's why they gave us those numbers. They said to call if anything happened."

I hesitated. The Dixie Reapers had been nothing but helpful. They'd given us a place to stay, set me up with a job, enrolled the boys in school. But they were still an MC. Still men who lived outside the law in ways I didn't fully understand. Trading one club's protection for another's felt like slipping backward.

"He's right, Mom," Levi said, pushing his glasses up his nose. "Hammer would help us. He watches you at the diner all the time."

I blinked, surprised. "What do you mean, he watches me?"

Even if he was a regular at the diner, that didn't mean he'd been there for me. A lot of people in town ate there nearly every day.

Levi exchanged a look with Chase. "The older guy with the silver beard. For the last week, he's come in almost every day you work. Sits in the same booth. Always watching the door and windows. We didn't realize you weren't aware he was there."

Chase nudged him. "She's busy at work. If he's not in her section, then she doesn't really have time to go socialize."

"How do you know that?" I asked. I worked while they were in school most of the time.

"Jessie told me," Levi said.

"And you," Chase added. "He watches you too."

I felt a flush creep up my neck. Of course I'd noticed Hammer's appearance the other day, his quiet presence in the corner booth. I'd attributed it to routine. The idea that he'd been there deliberately, keeping an eye on me...

"Jessie said Hammer's been making sure no one bothers you. And Tank said they've been rotating shifts, different guys checking different times." Chase smiled a little. "They're good men, Mom."

My mouth went dry. I mean, yeah. A few had come through the diner and asked how we were doing, but the way Chase worded it made it seem more... deliberate, like they'd been standing guard. "They've been watching us?"

"Protecting us," Levi corrected. "That's what Tank told Chase."

I sank back in my chair, processing this information. All these weeks I'd thought we were establishing independence, building a new life. Instead, we'd been under surveillance -- benevolent perhaps, but surveillance nonetheless.

"Mom," Chase said, his voice gentler than I'd heard it in months as he righted his chair and sat back down. "I know you hate asking for help. I know you're afraid of getting mixed up with another club. But the Reapers aren't like Dad's club."

"You don't know that," I whispered.

"Actually, I do." He leaned forward. "I've been at the garage. I've seen how they treat their women, their kids. It's different. Hammer's granddaughter came by the other day with her son, Kellen. You should have seen how those guys melted while talking to that kid. And if Amity needed anything, whoever was closest would jump like she'd given an order."

I thought of Hammer in the diner, his quiet presence, the way he'd left me a generous tip. His words before he'd left the other day. "*Your boys are safe here, Amelia. And so are you.*"

"The numbers are right there," Levi said, nodding toward the refrigerator. "We can't wait for Dad to find us. It's time to ask for help."

Chase reached across the table, taking my hand in his. His palm dwarfed mine now, calloused already from whatever work he'd been doing at the garage. "You've protected us our whole lives, Mom. Let someone help protect you for a change."

Tears pricked at my eyes. When had my boys become so wise? When had they grown into these young men, capable of seeing truths I'd been too afraid to acknowledge? And how could they possibly feel like I'd protected them? I'd failed them so many times.

I stood, crossed to the refrigerator, and stared at the list of numbers. My fingers hovered over

Hammer's name, hesitating only briefly before I plucked the paper from under its magnet. My hands had stopped shaking, I realized. The paralyzing fear from earlier had receded, replaced by something stronger -- determination.

"You're right," I said, turning back to my sons. "We can't wait for Piston to find us."

I reached for the phone, dialing the number. As it rang, I caught my reflection in the microwave door -- pale, frightened, but standing straight. No longer running. This time, I was facing the threat head-on.

"Hello?" The gruff voice on the other end was instantly recognizable.

"Hammer, it's Amelia Decker," I said, my voice steadier than I'd expected. "I need your help. A Devil's Minions Prospect was watching the diner today."

The momentary silence felt endless before he replied, "Stay put. Lock your doors. I'll be there in ten minutes." A pause, then, more softly, "You did the right thing calling, Amelia."

As I hung up, I realized with startling clarity that for the first time since leaving Florida, I believed those words might actually be true.

Chapter Eight

Amelia

I heard a vehicle long before I saw it, the deep rumble echoing between the buildings like distant thunder. I'd expected Hammer to show up on his bike, but instead, a big truck pulled in. My fingers curled into fists at my sides as I stepped onto the landing outside my apartment. A slight breeze blew as I watched. I'd called him in panic, and now he was here -- my reluctant savior, wrapped in leather and denim.

He pulled up by the stairs, the engine's growl cutting off abruptly as he turned the key. The sudden silence felt heavier than the noise had been. Hammer swung open the door and stepped out, his movements unhurried yet purposeful. His leather cut bore the Dixie Reapers patch I'd come to both fear and respect -- so different from the Devil's Minions emblem that had haunted my nightmares for years.

"You're alone?" he asked, his deep voice carrying up to me as he surveyed the area, eyes scanning every shadow.

I nodded, wrapping my arms around myself despite the lingering heat of the day. "The boys are inside. Levi's watching through the window."

Hammer climbed the metal stairs, each step deliberate. Up close, the lines etched around his eyes seemed deeper, his beard more silver than I'd noticed in the diner. Tattoos crawled up his forearms, faded with age but still bold against his tanned skin.

"Tell me exactly what you saw," he said, stopping a respectful distance away.

Words tumbled out of me then, my voice unsteady at first but gaining strength as I recounted the Prospect watching the diner, how I'd recognized the Devil's Minions colors instantly, how I'd fled with the boys from school.

"He was young," I said, "Maybe twenty-two, twenty-three. Thin, dark hair. Watching me like... like he was memorizing everything." I swallowed hard. "Like Piston told him to."

Hammer's expression remained impassive, but something in his expression hardened at Piston's name.

"There's more," I admitted, my hand unconsciously rising to my throat where phantom fingers still seemed to press. "This wasn't our first attempt to escape. Last time, Piston... he got drunk. Angrier than usual."

I closed my eyes briefly, the memory washing over me like ice water. Piston's face twisted with rage, his breath hot with whiskey as he'd pinned me against the wall. "You think you can take my sons?" he'd snarled, his hand closing around my throat until black spots danced before my eyes. "You try to leave, and I'll make sure those boys watch while I teach you your place."

"He threatened me, said he'd make the boys watch while he hurt me," I told Hammer, my voice dropping to a whisper. "I have no doubt he'll kill me if he gets his hands on me again."

Hammer's weathered face remained still as stone, but his eyes -- those deep brown eyes that had watched me in the diner -- flashed with something dangerous.

"If a Prospect is here, others won't be far behind," he said finally. "Piston's reaching out, testing. Seeing if the rumors about you being here are true."

A chill ran through me despite the warm evening. "What do we do?"

Hammer studied me for a long moment. "The Dixie Reapers protect their own, Amelia. But there are rules."

"Rules," I repeated, the word bitter on my tongue. Rules had governed my life with Piston too.

"To get full protection from the club," Hammer continued, his voice level, "you need to be family. Blood relation, or an old lady of a member."

I stared at him, understanding dawning slowly. "You're saying I need to… to belong to someone in the club for protection?"

Hammer's jaw tightened. "Not belong to. Be with. There's a difference."

I laughed, a harsh sound with no humor in it. "Is there? Really?"

"Yes," he said simply. "The women of the Dixie Reapers are respected, Amelia. Protected. Not owned. But the club won't go to war with another MC for someone who isn't family."

I turned away, looking out over the street. Chase and Levi were watching through the window. I could feel their eyes on us, their worry a tangible thing. They'd already lost so much -- their childhood, their sense of safety. I couldn't let them lose more.

"How long do we have?" I asked, still not facing him. "Before they come for us?"

"Hard to say. Could be days. Could be hours. But you won't face them alone. We can move you tonight. Somewhere safe until we figure this out."

I turned back, meeting his gaze directly. "And then what? We just keep running? Keep hiding?" My voice trembled with sudden anger. "I'm so tired of being afraid, Hammer. So damn tired of looking over my shoulder, of checking locks three times, of jumping every time a motorcycle drives by."

His expression softened almost imperceptibly. "I know."

Two simple words, but somehow I believed he did know. That he understood what it was to live with fear as a constant companion.

I took a deep breath, steeling myself for what I was about to say. The thought had formed the moment he'd mentioned old ladies, crystallizing with sudden clarity. It was desperate. Possibly insane. But I was done running.

"You said I need to be an old lady for protection," I said, my voice steadier than I felt. "Then let me be yours."

Hammer went utterly still, his expression frozen. For a heartbeat, shock registered in his eyes before his features rearranged themselves into that unreadable mask. But I'd seen it -- that moment of complete surprise.

"You don't know what you're asking," he said finally, his voice rougher than before.

"I do." I stepped closer, close enough to catch the scent of leather and motor oil that clung to him. "You've been watching over me at the diner. The boys told me. You've been keeping an eye on us all along."

"That's not --"

"It is," I insisted. "And I'm not asking for love, Hammer. I'm not even asking for anything real. I'm asking for protection for my boys." My voice cracked slightly. "I'm asking you to help us stop running."

Hammer's gaze bored into mine, searching for something I couldn't name. The silence between us stretched taut as a wire, the only sound the distant hum of traffic and the soft whisper of wind through the trees lining the street.

"You think it's that simple?" he asked finally.

"Nothing about this is simple," I answered. "But my boys need safety more than I need pride." I held his gaze, refusing to look away. "Please, Hammer. Let me be yours."

His jaw tightened, muscles working beneath his beard as he processed my words. For a moment, something raw and unguarded flashed across his face -- including something that might have been longing -- before he forced himself back into that unyielding mask I'd grown familiar with.

"Pack your things," he said finally, his voice giving away nothing of what he might be feeling. "Just the essentials. We're moving you tonight."

I backed toward my open door, tugging the hem of my cardigan tight around my ribs. The air had cooled, or maybe it was just the chill spreading through me at Hammer's non-answer. He hadn't agreed to my proposition, but he hadn't laughed in my face either. That had to count for something.

"I'll wait here while you pack," Hammer said, his voice low enough that only I could hear. "Ten minutes, Amelia. Grab what you need for tonight. We can come back for the rest later."

I nodded, my throat too tight for words. "The boys --" I started.

"Will be safe," Hammer finished. "You have my word."

His word. How many times had Piston given me his word, only to break it with the next bottle of Jack? But something in Hammer's steady gaze made me believe him, made me trust despite years of learned wariness.

Chase and Levi waited by the window, both springing back as I entered the apartment. Chase's face was tight with anxiety, Levi's pale behind his glasses.

"What did he say?" Chase demanded immediately. "Is he going to help us?"

I closed the door but didn't lock it, knowing Hammer stood just outside. "We're leaving tonight. Just for a while, until they figure out what to do about the Prospect."

"But the diner -- school --" Levi began.

"Will still be here when it's safe," I said, moving quickly to the boys' room. "Pack only what you need for a few days. Clothes, toiletries, any medication. Chase, make sure Levi gets his inhaler."

"Mom." Chase followed me, his voice dropping. "What aren't you telling us?"

I paused, my hands stilling on the duffel bag I'd pulled from under my bed. The duffel we'd used to flee Florida, that I'd kept ready in case we needed to run again. "I asked Hammer to make me his old lady," I said quietly. "For protection."

Chase's eyes widened, his jaw tightening in a way that reminded me painfully of his father. "You what?"

"It's the only way to get full club protection." I resumed packing, stuffing clothes into the bag without folding them. "The Reapers only go to war for family."

"But you barely know him," Chase protested.

I gave my son a weary smile. "I barely knew your father when I got on the back of his bike. At least this time, I'm choosing someone who might actually be decent."

"You don't have to do this," Chase said, his voice softening. "We can find another way."

I zipped the duffel closed with more force than necessary. "There is no other way. Not with a Devil's Minions Prospect already in town, not with your father looking for us." I met my son's troubled gaze. "I've spent your entire life making the wrong choices, Chase. Let me make one right one."

He held my gaze for a long moment before nodding reluctantly. "I'll help Levi pack."

As Chase moved to their room, I sank onto my bed, the reality of what I'd just proposed to Hammer crashing over me like a wave. Become his old lady. Let a man claim me again, even if only in name. Trade one leather cut for another.

But it wasn't the same. It couldn't be. Hammer's eyes held none of the cruel possessiveness that had always lurked in Piston's. His hands, when they'd brushed mine at the diner, had been gentle. And he'd come when I called -- not to control, but to protect.

I checked the window one last time, catching only the briefest movement at the end of the alley -- a dark figure turning the corner, disappearing from sight. Another trick of my anxious mind, I was sure.

Gathering my courage, I picked up the duffel and moved to check on the boys. Ten minutes had nearly passed. Hammer would be waiting, his patience wearing thin. I had no idea where he planned to take us or what would happen once we arrived. All I knew was that I'd offered myself as payment for my children's safety, and I didn't regret it. Not if it meant Chase and Levi would never have to fear their father again.

"Ready?" I called to the boys, hefting my duffel over my shoulder. The familiar weight of it -- this bag that had carried our desperate hopes out of Florida -- felt like both a burden and a security blanket.

Chase emerged from their bedroom, his own backpack slung over one shoulder, Levi's in his other hand. Levi trailed behind him, clutching his laptop to his chest like a shield.

"We can come back for the rest, right?" Levi asked, looking around our small apartment. In just a few weeks, we'd managed to make this place feel like home -- more than any place we'd had in Florida.

"Yes, baby. This is just temporary." I hoped I wasn't lying to him.

I opened the door to find Hammer exactly where I'd left him, leaning against the railing, scanning the street below. He straightened when he saw us, nodding once at the boys before taking my duffel.

"My truck's downstairs," he said, his voice a low rumble. "We'll leave your car here for now."

"Where are we going?" Chase asked, stepping protectively closer to Levi.

Hammer's gaze shifted to my older son, assessing him with a look that wasn't unkind but wasn't particularly warm either. "Somewhere safe."

"That's not an answer," Chase pressed, and I tensed, ready to step between them if needed.

But Hammer just nodded, something like respect flickering across his face. "The compound. You'll have a duplex to yourselves."

The Dixie Reapers' compound. My stomach twisted with a mixture of relief and apprehension. We'd be surrounded by bikers again, but this time ones sworn to protect us rather than control us. At least, that's what I needed to believe.

"Let's go," Hammer said, already moving toward the stairs. "Stay close."

We followed him down to the street. It remained quiet, the only movement coming from a stray cat slinking along the curb.

Hammer's truck was parked at the bottom of the stairs as he'd said -- a massive black pickup that looked like it could plow through a brick wall without slowing down. He opened the passenger door for me, his hand briefly touching the small of my back as I climbed in. The casual contact sent an unexpected shiver up my spine.

The boys piled into the back seat, Chase sitting directly behind me as if to guard my back. Hammer slid behind the wheel, his large frame making even this beast of a truck seem almost small.

"Seat belts," he said, not starting the engine until he heard three clicks of compliance.

As we pulled away from the curb, I couldn't help glancing back at our apartment above the diner. The windows were dark now, no trace of the life we'd just abandoned visible from the street.

Hammer drove in silence, constantly checking the mirrors as we wound through side streets instead of taking the main road. My pulse quickened each time we passed a parked motorcycle, but I didn't see any bikers who bore the Devil's Minions colors. In the back seat, Levi had opened his laptop, the blue glow illuminating his face as his fingers flew across the keyboard.

"What are you doing?" I asked, twisting to look at him.

"Checking traffic cameras," he replied without looking up. "Making sure we're not followed."

Hammer's gaze flicked to the rearview mirror. "You can do that?"

Levi shrugged. "It's not that hard if you know what you're doing. Just need a signal, and your truck has Wi-Fi."

A ghost of a smile touched Hammer's lips before vanishing. At least he was taking this in stride. Not that I'd ever had a car with Wi-Fi before, but I'd imagine Levi had needed a password. Of course, knowing my son, he'd figured it out on the first try. "I heard you were good with computers. Didn't realize how good."

Pride warmed my chest despite the circumstances. My quiet, thoughtful son had skills that even these hardened bikers respected. Chase leaned over, watching Levi's screen with narrowed eyes, his protective instincts never switching off.

"See anything?" Chase asked.

"Nothing yet," Levi murmured.

We turned onto a gravel road I didn't recognize. Trees crowded close on either side, branches scraping against the windows like skeletal fingers.

"How much farther?" I asked, breaking the heavy silence.

"Ten minutes," Hammer replied, his hands steady on the wheel. "The compound's rear entrance is isolated. Good for security."

I nodded, fidgeting with the hem of my cardigan. The question I'd asked him -- my desperate proposition -- hung between us, unacknowledged but impossible to forget.

"What happens when we get there?" I finally asked.

Hammer's gaze remained fixed on the road. "You'll stay in one of the duplexes we keep for emergencies. Club members will take shifts patrolling the perimeter. No one gets in without going through the gate, and the gate's always manned."

It sounded like a prison. Or a fortress. I wasn't sure which scared me more.

"And us?" Chase asked from the back seat. "What, we just stay locked up until you decide it's safe?"

Hammer looked at Chase in the rearview mirror.

"For tonight, yes. Tomorrow we'll figure out school, work, everything else."

"And my mom's… offer?" Chase's voice hardened on the last word.

I closed my eyes, heat rushing to my face. Of course he'd bring it up. Chase had never been one to dance around difficult subjects.

The truck slowed as Hammer took a sharp turn onto an even narrower road. "That's between me and your mother."

"Like hell it is," Chase shot back. "It affects all of us."

"Chase," I warned, turning to give him a look.

He huffed and sat back in the seat. I had a feeling I hadn't heard the end of it with him. I knew he worried about me, but even he'd told me Hammer was a nice guy. I didn't understand why he suddenly seemed so concerned.

I watched the man next to me, and wished I knew what he was thinking. If we were staying at a duplex tonight, did that mean he wasn't accepting my offer? Or did he simply want more time to think it over?

The unanswered questions hanging over me felt like an oppressive weight. I hated things being so up in the air.

Chapter Nine

Hammer

The duplex smelled of fresh paint and the industrial cleaner Aura insisted on using whenever we prepped a place for someone new. Basic furniture filled the space -- a couch, coffee table, kitchen table with four chairs, beds in each room. Nothing fancy, but solid. Safe.

Chase shouldered past me, walking into the duplex. The kid moved with the coiled tension of someone expecting a fight. After being here a few weeks, I'd hoped some of that tension would have eased. Then again, having the Devil's Minions find them had probably kicked the boy back into his hypervigilant state. I recognized the look in his eyes -- had seen it in brothers just back from war zones, in women who'd escaped men like Piston, and in men like me who'd just gotten out of prison. I'd been the same way during those first months of freedom. The kid was living in survival mode.

"Your room's on the right," I told him, nodding toward the hallway. "Your brother's is on the left."

Chase didn't respond, just headed down the hall with his bag. I couldn't blame him for the cold shoulder. His mother had offered herself to me as payment for protection. What sixteen-year-old wouldn't hate that arrangement?

Levi slipped past us both, laptop clutched to his chest like it held state secrets. The younger boy hadn't spoken two words since we'd arrived at the compound. Just watched everything with those analytical eyes behind his glasses, taking in details, assessing. Smart kid. Dangerous kid, in his own way. The quiet ones usually were.

Amelia began opening kitchen cabinets and taking stock of what was available, her movements efficient but tentative. I watched her for a moment, the way she stretched to reach the upper cabinets, how her ponytail swung with each movement. She wore jeans and a simple T-shirt, both well-worn but clean. The sweater she'd had on had been removed at some point. No makeup hiding her features today, just the natural flush of exertion on her cheeks and the hint of shadows under her eyes from constant worry.

I stepped outside to give her space, without having her feel like I was staring her down. Outside, the compound hummed with its usual activity. A Prospect washed bikes near the clubhouse. Tank's booming laugh carried from the garage. Everything normal, except for the guards I'd asked Savior to double at the gate and the brothers he'd stationed around the perimeter. Devil's Minions wouldn't be stupid enough to come onto Dixie Reapers' territory, not yet, anyway. They'd sent the Prospect to make sure Amelia was actually here, and they'd watch her, gather intel. But Piston wasn't entirely stupid. He wouldn't make a move yet.

When I went back inside, Amelia was checking out the books on the shelves in the living room. It was something the old ladies had added over the last few years. This place had been used for multiple things... safe zone for women we rescued, family visiting from out of town, and even for the Prospects on occasion.

"Need to show you the security features," I said, moving toward the front windows. Better to focus on practical matters than the way her scent -- something floral mixed with coffee -- had invaded my senses. "Every window and door has an alarm. Code is 9241. Don't share it with anyone but your boys. Once you're gone from here, Savior will change it again."

She nodded, following me as I pointed out the surveillance cameras visible through the windows.

"That one covers your front door. Another in back. Gate's manned 24/7. No one gets in or out without us knowing." I glanced toward the hallway, lowering my voice. "If something happens, if you feel unsafe for any reason, you hit this."

I showed her the panic button installed beside the front door, disguised as a light switch. "Signal goes directly to Wire and to my phone."

"And the boys' school?" she asked, her voice steadier now that we were discussing logistics rather than the elephant in the room.

"Tank's wife knows someone there. She'll keep an eye on them. Plus, I've got Prospects watching the campus." I hesitated, then added, "Chase seems to like the garage. He could work there after school if he wants. Safer than having him wander."

Something softened in her expression. "He told me he's been learning about engines."

"Kid's got a knack for it." I moved toward the kitchen, needing space from her grateful look. "Phone's hooked up. Important numbers are programmed in. Mine's number six on speed dial, but Savior is number one and Saint is number two."

The boys emerged from their rooms, Chase positioning himself slightly in front of Levi, his stance wide and protective. My respect for the kid notched higher. He might be a pain in my ass with his attitude, but he looked after his brother.

"You got cameras inside too?" Chase asked, eyes narrowed.

"No," I said firmly. "Your privacy matters. Just outside, for security."

Levi spoke for the first time since they'd arrived. "The Wi-Fi password?"

I couldn't help the slight twitch of my lips. Kid had priorities. "Figured you'd already know it, but to answer your question, it's written on the router in your mom's room. It's secure. Encrypted."

Levi nodded, seemingly satisfied, and disappeared back into his room.

I turned to leave, suddenly aware of how much space I took up in the small duplex. My shoulders nearly brushed the doorframe, my boots loud on the laminate flooring. Amelia looked small standing in the middle of the living room, her fingers twisting the hem of her shirt.

"Hammer," she said quietly as I reached for the door. "About what I said before…"

I held up my hand, stopping her. "Not now. Let's get you settled first."

Her lips pressed together, but she nodded. Relief and disappointment warred in her expression.

"I'm just down the road if you need anything," I added, my voice gruffer than I intended. "Aura, my daughter, will probably stop by later. She's excited to meet you properly. Unless you've already met?"

"No, I haven't. And thank you," she said, those two simple words carrying the weight of everything she couldn't say.

I nodded and stepped outside, taking my first deep breath since entering the duplex. The responsibility of her offer pressed on my shoulders like a physical weight. She'd offered herself to me for protection. Part of me -- the part that had been alone too long -- wanted to accept. But another part knew she was offering out of desperation, not desire. And I was too old, too jaded, and too damn honest to take advantage of that.

For now, I'd focus on keeping them safe. The rest could wait.

I heard Aura's bike before I saw it, the distinctive rumble of her Sportster cutting through the compound's afternoon noise. She'd customized that engine herself, insisted on doing the work alone even though I'd offered to help. Stubborn girl. She pulled up outside the duplex, killing the engine with a practiced flick. Some dads might've worried about their daughters riding, but Aura handled that bike like it was an extension of herself. She'd been riding for more than five years now, and she was better than half the brothers in the club.

I stood on the porch, watching as she removed her helmet and hung it on her handlebars. Her dark hair fell loose around her shoulders, and the afternoon sun caught the colorful tattoos covering her left arm. My girl had always been fearless, from the day I'd found her at sixteen, nearly broken by the men who'd trafficked her, but never surrendering her spirit.

Aura spotted me and waved before hurrying up the steps. She shoved past me. She didn't knock -- just rapped twice on the door frame before pushing it open. "Hello? Anyone home?"

I shook my head, smiling despite myself. No one could resist Aura when she decided to befriend them. Amelia and her boys didn't stand a chance.

I peered inside just in time to see Aura wrapping Amelia in a hug. The older woman stiffened for a moment before relaxing, uncertainty written across her face.

"I'm Aura," my daughter announced, pulling back to beam at Amelia. "Hammer's kid. Well, adopted, but he's still stuck with me." She winked at me over her shoulder.

"Nice to meet you," Amelia said, her voice soft but genuine. "I'm --"

"Amelia," Aura finished for her. "And these must be Chase and Levi." She turned to the boys. Without hesitation, she moved to hug them too. Chase froze like he'd been shot, arms hanging awkwardly at his sides. Levi looked bewildered by this hurricane of a woman who'd blown into their space.

"I thought we should celebrate your first night properly," Aura continued, undeterred by their reaction. "I could cook dinner for everyone! We could eat at our place -- we have a bigger table."

I snorted. "If by 'cook' you mean 'set off the smoke alarm,' then sure."

Aura spun around, pointing an accusing finger at me. "That was one time!"

"Three times," I corrected. "Last month alone."

"The recipe said 'high heat'!"

"Not 'inferno.'"

A small sound caught my attention -- Levi, hiding a smile behind his hand had let out a soft laugh. The kid had barely shown any emotion since they'd arrived, and here he was, laughing at our bickering. Even Chase's rigid posture had softened slightly, as he looked between Aura and me with something like curiosity.

"We could order pizza," I suggested, leaning against the doorframe. "Safer for everyone."

"Pizza?" Levi perked up immediately.

Aura threw her hands up in mock surrender. "Fine, pizza it is. But I'm picking the toppings."

"No pineapple," Chase said, the first words I'd heard from him that didn't sound hostile.

Aura gasped dramatically, pressing a hand to her

chest. "A pineapple hater? In my presence? We need to fix this travesty immediately."

Chase's lips twitched toward a smile. "Not happening."

"Half and half," Amelia suggested, the tension in her shoulders visibly easing as she watched the exchange. "Pineapple for Aura, none for Chase."

"A diplomat," Aura said, grinning at Amelia. "I like you already."

"Just order several," I said. I knew damn well those boys could eat and would if given the chance. At the garage, the guys were always having to tease Chase into eating more. Even when we could see how badly he wanted the food, he always held himself back.

I watched as Aura moved around the duplex, while chatting easily with everyone. She asked Levi about his computer setup, listening intently as he launched into an explanation filled with technical terms I couldn't follow. She got Chase talking about engines, drawing him out with questions about what he'd learned at the garage. The transformation in both boys was subtle but unmistakable -- they were relaxing, engaging.

Aura had that effect on people. Maybe because she'd been broken once too, had survived her own hell before finding her way to us. There was an authenticity to her that cut through bullshit and facades. The same way she'd called me "Dad" within a week of my taking her in, refusing to be intimidated by my gruff exterior. "You're stuck with me now," she'd declared. "Might as well get used to it."

"So what do you do around here?" Amelia asked Aura as they folded clothes into a drawer.

"I work at the garage part-time and help out at the tattoo shop sometimes too," Aura replied. "And

I'm finishing my degree in social work online. When I'm not driving this old man crazy." She jerked her thumb toward me.

"Full-time job, that," I said dryly.

Aura stuck her tongue out at me, the small stud in it catching the light. "Like you'd know what to do without me."

The truth in her teasing hit deeper than she knew. Before Aura, my life had been the club, the garage, and the empty spaces between. She'd filled those spaces with noise and light and relentless optimism. I'd saved her life once, but she'd saved something in me too.

"Let's eat at my place," I said, watching Chase help Aura reach a high shelf. "More room. Same pizza. Seven o'clock."

"Perfect!" Aura exclaimed. "That gives us time to finish unpacking."

I didn't have the heart to tell her they'd only brought one bag each. They weren't exactly moving in.

She looked at Levi. "Think you could help me set up a better security system for my laptop? Someone keeps hacking in and changing my desktop background to pictures of cats."

Levi's eyes narrowed. "That's pretty easy to prevent."

"My hero," Aura said, linking her arm through his and guiding him toward his room, chattering about firewall protocols the whole way.

Amelia moved beside me, her voice low enough that only I could hear. "She's wonderful."

I nodded, pride swelling in my chest. "She's something, all right."

"You've raised her well."

"She raised herself," I corrected. "I just gave her

space to do it."

Amelia studied me for a moment, those brown eyes seeing more than I wanted her to. "I doubt it was that simple."

It hadn't been. Nothing about saving a traumatized sixteen-year-old girl from human traffickers was simple. Nothing about helping her heal, watching her nightmares, teaching her to trust again had been easy. But I wasn't about to say all that with her kids within earshot.

"Seven o'clock," I repeated instead, touching the brim of an invisible hat before turning to leave.

As I walked out to the truck, I heard Aura's laughter floating through the open windows of the duplex. The sound always hit me square in the chest, a reminder of how close we'd come to never hearing it at all. Some people were worth saving, worth protecting. Aura was one. Amelia and her boys were too.

* * *

My living room had never felt small until I watched Amelia and her boys file in behind Aura. Suddenly, the space I'd occupied alone for years, and later with Aura, seemed cramped, the worn leather furniture and scattered motorcycle memorabilia marking it as unmistakably mine. I'd shoved some laundry into my bedroom and cleared beer bottles from the coffee table but hadn't thought to do much else. It wasn't like I'd been planning a dinner party when I'd woken up yesterday. Now I had two teenagers, their mother, and my daughter crowding around while Aura carried in pizza boxes, her voice filling the silence with cheerful chatter that bounced off the walls.

"Plates are in the kitchen," I said, gesturing vaguely toward the adjoining room. "Drinks in the fridge."

Chase stood awkwardly by the door. Levi had already gravitated toward my bookshelf, fingers trailing over spines with reverent curiosity.

"You can look at them," I told him, noting his surprise. "Books are meant to be read."

Levi pulled one out -- an old motorcycle repair manual. "Thanks," he said quietly.

Amelia hovered between the kitchen and living room, as if unsure where to plant herself. She wore jeans and a simple shirt, her brown hair loose around her shoulders instead of in the ponytail she'd worn earlier. The casual look suited her, softened her edges in a way that made my chest tighten unexpectedly.

"I ordered five different pies," Aura announced, setting the stack of boxes on the coffee table. "Because I have no idea what anyone likes except Dad, and he'll eat anything that doesn't eat him first. Well, and of course, Chase's aversion to pineapple."

"Not true," I grunted, moving to help her. "I draw the line at that anchovy disaster you brought home last month."

"Philistine," she teased, bumping her hip against mine as she passed.

The sudden rumble of a motorcycle outside made everyone tense except Aura and me. I recognized the engine -- my son's Harley, customized with the same pipes I'd had on my first bike. The heavy tread of boots on my porch was followed by the door swinging open without a knock. Sam strode in, his massive frame filling the doorway, dark eyes sweeping the assembled group with surprise.

"The fuck is this, Dad? Intervention?" He grinned to soften the blunt words, but his gaze lingered on Amelia and her boys with undisguised curiosity. His cut bore the same Dixie Reapers patch as mine, though his was newer, the leather not yet weathered by decades of sun and rain. He'd patched in not too long ago and now went by Ghost.

"Pizza night," I said, as if I regularly invited strangers over for dinner. "Amelia and her sons, Chase and Levi. They're staying in one of the duplexes." I gestured to my son. "This is Sam, but outside the walls, he goes by Ghost."

Understanding flickered across Sam's face. He and Aura exchanged a look I couldn't quite interpret before he stepped fully into the room, shutting the door behind him.

"Nice to meet you," he said, his voice deliberately casual as he grabbed a slice directly from the box. "Heard we might have visitors. Didn't expect dinner with Dad." He took a massive bite, cheese stretching from the pizza to his mouth.

Aura rolled her eyes. "Use a plate, you animal."

"What for? Just means more dishes," Sam replied through his mouthful.

"And this is why you're still single," Aura shot back, handing plates to Amelia and the boys.

The easy banter between them broke some of the tension. Chase accepted his plate with a mumbled thanks, selecting a slice of meat-lovers pizza. Levi chose plain cheese, perching on the edge of the couch like he might need to bolt at any moment. Amelia took supreme, her movements graceful as she navigated the unfamiliar space.

"What are we watching?" Sam asked, dropping onto the floor and leaning back against the couch.

"Something with explosions," I suggested. "*Die Hard*?"

"The boys probably want something more

current," Amelia said, looking to Chase and Levi.

"*Die Hard*'s classic," Chase replied with a shrug. "I'm good with that."

I raised an eyebrow, surprised by his taste. Maybe the kid wasn't so bad after all.

We arranged ourselves in the living room as I found the DVD -- one of the few physical copies I still kept around. Aura curled into one end of the couch, Sam sprawled on the floor beside her, while Amelia perched at the opposite end of the couch, maintaining a careful distance from everyone. The boys settled on the floor with their plates, Chase positioned so he could see both the TV and his mother, ever vigilant. I took my recliner, the worn leather creaking a familiar welcome beneath my weight.

The movie provided a buffer against conversation, filling the silence with gunfire and one-liners that had Chase smirking occasionally. I found myself watching the others more than the screen -- Aura mouthing along to her favorite lines, Sam absently spinning his rings as he watched, Levi's analytical expression as he dissected the plot, Amelia's occasional sideways glances in my direction when she thought I wasn't looking.

For a brief moment, the scene almost felt... normal. Like we weren't a random collection of broken people thrown together by circumstance and danger. Like this was just a regular family movie night instead of a fragile truce built on pizza and Bruce Willis.

"So, Levi," Sam said during a quieter scene, "Aura tells me you're good with computers."

Levi nodded, pushing his glasses up his nose. "I like coding."

"You ever think about cyber security? Club could use someone with those skills."

"Sam," I warned, not wanting him recruiting the kid for club business.

He held up his hands. "Just saying. Kid's got talent, or so I've heard."

Levi looked intrigued, but Chase shot Sam a suspicious glare. Always the protector. Always on guard. I knew that stance all too well -- had adopted it myself with Aura when she'd first come to live with me, watching for threats around every corner.

The conversation drifted back to the movie as plates emptied and bodies relaxed deeper into furniture. Even Amelia seemed less tense, a small smile playing at her lips during the funnier scenes. I caught myself staring more than once, drawn to the way the tension had eased from her shoulders, how her eyes crinkled slightly at the corners when she smiled.

"Anyone want more pizza?" Aura asked during a lull in the action.

Murmurs of satisfaction and decline circled the room. Chase set his empty plate on the coffee table, then turned those penetrating green eyes directly on me. His jaw tightened, and something in his expression set alarm bells ringing in my head.

"So are you going to claim my mom as your old lady for real?" he asked, his voice slicing through the room's comfort like a blade.

Exactly what I'd been wondering too. Her request had blindsided me, and I still wasn't able to wrap my head around it. Did I want to claim her and the boys? Start a family? Hell, I already had one, but this was different.

The sudden silence was deafening. Aura's eyes widened to saucers, her mouth forming a perfect "O" of shock. Sam muttered "oh shit" under his breath, setting down his beer with exaggerated care. Levi froze mid-bite, a slice of pizza suspended halfway to his mouth.

Amelia paled, her gaze dropping to her lap, where her fingers twisted together in a white-knuckled grip. "Chase," she said softly, a warning and a plea wrapped in a single word.

The kid didn't back down, gaze still locked on mine. "I want to know what's happening. You brought us here for protection, but I need to understand the terms."

Terms. Like his mother was a contract to be negotiated. Like she was a transaction. The implication sent a flare of anger through me before I caught the undercurrent in his tone -- fear, protectiveness, a desperate need to make sense of the chaos his life had become.

My jaw tightened as I set down my own plate. The room felt suddenly airless, all eyes on me, waiting for my response. How the hell had a simple pizza night devolved so quickly? But I knew the answer. Nothing about this situation was simple. Nothing about Amelia's desperate offer or my conflicted response could be wrapped up neatly like a Hollywood ending.

"Amelia," I said, my voice rougher than I'd intended. "Think we should talk. Outside."

She nodded, rising from the couch with forced composure. Her chin lifted slightly, pride straightening her spine despite the embarrassment staining her cheeks. Without a word, she followed me through the kitchen toward the back door.

Behind us, I heard Aura's stunned voice: "What the actual fuck did I miss?"

The screen door swung shut behind us, cutting off Sam's low response. The night air was cool against my face as we stepped onto the back porch. The compound spread out before us, security lights illuminating patches of ground while leaving others in shadow. Somewhere in the distance, a motorcycle engine revved.

I turned to face Amelia, knowing whatever I said next would change things between us. Knowing her sons were probably pressed against the windows, watching. Knowing my own kids were likely doing the same.

The time for avoiding had passed. Now, we needed to talk.

Chapter Ten

Hammer

I leaned against the porch railing, the weathered wood creaking under my weight. Amelia stood a few feet away, arms crossed over her chest, moonlight catching the strands of her hair as she waited for me to speak. The question her boy had thrown out hung between us like smoke -- thick, suffocating, impossible to ignore.

Crickets chirped in the darkness beyond the porch light's reach. The familiar sounds of the compound at night should have been comforting, but everything felt off-kilter since Amelia had made her desperate proposition.

"Your boy doesn't pull punches," I finally said, breaking the silence.

Amelia sighed, her shoulders drooping slightly. "Chase has been the man of the house for years. Mostly because his father was just an abusive asshole. He's protective." She stepped closer, her voice dropping. "I'm sorry he put you on the spot like that."

"Don't apologize for him looking out for you." I straightened, turning to face her fully. "But we do need to talk about what you proposed earlier."

Her chin tilted up, defiance and vulnerability warring in her expression. "I meant what I said, Hammer. I'll be your old lady in exchange for protection."

"It's not that simple," I said, rougher than I intended. I softened my tone. "Being someone's old lady in this club isn't just for show. It's not something we take lightly."

"I understand --"

"No, you don't." I cut her off, needing her to

grasp the weight of what she was offering. "The Dixie Reapers have a code. When we claim a woman, it's serious. It's a commitment."

The porch light cast shadows across her face, highlighting the wariness in her eyes. She'd learned to be cautious, to expect the worst. Piston had taught her that lesson through pain. I wanted to reach for her hand, to offer some comfort, but kept my distance. She needed to hear me out first.

"In this club, there's no cheating," I continued. "No sleeping around. If you become my old lady, that means something to every man who wears this patch." I tapped my cut. "They'll expect me to handle my business, and they'll expect you to be loyal."

"Piston didn't believe in fidelity," she said quietly. "At least, not for himself."

"I'm not Piston." The words came out harsher than I'd meant, edged with anger at the man who'd hurt her, not at her. "We don't operate that way here. One woman, one man. And divorce isn't an option."

Her eyes widened slightly. "What do you mean?"

"I mean if we do this, we're in it for good. The club doesn't recognize divorces. It's a life commitment." Of course, her being my old lady was the same as marriage in this place. To my brothers anyway. The women sometimes had a different point of view.

Of course, I left off the part where at my age, a lifetime could mean as few as ten years. She'd still be young enough to start fresh and fall in love with someone more appropriate.

Amelia absorbed this, her fingers twisting the hem of her shirt. I could almost see the wheels turning in her head, weighing the cost of safety against the burden of another permanent bond.

"What about..." She hesitated, a flush creeping up her neck. "Physical expectations?"

There it was. The question I'd been dreading. My jaw tightened as I turned slightly away, staring out into the darkness beyond the porch. Now that I was in my sixties, I wasn't the man I'd been at thirty. Hell, not even the man I'd been at fifty.

"I won't force anything," I said gruffly. "I'm not that kind of man. But you should know... sometimes the equipment doesn't work like it used to." The admission burned in my throat, pride making the words difficult. "Age catches up with everyone eventually."

Silence stretched between us. I kept my gaze fixed on the distant security lights rather than watch her reaction. Damn it all to hell. I hadn't planned on discussing my occasional dick problems with a woman I barely knew, but she deserved honesty.

"Hammer." Her voice was softer than I expected. "Look at me."

I turned, bracing myself for pity or disgust. Instead, her expression held something closer to relief.

"After Piston," she said carefully, "the idea of... physical demands... it's not something I'm eager for. If anything, knowing there might be... limitations... makes this easier."

I blinked, taken aback by her candor. "You're not concerned?"

"I'm not looking for a lover, Hammer. I'm looking for safety. A companion, and for someone who won't hurt me or my boys." She stepped closer, close enough that I could smell the faint scent of coffee that clung to her from the diner. "If we eventually become more... intimate... we'll figure it out. But it's not a deal-breaker for me."

Something loosened in my chest -- a tension I hadn't realized I was carrying. It still bothered me, this arrangement based on necessity rather than desire, but knowing she wasn't expecting sexual miracles eased one of my concerns.

"Besides," she added with a small, hesitant smile, "there's more to a relationship than just... that."

I studied her face in the dim light, searching for any sign of deception. All I found was tired honesty and cautious hope. This woman had endured hell with Piston, had risked everything to protect her boys, and now stood before me offering herself as collateral for their safety. The weight of that responsibility settled on my shoulders, heavier than my cut had ever felt.

"If we do this," I said slowly, "it's real to the world. You wear my patch, you're under my protection. The club will treat you as my woman. Your boys will be considered my responsibility. And we'll sleep in the same bed, whether or not anything happens other than sleeping. Are you prepared for that?"

She nodded, a single decisive movement. "Yes."

The simple answer hung between us, neither of us quite believing we were having this conversation. A frog croaked loudly from somewhere nearby, the sound almost comically ordinary against the gravity of the moment.

"All right then," I said, still not entirely convinced this wasn't a massive mistake. "But there's more we need to discuss."

Amelia shifted her weight, angling her body slightly away from me. Her gaze drifted toward the house where her boys were with Aura and Sam. When she looked back at me, her expression had hardened with maternal determination.

"What about my boys?" she asked, her voice steady but thin with tension. "Before we go any further, I need to know how you'll treat them."

The question didn't surprise me. If anything, I'd have thought less of her if she hadn't asked. She crossed her arms over her chest, a physical barrier between us as she waited for my answer. Every line of her body screamed protection -- a mother bear ready to fight for her cubs.

"That's fair," I said, giving her question the respect it deserved. "What exactly are you worried about?"

"Piston..." She hesitated, her jaw tightening. "He was cruel to them. Used them against me. Terrorized them when he was angry or drunk or just bored." Her voice dropped. "Chase tried to protect me from the time he was twelve, but when he was fourteen Piston put him in the hospital. Three broken ribs and a concussion."

Rage flared hot in my chest. No wonder the kid was so vigilant, so protective. He'd been in the trenches, fighting a war he was too young to understand against an enemy he had no hope of defeating.

"I need to know you won't hurt them," Amelia continued, watching my face with the careful assessment of someone who'd learned to read moods to survive. "That you won't treat them like they're in your way or use them to control me."

I straightened up from the railing, meeting her gaze directly. This wasn't a moment for casual postures or half-truths. "I have never laid a hand on a child in anger," I said, my voice steady and firm. "Not my own, not anyone else's. And I never will."

She didn't flinch from my stare, measuring the truth in my words. "Even when Chase challenges you? Because he will. It's how he protects himself -- how he protects all of us."

"The boy's earned the right to be cautious," I acknowledged. "I don't expect blind obedience or instant trust. That would be foolish of me."

I thought of my own journey with Aura and Sam. Fatherhood hadn't come naturally to me, but I'd learned. Made mistakes. Grown. The memories of Aura's early days with me -- her nightmares, her distrust, her slow journey toward healing -- flooded back.

"I raised a daughter who came to me traumatized," I continued. "And a son who tested every boundary I set, even though he was already a grown-ass adult. I'm not perfect. I get angry. I say things I regret sometimes. But I don't solve problems with my fists, especially not with kids, or with women."

Amelia's posture relaxed slightly, but her eyes remained watchful. "And how would you discipline them?"

"They're not little kids, Amelia. Chase is nearly a man, and Levi's not far behind. At their age, it's about guidance more than discipline." I shook my head. "But if you're asking if I'd hit them, the answer is no. Never. Not an option."

"And if they break rules? If they mess up?"

"Then there are consequences. Loss of privileges. Extra chores. Straight talk about making better choices." I shrugged. "Same as with any kid. Once I realized Aura was interested in motorcycles, her punishment was learning how to take a bike apart and put it back together. No phone calls, no TV. Taught her a skill and made her think twice about lying to me."

A ghost of a smile touched her lips before fading. "You'd be firm with them?"

"When needed." I nodded. "I won't pretend to be a pushover. Rules matter, especially in our world. But there's a world of difference between being strict and being unreasonable or abusive. They need room to grow, and that means making mistakes. It's how people learn, even adults."

She absorbed this, her gaze dropping to the weathered boards of the porch. I watched emotions flicker across her face -- hope, doubt, calculation. She was weighing risks, measuring the cost of trusting me against the benefit of protection.

"I've seen how you are with Aura," she said finally. "And with Sam. They respect you, but they're not afraid of you."

"Fear doesn't build respect," I said. "Just resentment."

Amelia's shoulders relaxed, dropping from their defensive hunch. "Chase needs someone to look up to. Someone who isn't..." She trailed off.

"Someone who isn't Piston," I finished for her.

She nodded, her eyes suddenly bright with unshed tears. "And Levi needs someone who sees his value. His father always treated him like he was weak because he prefers computers to fighting."

"The kid's smart as hell," I said. "That's not weakness. That's just a different kind of strength. Wire and his family are practically gods not only in this club, but among others as well. Just don't tell him I said that because I'll fucking deny it."

"So you'll..." She hesitated. "You'll help guide them? Be a positive influence?"

I ran a hand through my silver hair, feeling the

weight of what she was asking. Being an old lady was one thing. Becoming a father figure to two damaged teenagers was something else entirely. But looking at her -- this woman who'd survived hell to protect her sons -- I couldn't find it in me to say no.

"I'll do my best," I promised, wondering if I could actually deliver on that. I hadn't exactly had a hand in raising Sam. Hopefully I sounded more confident than I felt. "Can't guarantee I won't screw up sometimes. But I'll treat them with respect. Give them boundaries and safety. Show them there are men in this world who keep their word."

The tension drained from Amelia's body like water through a sieve. She nodded, her decision visibly solidifying behind her eyes. "Then I still want to do this," she said firmly. "I want to be your old lady."

Despite everything, despite knowing this was an arrangement born of necessity rather than love, something in me responded to her certainty. A warmth I hadn't expected spread through my chest. Maybe she wasn't the only one who needed a companion.

"All right then," I said. "I'll talk to Savior tomorrow. Make it official with the club."

I hoped she didn't come to regret this. I stared out at the darkened compound, listening to the crickets chirp and the sound of a motorcycle somewhere farther down the road. Normally, those sounds would make me feel calm. Tonight, they didn't do shit for the turmoil inside me.

"What will you tell them?" she asked.

"The truth," I replied. "That you're under my protection now. That anyone who has a problem with that can take it up with me." I paused. "The details of our arrangement stay between us."

She nodded, relief evident in the slight tremble of

her exhale. "Thank you, Hammer."

Those simple words of gratitude hit harder than they should have. I wasn't used to being thanked for doing what needed to be done. I looked away, uncomfortable with the naked appreciation in her eyes.

"Don't thank me yet," I muttered. "You might regret signing up with a grumpy old biker."

She shook her head. "I know what I'm getting into."

Did she? Did either of us? My stomach knotted with conflicting emotions -- relief that she still wanted this arrangement despite my blunt honesty, worry about what I was committing to, and an unexpected flutter of something that felt dangerously like anticipation.

I was sixty-one years old, had seen too much, done too much. I'd long ago accepted that my remaining years would be spent alone except for occasional visits from Aura and Sam. Assuming Aura ever moved out. Now suddenly I had an instant family -- a woman and two teenage boys with their own set of trauma and baggage.

If Satan himself had appeared and offered me a deal like this a week ago, I'd have told him to go fuck himself. Yet here I stood, agreeing to it all, because something in Amelia's determined brown eyes made me want to be the man she needed me to be.

The sudden rustling from the bushes near the porch shattered our moment of understanding. My body tensed instantly, decades of survival instincts kicking in before my brain could process the sound. I moved without thinking, positioning myself between Amelia and the potential threat, my hand automatically reaching for the gun that wasn't there -- I'd left it inside, not expecting trouble in our own compound.

"Stay behind me," I growled, my voice dropping to a harsh whisper.

Amelia froze, her eyes widening as they fixed on the dancing shadows beneath the ornamental shrubs that lined my porch. The rustling came again, followed by what sounded suspiciously like a muffled curse.

"Who's there?" I demanded, moving toward the edge of the porch, every sense on high alert. My mind raced through possibilities -- a Prospect overstepping boundaries, one of Piston's men somehow breaching our security, an animal. But animals didn't swear.

No answer came, but the bushes trembled slightly. I descended the three wooden steps with deliberate slowness, my feet making no sound on the weathered boards. Years in prison had taught me to move silently when needed, to approach threats without telegraphing my intentions.

"Hammer --" Amelia started, her voice tight with apprehension.

I held up one hand, signaling her to stay put. The security lights cast long shadows across the yard, but the area beneath the bushes remained stubbornly dark. As I approached, I caught the faintest gleam of something reflective -- metal, or maybe glass.

In one swift motion, I lunged forward, grabbing a fistful of branches and yanking them aside to reveal the source of the disturbance. Two figures huddled in the shadows, caught in the act of eavesdropping.

"What the actual fuck?" I snarled, recognizing them immediately.

Atlas crouched closest to me, his lanky frame folded awkwardly in the dirt, a pair of earbuds dangling around his neck. Beside him, Lavender kneeled in the mulch, her purple-streaked hair instantly recognizable even in the dim light. Wire's kid and his mother, of all people.

"Hey, Hammer," Atlas said, a sheepish grin spreading across his face. "Nice night, huh?"

"Don't 'nice night' me, boy," I growled, anger surging through me. "What the hell are you doing hiding in my bushes?"

Lavender at least had the decency to look embarrassed, a flush creeping up her neck as she brushed dirt from her knees. "We were just passing by," she offered lamely.

"With listening devices?" I pointed to the small directional microphone partially hidden in Atlas's jacket.

"Research project," Atlas tried, the lie so transparent it would have been comical under different circumstances.

I reached down, grabbed the front of his shirt, and hauled him to his feet. "Try again."

Atlas's easy smile faltered under my glare. "Okay, okay. We might have been… gathering intel."

"Eavesdropping," I corrected flatly.

"Such a harsh word," Atlas muttered.

Behind me, I heard Amelia's sharp intake of breath as she realized what was happening. I glanced back to see her standing rigid on the porch, her face flushing dark with embarrassment as she processed how much of our private conversation these two might have overheard.

"Inside," I ordered, releasing Atlas's shirt with a small shove toward the steps. "Both of you."

Lavender rose with as much dignity as she could muster, brushing leaves from her jeans. "Hammer, it's not what you think --"

"Save it," I cut her off. "You can explain to my

face instead of sneaking around like teenagers."

"Technically, I *am* a teenager," Atlas pointed out, then immediately held up his hands in surrender when I turned my glare on him. "Right, inside. Going now."

I waited until they'd trudged up the steps, Amelia stepping aside to let them pass. The flush of embarrassment hadn't left her face, and she wouldn't look at me. This was exactly what she didn't need -- more people knowing the private details of our arrangement, especially the parts about my aging equipment.

"I'm sorry," I murmured to her as I climbed the steps. "I'll handle this."

She nodded stiffly, arms wrapped around herself protectively. "How much did they hear?"

"We'll find out," I promised, holding the door open for her.

Inside, Atlas and Lavender stood awkwardly in my living room, the movie still playing on the TV while Aura, Sam, and the boys stared at them in confusion. Aura raised an eyebrow at me in silent question.

"Everyone out," I commanded. "Except these two." I pointed at Atlas and Lavender.

"Dad?" Aura started.

"Not now, sweetheart. Family movie night's over." My tone left no room for argument.

Aura's eyes narrowed, but she nodded. "Come on, guys. Let's get you back to the duplex." She ushered Chase and Levi toward the door, Sam following behind with a curious backward glance.

When the door closed behind them, I turned to our unwanted audience. "Sit."

They sat on the edge of my couch, looking about as comfortable as prisoners awaiting sentencing.

Which, in a way, they were.

"Start talking," I demanded, remaining standing to maintain the advantage of height. "And don't bother lying. I want to know exactly what you heard and why you were listening."

Atlas exchanged a glance with his mother before speaking. "We heard the Devil's Minions were looking for someone new in town. Wire -- Dad -- asked us to gather information. He figured they were looking for Ms. Decker and her sons. When we saw you and Ms. Decker go outside for a private talk, we thought..." He trailed off.

"You thought you'd stick your nose where it doesn't belong," I finished for him. I hadn't thought to call Wire when I'd gone to pick up Amelia. Although, I had told the Pres and I'd assumed he'd tell whoever needed to know.

"It's our job to know things," Lavender said, her voice steady despite her clear discomfort. "Information keeps the club safe."

"So how much did you hear?" Amelia asked quietly from where she stood near the door, as if ready to bolt at any moment.

Atlas had the grace to look down. "Pretty much everything."

My stomach knotted tighter. Everything. My admission about erectile issues. Our agreement about her being my old lady for protection. Everything.

"That information doesn't leave this room," I said, my voice deadly quiet. "Not a word. To anyone."

Atlas nodded quickly, but something in his expression set off warning bells in my head. The kid was Wire's son, after all, with all of his father's hacking skills and his mother's flair for drama. Worse, he had none of Wire's discretion.

"I mean it, Atlas," I pressed. "Not a whisper. Not a text. Not a hint on any of those computer systems you're so good at breaking into."

"I wouldn't --" he started to protest.

"You would," I cut him off. "Without even realizing it. You think everything's a game, kid. This isn't. This is Amelia's life. Her boys' safety."

Lavender placed a restraining hand on her son's arm. "We understand, Hammer. This stays confidential."

But the damage was already done. These two knew about our arrangement -- knew it wasn't a love match, knew about my physical limitations, knew everything. And in a club like ours, information was as valuable as currency. Not to mention, bikers gossiped worse than little old ladies.

"Go," I said finally. "And if I hear one word about this circulating, I'll know exactly where it came from."

They left quickly, Atlas casting one last curious glance at Amelia before his mother hustled him out the door. When they were gone, I turned to find Amelia staring at me, her face a mixture of embarrassment and concern.

"How bad is this?" she asked softly.

I wished I could reassure her, but honesty had become the foundation of whatever we were building. "Bad enough," I admitted. "Atlas is brilliant with computers, but he's got a mouth on him. And access to every security system in the compound."

"So he could… what? Tell everyone about us?"

"About everything," I confirmed, my stomach turning at the thought of the whole club knowing my business. Knowing I'd agreed to claim a woman who didn't really want me. Knowing about my damn dick problems.

Amelia sank onto the couch, shoulders slumping. "Great. We haven't even made it official, and I'm already causing you problems."

"Hey." I moved to sit beside her, not touching but close enough that she could feel my presence. "This isn't on you. Those two shouldn't have been snooping. Especially Lavender. You'd think a grown-ass woman would know better."

She nodded, but the worry didn't leave her eyes. Her gaze drifted to the window where Atlas and Lavender had disappeared into the night. "What do we do now?"

I had no easy answer. All I knew was that our private arrangement had just gained an audience, and I couldn't shake the feeling that our carefully constructed plan was already beginning to unravel.

Chapter Eleven

Hammer

Amelia hadn't been ready to go back to the duplex, so I'd handed her the TV remote and hidden myself in my home office. Not that I used it frequently, but Savior had assigned me tasks that were less on the physical side. Sadly, it had required me to learn more about computers than I'd ever wanted to know.

The computer screen cast an eerie blue glow across my office, the only light besides the security light outside my window. My eyes burned from staring at records for the past hour. The Amelia situation had my mind spinning, and work was my only refuge. I scrolled through the club's financial statements, checking supply orders against payments, when a file I didn't recognize appeared in my email. "Marriage Certificate - Hammer and Amelia Decker" stared back at me in bold text. My finger froze over the mouse. What the hell was this?

I clicked the file open, my heartbeat suddenly loud in my ears. A legitimate-looking marriage certificate filled my screen, complete with the state seal and official signatures. My name -- not my road name, but my legal name -- sat next to Amelia's, both our signatures at the bottom. Signatures I sure as fuck didn't remember providing.

"What the fuck?" I growled, leaning closer as if proximity might reveal this as some elaborate prank.

But the document looked genuine. The county clerk's signature, the date stamp from just three hours ago, the official seal watermarked in the background -- all of it perfect. Too perfect.

My weathered hands gripped the edge of the desk until my knuckles whitened. This wasn't just a prank. This was forgery. This was identity theft. This was illegal as hell. And I had a pretty Goddamn good idea who was behind it.

The rage building in my chest felt like molten lead. I'd been violated in a way that went beyond physical -- someone had stolen my identity, my agency, my right to choose. After spending years behind bars with no freedom, I guarded what little control I had left with fierce determination. And now this punk kid had decided to play God with my life.

"You like it?" Atlas's voice came from the doorway, casual as if he'd just asked about the fucking weather.

I turned slowly, forcing my hands to release their death grip on the desk. Atlas lounged against the doorframe, a satisfied smirk playing on his lips. His lanky frame cast a long shadow across my office floor, but he looked smaller somehow -- younger and stupider than I'd ever noticed before.

"You've got five seconds to explain why I shouldn't drag your ass to Savior for this," I said, my voice deadly quiet. "And how the fuck did you get into my house?"

Atlas sauntered into my office like he owned it, dropping into the chair across from my desk. That confidence of youth -- the kind that made him think he was untouchable. I'd seen it before. Hell, I'd had it myself once, before life and prison beat it out of me.

"You needed the push," he said, folding his arms behind his head. "Besides, you two are good together."

"It's forgery," I growled. "It's illegal. It's a fucking breach of trust."

"It's protection," Atlas countered, leaning forward now, his expression growing serious. "I heard everything, remember? She asked to be your old lady.

You agreed to talk to Savior. This just… expedites things."

"This just commits multiple felonies," I corrected him, shoving back from the desk and standing. I might not be in my prime, but I still towered over the kid. "Marriage fraud. Identity theft. Forgery. Hacking government systems. You want me to continue?"

Atlas shrugged, but I caught the slight wariness that crept into his posture. "The Devil's Minions have people everywhere. Mom and I did some digging. They've got contacts in three state DMVs, two sheriff's departments, and at least one county clerk's office. This makes it official in every database they might check. Makes her untouchable."

My jaw clenched so tight I thought it might crack. The worst part was the little shit had a point. A legal marriage certificate offered Amelia protection that went beyond the club's reach. It changed her name in official records. It created a paper trail that would make it harder for Piston to kidnap her.

"You had no right," I said, the words grinding between my teeth.

"Never claimed to," Atlas replied, his cockiness returning. "But it's done now. And it's solid work. Mom helped with the backdating and the digital fingerprints. Even if someone investigates, they'll find a properly filed license from last week, witnesses, everything."

"Witnesses?" The word came out harsher than I intended.

"Ghost and Aura," Atlas said, nodding as if this made perfect sense. "Your son and daughter. We didn't forge their signatures -- they gave permission."

That revelation hit like a sucker punch. Sam and Aura knew about this? Were part of it? The betrayal cut deeper than I wanted to admit. It wasn't the first time I'd felt the sting of betrayal, but from my own kids? That fucking hurt.

"This isn't a fucking game, kid," I said, my voice dropping lower. "These are people's lives. My life. Amelia's life."

"Exactly." Atlas nodded, his expression earnest now. "Piston will kill her if he finds her. You know it, I know it, the whole club knows it. This gives her the best chance at staying safe. Now, if he comes for her -- no, *when* he comes for her -- you have a legal right to protect her and her sons."

I turned back to the screen, staring at the certificate. My name next to hers. Husband and wife. The words felt foreign, almost ridiculous. I hadn't been married in all my sixty-plus years and never thought I would be.

"What gives you the right to decide this for us?" I asked finally.

Atlas sat forward, his usual smugness replaced by something that looked almost like sincerity. "Look, I've seen the way you look at her when she's not watching, and I don't just mean tonight. I've been observing the two of you for the last few weeks."

"You don't know what you're talking about," I muttered, uncomfortable with the direction this conversation had taken.

"Maybe not," Atlas conceded, rising from the chair. "But I know what I saw. And I know what needs to be done to keep her and those boys safe. The certificate's legit, Hammer. In every database that matters. As far as the state is concerned, you two got married last week."

I rubbed a hand over my face. The anger was still there, burning beneath the surface, but it had begun to mix with a grudging acknowledgment that the kid's hacker skills might have actually helped. If Piston was searching records for Amelia Decker, he wouldn't find her anymore. She was Amelia Williams now, at least on paper. The fucker might know she was in this town, but he wouldn't be able to find her exact location. He'd know where she worked, but even if someone followed her to the compound, he'd have no way of finding out which house she lived in.

"You pull something like this again," I said finally, my voice low and controlled, "and there won't be a computer system in the world that can protect you from me. We clear?"

The threat wasn't empty, and Atlas knew it. His Adam's apple bobbed as he swallowed. "Crystal," he said, some of the smugness finally leaving his expression.

"I still need to tell Amelia," I said, turning back to the screen. "This affects her more than anyone."

"I figured you would," Atlas said, backing toward the door. "That's why I came to you first. Thought you should be the one to break the news to your wife. Oh. And as for how I got in, you left your back door unlocked. I snuck past Amelia and came straight here."

Before I could respond, movement in the doorway caught my attention. My stomach dropped as I saw who stood there, her expression a mixture of confusion and concern. *Shit*. My heart thundered in my chest and I scrambled to come up with something to say.

Amelia. Her gaze flicked between me and Atlas then back again. How much had she heard? The office suddenly felt too small, the air too thick with tension and unspoken words. Atlas had the sense to straighten up, the smirk fading from his face as he recognized the gravity of the situation.

"I heard shouting," Amelia said, her voice soft but steady. "Is everything okay?"

I struggled to find the right words. How exactly do you tell a woman you've barely known for weeks that you're suddenly legally married to her because some hacker kid decided to play matchmaker?

"Show her," Atlas said, nodding toward my computer screen.

I hesitated, then turned the monitor so Amelia could see it. She stepped closer, her forehead creasing as she took in the document. For a moment, she just stared, her expression unreadable. Then she raised her eyes to mine, a question in them that I couldn't quite interpret.

"What is this?" she asked, though I suspected she already knew.

"According to every government database in the country," I said, not bothering to hide the edge in my voice, "we've been married for a week."

Her gaze shifted to Atlas, who had the decency to look slightly less smug now. "You did this?" she asked him.

Atlas nodded, shoving his hands into his pockets. "Heard you needed protection. Marriage is the strongest legal bond there is. Changes your name in every system. Makes you harder to find. And harder for you to disappear."

I knew that last part was the most important right now. Watching Amelia, I expected anger, outrage, perhaps tears. What I didn't expect was the slow nod of acceptance that came instead. Amelia moved to my side, close enough that I could smell the faint trace of floral shampoo in her hair. To my surprise, she placed her hand gently on my forearm, her fingers warm through the fabric of my shirt.

"It's fine," she said softly. "It doesn't change anything."

The simple touch sent an unexpected jolt through me. When was the last time a woman had touched me with such casual intimacy? Her hand on my arm felt both foreign and oddly right, like a puzzle piece I hadn't realized was missing.

"Fine?" I repeated, my voice rougher than I intended. "Amelia, this isn't just some club ceremony. This is a legal document. It means --"

"It means I'm officially under your protection," she finished. "It means Piston can't find me under my old name. It means my boys are safer." She squeezed my arm gently. "Isn't that what we agreed to anyway?"

Her calm acceptance left me off-balance. I'd been prepared to fight, to defend her honor against this invasion of privacy. Instead, she was the one steadying me.

Atlas watched our interaction, his earlier satisfaction returning. "See? You two are good together. I told you."

I shot him a glare that would have made most men shrink back, but the kid just grinned wider. In that moment, he reminded me so much of his father it was almost painful -- Wire had always been too smart for his own good too.

"How did you even pull this off?" Amelia asked him, her hand still resting on my arm like it belonged there.

Atlas leaned against the desk, his enthusiasm for explaining his technical prowess overriding any remaining caution. "Mom helped with the state database access. We created the original filing last week -- backdated, of course -- with all the proper digital signatures. Then we inserted it into the county records database with a timestamp and clerk verification."

"And the witnesses?" I asked, still trying to process that Sam and Aura had been part of this conspiracy.

"Your kids signed digitally," Atlas confirmed. "Ghost -- I mean Sam -- said, and I quote, 'About damn time the old man has someone to keep him in line.'"

The betrayal stung anew. My own children had gone behind my back, played a part in this deception. But beneath the sting was something else -- a warmth I didn't want to acknowledge. They wanted this for me. Wanted me to have someone.

"What about my boys?" Amelia asked, the first hint of concern entering her voice. "How does this affect them legally?"

Atlas shrugged. "They're minors. Their mother got married. Nothing really changes for them officially. Except now they're Hammer's stepsons and not just the kids of his girlfriend."

Amelia nodded, her expression thoughtful. The practicality of her response struck me again. She wasn't caught up in the violation of it all -- she was focused on what mattered. Protection. Safety. Her boys.

I considered our options. The certificate was done. The hack was complete. Fighting it might actually create more problems than it solved -- draw attention, leave digital traces that could be followed. And despite my anger at the invasion, I couldn't deny the effectiveness of what Atlas had accomplished. Amelia Decker had disappeared. Amelia Williams now existed in her place.

"Amelia," I said, turning to face her fully. "We need to talk about what this means for us. For real."

She nodded, her hand finally leaving my arm. I felt its absence immediately, like a cool draft where warmth had been.

"It means we need to make this look legitimate," she said, her voice steady despite the gravity of what she was suggesting. "For the protection to work, we need to appear to be an actual couple."

"You'd need to live at my place," I said bluntly. "Not the duplex. And while that was only supposed to be for tonight anyway, it means you definitely have to move in here tomorrow."

"I know." Her gaze didn't waver. "I'll explain it to the boys. Chase might be difficult at first, but he'll understand eventually."

"I'll help you and the boys pack in the morning," I told her, the decision solidifying as I spoke the words.

Atlas watched our exchange with undisguised satisfaction, like a kid who'd just gotten away with something major. Which, I supposed, he had.

"I should go," he said, inching toward the door. "Dad's probably wondering where I am."

"Tell your father we'll be having words," I growled, but with less heat than before. Part of me -- a part I wasn't ready to examine too closely -- was almost grateful for the kid's interference.

Atlas gave a mock salute and slipped out, leaving Amelia and me alone with the glowing screen between us. The marriage certificate seemed to take up more space than it should, its official seals and signatures a weight I could almost physically feel.

I turned back to the computer, staring at the document that had so fundamentally altered our arrangement. My gaze lingered on our names, side by side in official print.

"We can figure this out," Amelia said quietly, mistaking my silence for regret. "Take it one day at a time."

I nodded, unable to articulate the confusion of emotions churning inside me. And I had the feeling this forced arrangement might not be the worst thing that had ever happened to me.

"One day at a time," I agreed, closing the file and shutting down the computer.

Tomorrow, Amelia and her boys would move into my home. Tomorrow, I would officially have a "wife" for the first time. Tomorrow, everything would change.

But tonight, as I gave Amelia a ride back to the duplex where her sons waited, all I could think about was the gentle pressure of her hand on my arm, and how it had anchored me when I needed it most.

Chapter Twelve

Amelia

The dresser drawers felt too empty as I unpacked our meager belongings. I should have bought more things, but life had been so chaotic and uncertain, I hadn't wanted to risk leaving things behind if we had to suddenly run again. My clothes barely filled a quarter of the space Hammer had cleared for me, hanging limp and lonely in the closet like they knew they didn't belong. I smoothed my hand over the bed -- our bed now, according to a marriage certificate neither of us had actually signed. The thought sent a flutter of unease through my stomach as I tucked freshly washed sheets around the mattress, determined to at least make myself useful in this strange new arrangement.

"Mom?" Levi appeared in the doorway, his laptop clutched to his chest like a shield. "Where should I set up my computer?"

"Didn't Hammer say you had a desk in your room?"

Levi nodded, hesitating. "This is weird, right? Like, really weird."

I forced a smile I didn't feel. "It's a new start for us, baby. Something we've needed for a while."

He disappeared down the hall, his footsteps fading. I listened for Hammer's low rumble, the soft exchange of voices. He'd been almost painfully polite all morning, helping us move our few possessions, showing the boys their rooms, giving me space in his closet and dresser. The perfect gentleman. The perfect stranger who was now my husband.

I scrubbed the bathroom until my fingers were raw, reorganized his kitchen cabinets, and vacuumed every inch of carpet. By noon, I'd almost exhausted myself enough to forget how awkward breakfast had been -- Hammer reading his newspaper, Chase sullen and silent, Levi hunched over his cereal. The only sound had been spoons against bowls and the occasional rustle of paper.

I was elbow-deep in scrubbing the oven when the front door slammed open. Chase's voice, actually animated for once, followed by female laughter I recognized as Aura's. I straightened up, wiping my hands on a dishcloth as they tumbled into the kitchen.

"Mom, Aura's going to show us the garage," Chase announced. "She says Hammer has everything we need to work on pretty much any vehicle."

Aura grinned at me, dropping an easy arm around Chase's shoulders. At sixteen, my son towered over her, but something about Aura's confidence made her seem larger than life. "Hope you don't mind," she said. "Thought the boys could use a proper tour of the house and the compound."

Before I could respond, Levi appeared, drawn by the commotion. "Can I come too?"

"Hell yeah," Aura replied, grabbing him in a side hug. "The more the merrier. You ever seen the inside of a Harley engine?" When Levi shook his head, her grin widened. "You're in for a treat, kid. Dad has been working on one in the garage for a while now."

They were out the door in a whirlwind of energy, leaving me alone with my rubber gloves and oven cleaner. I sank onto a kitchen chair, suddenly exhausted by the effort of pretending everything was normal. The boys hadn't smiled like that in ages. Not with me. Not in our old life.

I found them an hour later in Hammer's garage, a cavernous space that smelled of oil and metal. From the doorway, I watched unseen as Aura demonstrated something on a gleaming motorcycle, her tattoo-covered arm gesturing expressively while Chase and Levi leaned in, completely absorbed. Their faces were smudged with grease, Levi's glasses slightly askew, but they were happy.

"They're naturals." Hammer's voice came from behind me, making me jump.

I hadn't heard him approach, hadn't realized he was home. He stood at my shoulder, his bulk blocking the sunlight, casting me in his shadow.

"Aura's good with them," I said, shifting slightly to put space between us.

He nodded, his gaze fixed on the scene in the garage. "She never had brothers. Always wanted some. I guess Sam doesn't count since he's nearly twice her age."

"And now she has two younger siblings," I replied.

Hammer's expression didn't change, but something in his posture tightened. "Right."

That evening, I cooked like my life depended on it. Pot roast, mashed potatoes, fresh rolls, green beans with almonds. I'd used most of my tip money from the diner on groceries, determined to prove my worth. The boys set the table without being asked, still buzzing with excitement from their afternoon with Aura. They chattered about engines and tools, words I barely understood flowing easily between them.

Hammer arrived late, just as I was taking the roast from the oven. He'd been at a club meeting, or so he'd said, though I suspected he was avoiding coming home to the awkward domestic scene I'd created. His eyes widened slightly at the spread on the table, something unreadable flickering across his weathered face.

"Figured everyone would be hungry after working so hard all day," I said, trying to sound casual.

"Starving," Chase confirmed, already loading his plate.

Hammer nodded his thanks, taking his seat at the head of the table. I noticed he'd showered at the clubhouse -- his silver hair was still damp, his beard freshly trimmed. He'd changed clothes too, wearing a clean T-shirt instead of the work clothes he'd had on earlier. The effort touched something in me, a flutter of warmth I tried to ignore.

The next evening was the same -- Aura arriving after the boys were out of school to whisk them away to the garage, Hammer finding reasons to stay at the clubhouse, me cooking another elaborate meal that received quiet appreciation but little conversation. By the third day, the pattern was firmly established. Aura had become the pied piper, leading my sons into a world of motorcycles and mechanics that they eagerly embraced, while Hammer and I circled each other like wary animals, careful never to get too close.

I watched him sometimes when he thought I wasn't looking -- the way his large hands cradled his coffee mug in the morning, how his eyes crinkled at the corners when Aura made him laugh, the silver in his beard catching the light. I'd catch him watching me too, his gaze quickly shifting away when I turned.

On the fourth night, Aura seemed to have caught on to the tension. She'd brought a cake from town, insisting we needed to celebrate our first week as a "family." The word hung in the air between Hammer and me, loaded with meanings neither of us was ready to examine.

"You should've seen Levi today," she said, passing the potatoes to Chase. "Kid figured out what was wrong with that Softail we've been struggling with for days. Has an ear for engines, I swear."

Levi blushed, ducking his head at the praise. "It was just the timing. Didn't sound right."

"Bullshit," Aura said cheerfully. "It was impressive as hell and you know it. Dad, tell him."

Hammer nodded, the corner of his mouth lifting slightly. "Kid's got talent," he agreed. "Heard the knock right away."

The pride in Levi's eyes made my throat tighten. How long had it been since someone had appreciated his quiet intelligence instead of mocking it? Sure, he'd been more hands-on with the motorcycles than he'd been with anything before, but he was still more of a computer geek.

After dinner, Hammer disappeared to his office while I cleaned up. From the hallway door, I could see him hunched over his desk, lit up by his desk lamp, deliberately putting distance between us. I understood his reluctance -- this marriage wasn't what either of us had planned -- but the constant avoidance was starting to sting. We'd kissed accidentally the other day, just once, and he didn't seem to be interested in repeating it. It had only been a peck, over within an instant. Mostly because I'd done it without thinking. I hadn't even realized what I was doing until it was too late. Still… It apparently spooked him. I wasn't a naive girl anymore, hadn't been even when I'd met Piston. But somehow, Hammer's quiet distance hurt more than Piston's loud disdain ever had.

Later, I found him on the back porch, nursing a beer as he stared out at the dark compound. I stepped outside, the night air cool against my skin. Though I couldn't see his eyes in the shadow, I felt them on me, tracing my outline in the yellow porch light.

"Boys asleep?" he asked, his voice low and rough.

I nodded, wrapping my arms around myself. "Exhausted from the garage. Aura's working them hard."

"She likes having them around."

"They like her too." I hesitated. "They like you, too, even if they don't say it."

Hammer took a long pull from his beer, his throat working as he swallowed. "I've got an early start tomorrow," he said, not acknowledging my comment. "Club business."

"Right," I said, trying to hide my disappointment. Another day of him finding reasons to be anywhere but home with me. "I'll see you tomorrow, then."

As I turned to go inside, I caught his reflection in the window -- the way his gaze followed me, lingering longer than necessary. Maybe there was hope for us yet. Perhaps this arrangement could become something real, if only one of us would be brave enough to take the first step.

* * *

The next night, Aura made the announcement halfway through dinner, casually dropping it between bites of the lasagna I'd spent all afternoon perfecting. "So I was thinking," she said, twirling her fork in the air, "the boys haven't really seen much of town yet. Thought I'd take them out tonight, show them the non-biker side of things." She winked at Chase, who perked up immediately. "There's a pretty decent arcade, and I know for a fact Levi would destroy everyone at the racing games."

My fork froze halfway to my mouth. "Out? Tonight?" The thought of my boys beyond the compound's gates sent a chill through me. At least at school, there were protocols in place. I knew someone couldn't walk in and take them. But being out in public? The Devil's Minions Prospect was still out there somewhere, watching, waiting. "I don't think that's --"

"Don't worry," Aura cut in, reading my expression. "Sam's coming too. Full colors, full protection. Nobody's gonna mess with your boys while big brother Ghost is around."

I glanced at Hammer, looking for guidance, for reassurance. He nodded once, his beard shifting against his jaw. "Sam won't let anything happen to them," he said, his voice a low rumble that somehow soothed the panic rising in my chest. "And Aura's no slouch herself."

Aura grinned, flexing her tattooed arm. "Damn straight. Been kicking ass since I was sixteen."

Levi's eyes were already bright with excitement, his perpetual caution melting away at the prospect of a normal teenage outing. "Can we go, Mom? Please?"

How long had it been since my youngest had asked for anything with such open enthusiasm? Since either of my boys had looked forward to something so simple as an evening at an arcade? The realization that Piston had robbed them of these normal experiences made my decision for me.

"All right," I relented, setting my fork down. "But phones on, check in every hour, and --"

"Home by eleven," Chase finished for me, already on his feet. It looked like he'd known I was going to give him a curfew. "Thanks, Mom."

Within twenty minutes, they were gone -- Aura

herding my boys out the door with promises of dessert and video games, Sam waiting outside on his bike, his imposing figure a comfort rather than a threat. The front door closed behind them, and suddenly the house seemed unnaturally quiet, the silence heavy between Hammer and me.

I stared at the half-eaten lasagna, the scattered plates, anything to avoid looking directly at Hammer. For the first time since we'd moved in, we were truly alone. No kids as buffers. No easy excuses to retreat to separate corners.

"Guess we should clean up," I said, my voice too high, too bright as I stood and began gathering plates.

Hammer pushed back from the table, the chair legs scraping against the floor. "I'll help," he offered, carrying his and Aura's plates to the sink.

We moved around each other in the kitchen, a careful dance of proximity and avoidance. His broad shoulder brushed mine as he reached for a sponge, and I nearly dropped the glass I was holding. Every nerve ending seemed hypersensitive to his presence -- the subtle scent of motor oil and pine soap that clung to him, the quiet rhythm of his breathing, the warmth radiating from his body in the narrow space between the sink and counter.

"Boys seem to be settling in," he said after a stretch of silence, rinsing a plate before handing it to me to dry. "Chase knew his way around a carburetor today. Aura was impressed."

I nodded, focusing intently on drying the plate. "Levi too. Never seen him so interested in anything that wasn't connected to a power source before."

Hammer chuckled, the sound warm and unexpectedly intimate in the quiet kitchen. "Kid's smart. Thinks things through."

"And Chase?" I couldn't help asking.

Hammer's hands stilled in the soapy water. "He reminds me of me," he said quietly. "Always watching. Always ready for trouble. Carrying the weight of everyone else."

Something about the simple honesty in his voice made my chest tighten. I'd spent the last five days watching him with my boys -- the way he gave Chase space but stayed available, how he asked Levi thoughtful questions about his computer projects, respecting their boundaries while gradually earning their trust. It was so different from Piston's approach of demanding immediate obedience through fear.

"Thank you," I said, the words inadequate for everything I wanted to express. "For being patient with them. With all of us."

Hammer shrugged, passing me another dish. "Nothing to thank me for."

We continued washing up, the silence more companionable now. I became acutely aware of his movements -- the flex of his forearms as he scrubbed a stubborn bit of lasagna, the slight furrow of concentration between his brows, the careful way he handled my favorite coffee mug. This close, I could see the individual strands of silver in his beard, the crow's feet fanning from the corners of his eyes, evidence of a life fully lived.

"You've been good for them too," he said suddenly. "Aura. Even Sam. Having you all here, it's... different."

"Different good or different bad?" I asked, half-joking, half-terrified of his answer.

He paused and looked at me full-on. "Good. Definitely good."

I reached for the pot he'd been washing and his

large hand covered mine as I fumbled the pot. Neither of us pulled away. His skin was warm, rough with calluses, solid against mine. I froze, hardly daring to breathe as our gazes locked. Something shifted in his expression -- a softening, a hunger quickly suppressed.

"Amelia," he said, my name like gravel in his throat.

I don't know which of us moved first. Maybe we both did. One moment we were standing with our hands touching, the next his lips were on mine, tentative at first, then with growing urgency. His beard was softer than I'd imagined, tickling my skin as his mouth claimed mine. I gasped against him, my hands -- still damp from the dishes -- clutching his shirt, pulling him closer.

The kiss deepened, his tongue stroking mine, drawing a moan from somewhere deep in my chest. He clasped my waist, lifting me slightly to set me on the counter, positioning himself between my legs. I wrapped my arms around his neck, fingers threading through his silver hair, holding him to me like he was my lifeline, and maybe he was.

Then, abruptly, he pulled back, breathing hard. His eyes were dark with desire, but something else flickered there too -- doubt, hesitation.

"We shouldn't," he said, his voice rough. "This isn't -- I'm not --"

"Not what?" I asked, not letting him step away, my legs still loosely wrapped around his waist.

His jaw tightened. "I'm too old for you, Amelia. Too damaged. Got too much history." He shook his head. "Don't want to take advantage."

I couldn't help the laugh that escaped me, short and incredulous. "Take advantage? I'm thirty-six, Hammer, not sixteen. I know what I want." I reached for him again, but he stepped back, disentangling himself from my grasp.

"You want safety," he corrected, his voice gentler now. "Protection for your boys. That's why we're doing this."

"Maybe at first," I admitted. "But now I want…" I hesitated, struggling to put into words the tangled mess of emotions he evoked in me. Desire, yes, but also something deeper, more frightening. "I want you," I finished simply. "Age doesn't matter to me."

He shook his head, putting more distance between us. "It should. This isn't right."

"Why not? Because you're older? Because we didn't choose this marriage?"

"Because," he said, turning away to grip the edge of the sink, knuckles white with tension, "you deserve better than a worn-out old biker who can't even guarantee he'll be able to satisfy you."

The raw honesty in his voice made my throat tighten. I slid off the counter, moving to stand beside him, not touching but close enough to feel the heat from his body. "Hammer," I said softly. "Look at me."

He turned, albeit reluctantly. I reached up, my fingers tracing the outline of his beard, the strong line of his jaw, the furrow between his brows.

"I want this," I whispered. "I want you. Not because I need protection or because I'm grateful. Because when you look at me, I feel seen for the first time in years."

For a moment, I thought he might give in. His expression softened, his body leaning almost imperceptibly toward mine. Then he straightened, gently removing my hand from his face.

"I need time," he said, his voice strained. "If we do this -- if we really do this -- I want it to be right. Not rushed. Not confused with everything else."

Before I could respond, he stepped back, running a hand through his silver hair. "I should check in with Savior," he said, already moving toward the door. "Make sure the boys are okay. I'm sure Sam asked for backup to go with them, even if the kids don't realize it."

I watched him go, frustration and understanding warring within me. He was being honorable, careful, everything Piston had never been. But standing alone in the kitchen, my body still humming with unfulfilled desire, honor felt like a cold comfort.

* * *

I heard the shower running when I finally gathered enough courage to enter the bedroom. After our kitchen encounter, Hammer had disappeared to his office, then to the clubhouse, returning late enough that I'd almost given up waiting. Now, I stood frozen by the dresser, nightgown clutched to my chest, listening to the water beat against the tile and wondering how we were supposed to navigate this -- sharing a bed with a man I'd kissed hours ago, who had pulled away despite wanting more. The marriage certificate might be fake, but the tension between us was painfully real.

The bathroom door opened in a cloud of steam, and Hammer stepped out, a towel wrapped around his waist. We both froze, caught in an awkward tableau. Droplets of water clung to his silver chest hair, trailing down to his stomach, which was solid but softened slightly with age. Scars marked his skin -- some faded white with time, others still pink and angry. The Dixie Reapers patch tattooed over his heart seemed almost to pulse with each beat.

"Sorry," he muttered, grabbing clothes from his

dresser. "Thought you'd be in the kitchen or watching a movie."

I shook my head, clutching my nightgown tighter. "The boys just texted. They're on their way home."

He nodded, retreating back to the bathroom with a pair of sweatpants and a T-shirt. When he emerged again, fully clothed, some of the tension had left his shoulders, though he still avoided looking at me.

"I'll change in here," I said, nodding toward the bathroom he'd just vacated.

My nightgown was nothing special -- a knee-length cotton thing, modest as a nun's habit. I'd packed it without thinking, never imagining I'd be wearing it while sharing a bed with a man I was legally married to yet barely knew. In the mirror, I looked pale, my eyes too wide, my hair a tangled mess from when Hammer's fingers had threaded through it during our kiss. I brushed it quickly, trying to calm my racing heart.

When I came out, Hammer was already in bed, propped against the headboard, pretending to read a motorcycle magazine. The bed was king-size, plenty large enough for two people to sleep without touching. He'd positioned himself on the far right edge, leaving a vast expanse of mattress between where he lay and where I would sleep.

I slipped under the covers on my side, the sheets cool against my skin. We lay there like strangers, two islands separated by an ocean of Egyptian cotton. The ceiling fan whirred softly overhead, the only sound besides our carefully measured breathing.

"Boys get home okay?" Hammer asked finally, his deep voice startling in the quiet room.

"Yes," I replied, staring at the ceiling. "Aura

texted while I was in the bathroom, saying they were all going to clean up and head to bed."

He grunted in acknowledgment, turning a page in his magazine without looking at me. I wondered what it would be like to feel the texture of his beard against my palms again.

I shifted slightly on the mattress, turning to face him. "We should talk about earlier."

His jaw tightened visibly. "Nothing to talk about."

"You kissed me," I said softly.

"Mistake," he replied, still not looking at me. "Won't happen again."

The dismissal stung more than it should have. "Didn't feel like a mistake to me."

Hammer sighed, finally setting down his magazine. "Amelia," he said, my name somehow both gentle and firm on his lips. "This isn't what you signed up for."

"Actually, it is." I propped myself up on one elbow, facing him directly. "I offered to be your old lady, remember? That usually implies more than just sharing a mailing address."

His eyes met mine, dark with something unreadable. "You offered because you needed protection. Not because you wanted…" He gestured vaguely between us. "This."

"Maybe both can be true," I suggested, inching closer to him on the mattress. "Maybe I needed protection and maybe I'm attracted to you."

Hammer tensed visibly as the distance between us narrowed. "This isn't working," he grumbled, throwing back the covers. "I'll sleep on the couch."

I reached out instinctively, my hand catching his forearm. "Stay," I said, the word half command, half plea. It felt like he was running away from me. I just didn't understand why. If I said this was what I wanted, why did he insist on pushing me away? "Please. We don't have to do anything. Just… stay."

He hesitated, his weight half-on, half-off the bed, muscles corded with tension beneath my fingers. Finally, he sank back onto the mattress, though he maintained his position at the far edge. "Fine. But we sleep. Just sleep."

I nodded, retreating to my side. "Deal."

We lay in silence, backs to each other, an invisible line drawn down the center of the bed. Despite the distance, I was acutely aware of his presence -- the subtle dip of the mattress beneath his weight, the rhythm of his breathing gradually slowing as he drifted toward sleep. Eventually, my own eyes grew heavy, and I surrendered to exhaustion, the ghost of our kiss still tingling on my lips.

The next night followed the same pattern -- awkward preparations for bed, careful distance maintained, minimal conversation. The night after that was the same. By the fourth night after our heated kiss, frustration had begun to simmer beneath my skin. This man had kissed me like he was drowning and I was air, then retreated behind walls so thick I couldn't find a way through.

On the fifth night, I decided on a different approach. The modest nightgown stayed in the drawer, replaced by a soft tank top and shorts I'd bought during a quick shopping trip with Aura. Nothing overtly sexy, but more revealing than what I'd been wearing. When I emerged from the bathroom, Hammer's gaze flicked up, then quickly away, but not before I caught the flare of appreciation in them.

"New pajamas?" he asked, his voice carefully

neutral.

I shrugged, slipping under the covers. "Aura took me shopping. Said I needed to 'expand my wardrobe.'"

"Hmm," was all he said, but I noticed he kept his gaze firmly fixed on his magazine after that.

Small victories, I told myself as I settled in for another night of enforced distance.

The next night, I was bolder. As I reached to turn off the bedside lamp, I "accidentally" brushed against him, my arm grazing his chest. He stiffened immediately, his breath catching audibly.

"Sorry," I murmured, letting my hand linger a moment longer than necessary.

He cleared his throat, shifting away slightly. "No problem."

By the seventh night, subtle wasn't working. I waited until we were both in bed, the lights dimmed, before I spoke.

"Hammer," I said into the darkness. "We need to talk about what's happening between us."

He was silent so long I thought he might be pretending to sleep. Finally, he sighed. "Nothing's happening, Amelia. That's the point."

"Exactly," I agreed, turning to face his profile in the dim light. "Nothing's happening, but something should be. I know you want me. I felt it when you kissed me."

His jaw worked beneath his beard. "Wanting isn't the same as should."

"Why not?" I shifted closer, emboldened by the darkness. "We're adults. We're married, even if it wasn't our choice. We're attracted to each other."

"You don't know what you're asking," he said, his voice strained.

"I think I do." I reached out, my fingers tracing his arm through the thin fabric of his T-shirt. "I'm asking my husband to touch me. To want me. To stop fighting whatever this is between us."

Hammer caught my wrist, gently but firmly stopping my exploration. "I'm old enough to be your dad. Hell, my son is older than you," he reminded me. "I've been to prison. I've killed men. I'm not some fantasy of a bad boy with a heart of gold, Amelia. I'm just bad."

"If you were just bad," I countered, "you wouldn't be fighting this so hard. You wouldn't care about taking advantage. You wouldn't have helped me and my boys escape Piston. You wouldn't have saved Aura."

He released my wrist, turning away. "Go to sleep, Amelia."

The stonewalling continued each night, despite my increasingly direct attempts to break through. More revealing sleepwear was met with studious avoidance. Physical proximity earned me nothing but tense muscles and careful distance. Conversations about our relationship were deflected or cut short.

But I noticed other things too -- the way his gaze followed me when he thought I wasn't looking, how his breathing changed when I emerged from the bathroom in my tank top, the way he sometimes reached for me in his sleep before catching himself and pulling away. He wanted me. He just wouldn't let himself have me.

On our tenth night of sharing a bed post-kiss, but not really sharing it, I lay awake long after Hammer's breathing had deepened into sleep. In the dim glow of moonlight through the curtains, I studied his profile -- the strong nose, the full lips partially hidden by his beard, the furrow between his brows that didn't completely relax even in sleep. Something protective uncurled in my chest at the sight. This man, with all his scars and history, had offered shelter when we'd had nowhere else to go. Had given my boys a sense of security they'd never known with their own father. Had fought his own desire rather than risk pressuring me.

His restraint, which had first frustrated me, now seemed like its own kind of tenderness.

Still, as I watched the slow rise and fall of his chest, I knew I needed a new strategy. Subtle wasn't working. Direct approaches were being deflected. What I needed was something that would make it impossible for him to maintain this careful distance between us. Something that would force him to acknowledge what was growing between us, whether he wanted to or not.

As I drifted toward sleep, a plan began to form -- risky, perhaps, but I was tired of playing it safe. Tomorrow, I'd enlist Aura's help. Tomorrow, I'd stop trying to seduce Hammer and instead make him realize exactly what he stood to lose by keeping me at arm's length.

Tomorrow, the real battle would begin.

Chapter Thirteen

Amelia

Aura's plan required me to look the part, so I stood in front of the mirror scrutinizing the outfit she'd helped me pick -- dark jeans that hugged curves I'd hidden for years, a deep burgundy top that dipped just low enough to be interesting without being desperate, and leather boots with a modest heel. My hair fell in loose waves past my shoulders, and I'd even applied makeup for the first time since leaving Florida. The woman staring back at me looked like someone with confidence, someone who belonged on a biker's arm.

"Mom?" Chase called from the hallway. "We're gonna be late."

I took a deep breath, smoothing my hands down my jeans one last time. "Coming." My boys waited by the front door, both looking uncomfortable in the new clothes Aura had insisted on buying them. Chase wore dark jeans and a button-down shirt that made him look older than his sixteen years. Levi had chosen a simple black T-shirt and jeans, his glasses freshly cleaned, his blond hair combed neatly to one side.

"You look nice, Mom," Levi said, his voice sincere.

Chase nodded his agreement, though his eyes held questions he wouldn't voice in front of his brother. He knew something was up -- he always did. "Hammer already left," he informed me. "Said he had to help set up."

Of course he had. The man had been finding excuses to avoid me since our kiss in the kitchen. Well, tonight that would change.

The walk to the clubhouse took less than five minutes, but with each step, my pulse quickened.

Music spilled into the night air as we approached. Not the pounding bass that had characterized Devil's Minions parties, but something more classic rock, at a volume that still allowed for conversation. The scent of grilled meat and cigarette smoke mingled in the warm evening air.

"Stay close," I told the boys as we reached the entrance. It was an old habit, one born from years of navigating Piston's volatile gatherings.

Chase shot me a look. "We're not babies, Mom."

"Humor me," I replied, squeezing his arm gently.

The scene that greeted us inside the clubhouse was nothing like the Devil's Minions' gatherings I'd endured. No women dancing on tables, no men so drunk they could barely stand, no dark corners where questionable substances changed hands. Instead, groups clustered around tables, some playing cards, others engaged in conversation. A dartboard occupied one wall, with several members taking turns, cheering good shots and heckling bad ones. The bar was well-stocked but not the center of activity. Most importantly, I didn't see a single woman who looked uncomfortable or trapped.

What struck me most was the watchfulness in the room. Each man seemed aware of his surroundings, gazes regularly scanning the entrances, noting who came and went. But it wasn't the paranoid, aggressive surveillance of the Minions. This felt protective, alert -- men watching their brothers' backs, not watching for threats to their egos.

Aura hugged me, whispering, "He hasn't shown up yet. Perfect timing." Then louder, "Boys, Theo's by the pool table. I think he's been waiting for you."

Chase hesitated, glancing at me. I nodded, and

he and Levi moved cautiously toward the back of the room, sticking close together.

"You look hot," Aura announced, stepping back to appraise me. "Dad's gonna lose his mind."

I fidgeted with my top. "I feel ridiculous."

"You look confident," she corrected. "And sexy. Two things my dad is absolutely going to notice."

Before I could respond, a commanding presence approached from my left. He stood just over six feet, with a silver-streaked beard and hair, his leather cut adorned with patches that spoke of decades of membership. His eyes -- keen and assessing -- took my measure in a single glance.

"You must be Amelia," he said, his deep voice carrying easily over the music. "Hammer's old lady."

I straightened, meeting his gaze directly. "I am."

His weathered face broke into a surprising smile. "Venom," he introduced himself. "And this is my wife, Ridley."

A petite blonde woman stepped forward, her blue eyes sparkling with genuine warmth. Though she couldn't have been more than five-foot-four, she carried herself with an authority that made her seem taller.

"About damn time we met you properly," Ridley said, linking her arm through mine as if we were old friends. "Hammer's been keeping you all to himself."

I glanced at Aura, who winked before melting back into the crowd. "He's been... protective," I managed, the half-truth sticking in my throat.

Ridley laughed, the sound rich and genuine. "That's one word for it. Come on, honey. Let me introduce you to everyone while that stubborn man of yours is still busy out back."

Venom nodded his approval, and Ridley guided

me deeper into the clubhouse, her grip on my arm both friendly and firm. I couldn't help but compare her confident touch to the bruising way Piston had always dragged me around Minions' gatherings, parading me like a trophy one minute, ignoring me the next.

"That's Saint's old lady, Sofia," Ridley said, nodding toward a tall brunette who waved from her position at the bar. "She makes the best damn margaritas you'll ever taste. And the woman by the pool table is Tank's wife, Emmie."

As we moved through the room, I collected names and snippets of information -- Delphine, married to Zipper; Isabella, Torch's wife; Amity, Thunder's woman. I'd remembered someone mentioning Amity was Hammer's granddaughter. Each woman greeted me with curious but welcoming eyes, so different from the cold assessment or outright hostility I'd experienced from the Minions' women.

"The first thing you need to know," Ridley said, handing me a beer from a cooler, "is that we stick together. Old ladies look out for each other. Any problem with your man, any issue at all, you can come to any of us."

I took a sip, trying not to show my surprise. "Even if the problem is with your husband?"

"Especially then," she replied without hesitation. "The men have their brotherhood, their patches, their codes. We have our own circle. Sometimes they need reminding that we're partners, not possessions."

"The Minions didn't operate that way," I admitted quietly. "Women were... commodities."

Ridley's expression hardened. "Hammer told Venom about your ex. Just enough for us to understand." She squeezed my arm. "That shit doesn't fly here, honey. These men are alpha as they come, but they know the difference between protection and possession."

As if to illustrate her point, I watched as Tank lifted his wife's feet onto his lap when she sat beside him, massaging her ankles without being asked. Nearby, Saint listened intently to something Sofia was saying, his focus entirely on her despite the activity around them.

"Second thing," Ridley continued, "is that wearing an old lady patch means something here. You don't have to earn respect by being the loudest or toughest. You already have it because Hammer chose you."

"That simple?" I asked skeptically. I noticed she had on a property cut. Even though I was technically Hammer's old lady, I didn't have one yet. Had he even requested one?

"That simple," she confirmed. "Doesn't mean they won't test you -- especially the Prospects. But one word from you, and Hammer will shut that down quick."

If only he were showing that kind of interest at home. I pushed the thought away, focusing instead on the tangible sense of camaraderie surrounding me. For the first time since meeting Piston, I felt myself truly relaxing in a crowd. There was no need to watch for signs of Piston's mood darkening, no need to position myself for a quick exit if things got ugly. The vigilance that had become second nature began to ease, replaced by something that felt dangerously like hope.

"Look at your boys," Ridley said, nodding toward the back of the room.

Chase and Levi stood with a red-haired teenager who gestured animatedly as he spoke. Levi was actually smiling -- a genuine smile that reached his eyes -- while Chase's defensive posture had softened slightly, his shoulders no longer braced for impact.

"They'll fit in just fine," Ridley assured me, watching my face. "This place is good for broken things, Amelia. Helps them mend."

I wondered if she included me among those broken things. If she did, she wasn't wrong. But standing there, surrounded by women who'd carved out respect in a world dominated by leather and testosterone, I felt the first stirrings of something I hadn't experienced in years -- the sense that I might belong somewhere after all.

I watched my sons from across the room, noting how they instinctively positioned themselves -- Chase slightly in front of Levi, his body angled to block potential threats, Levi's shoulders hunched as if trying to make himself invisible. Even in this seemingly safe environment, they fell into their protective patterns, honed from years of living with Piston's unpredictable rage. The red-haired boy talking to them didn't seem to notice their tension, his animated gestures and bright smile at odds with my sons' guarded expressions.

"Those are Sarge's boys over there with your sons," Ridley explained, following my gaze. "Theo's been going on about motorcycles since he could talk."

Theo stood about Chase's height, his dark red hair perpetually tousled as if he'd just removed a helmet. His blue eyes shone with enthusiasm as he gestured toward something outside the window, clearly trying to engage my stoic sons in conversation. They hadn't mentioned having classes with anyone at the club. Of course, I didn't know for certain which ones were the same ages as Chase and Levi, if any were. Chase nodded occasionally, his posture rigid, one hand casually positioned so he could grab Levi if they needed to make a quick exit.

"And the quiet one?" I asked, noticing a lankier boy approaching with a laptop tucked under his arm. He looked familiar. Wait. Wasn't he the kid who'd married us using his computer?

"That's Atlas," Ridley said. Yeah, I definitely remembered him. But he was dressed differently today and I hadn't been able to place him right away. "Wire and Lavender's son. Smartest kid in the compound. Probably the state."

Atlas moved with a deliberate grace, his hair falling across thoughtful eyes as he joined the small group. Unlike Theo's exuberant energy, Atlas carried a calm confidence, setting his laptop on a nearby table before offering a simple nod to my sons.

"Let me get you another drink," Ridley offered. "Then you can tell me how you're settling in with that stubborn man of yours."

I reluctantly let her guide me toward the bar, though I kept my boys in my peripheral vision. Old habits died hard.

Across the room, Theo was gesturing excitedly, pointing at something on his phone screen. "That's my dad's Harley-Davidson Road King," I heard him say as we passed nearby. "Custom exhaust, blacked-out chrome. Thing sounds like a monster when it fires up."

Chase nodded politely, his expression neutral. "Cool."

"You ride yet?" Theo asked, undeterred by Chase's minimal response.

"No," Chase answered, shifting his weight slightly to maintain his protective position in front of Levi.

Atlas settled against the pool table, observing the interaction with quiet interest. "Hammer mentioned you were working at the garage," he said to Chase, his voice lower and more measured than Theo's enthusiastic chatter.

Chase's eyebrows lifted slightly, surprised to be the subject of conversation. "Just helping out. Learning some basics."

"Dad says he's good," Theo jumped in. "Says you've got a natural feel for engines."

A flicker of pride crossed Chase's face before he could suppress it. "Just following instructions."

I accepted the beer Ridley handed me, but my focus remained on the boys. Something was shifting in their posture -- just slightly, but enough for a mother who'd spent years reading their body language to notice. Chase's shoulders had lowered a fraction. Levi had edged out slightly from behind his brother's protective stance. "You into computers?" Atlas asked Levi, nodding toward the laptop he'd set down.

Levi's eyes lit up, though his voice remained cautious. "Yeah. I do some coding."

"What languages?"

"Python, mostly. Some JavaScript."

Atlas nodded approvingly. "Solid choices. I'm working on a security system for the compound. Could use another pair of eyes if you're interested."

For the first time since we'd arrived, Levi stepped fully out from behind Chase. "What kind of system?"

"Multi-layered. Camera feeds with facial recognition, passive network monitoring to detect unauthorized devices, predictive algorithms for potential threats." Atlas shrugged as if this was all perfectly ordinary. "Standard stuff."

"Standard?" Levi repeated, clearly impressed despite himself. "That's government-level security."

Atlas's mouth curved in a slight smile. "Government wishes they had our setup."

I couldn't help but smile as I watched Levi lean forward, genuinely interested. Atlas opened his laptop, angling the screen so Levi could see, pointing out something on the display. My youngest son moved closer, his usual hesitation temporarily forgotten in the face of technological fascination.

"You designed all this?" Levi asked, his voice carrying an unfamiliar note of admiration.

"With my dad," Atlas confirmed. "But this section here is all mine." He tapped the screen. "It's specifically scanning for any digital traces of Piston or Devil's Minions activity within a hundred-mile radius."

Chase's head snapped up at the mention of his father's name, his body tensing again.

"Relax," Atlas said, noticing Chase's reaction. "It's just a precaution. Hammer asked us to set up alerts if anyone from your dad's club starts nosing around digitally. Bank transactions, phone records, social media -- the system flags anything suspicious."

"Basically, if your dad so much as Googles your mom's name, we'll know about it," Theo added, leaning against the pool table. "Nobody gets past Wire, Lavender, and Atlas when they're on the case."

Some of the tension drained from Chase's frame, though his eyes remained wary. "Thanks," he said simply.

Theo grinned, clearly taking this as a breakthrough. "Hey, you guys want to see my dad's garage? I've been helping rebuild this sick Panhead from the sixties. Original paint job and everything."

"Your Panhead's a piece of junk," Atlas commented dryly.

"It's a work in progress," Theo corrected, unbothered by the criticism. "So, you in?"

Chase and Levi exchanged a look. To my surprise, it was Levi who nodded first. "Yeah, I'd like to see it," he said.

"I'll come too," Chase added, still playing the protector but now with a hint of genuine interest.

"Awesome!" Theo pushed off from the pool table. "And after, I can show you where the Prospects have been training. I'm gonna prospect as soon as I'm eighteen. My dad's teaching me everything I need to know."

"Which one is your dad?" Chase asked, curiosity finally overcoming caution.

"Sarge," Theo confirmed proudly. "Been patched in for like twenty years."

"And your mom?" Levi asked quietly.

Theo's expression softened slightly. "She's not around. But my aunt Katya's awesome. She's not technically my mom, but she's like my mom, you know? I call her Mom, anyway."

Chase nodded, something like understanding passing between them. "Yeah, I get that."

I sipped my beer, watching this exchange from my position by the bar, warmth spreading through my chest that had nothing to do with alcohol.

"Your boys are connecting," Ridley observed, following my gaze. "It's good. They need friends their own age who understand this life."

The boys moved toward the door, Theo leading the way with boundless energy, Atlas following at a more measured pace, laptop tucked back under his arm. Just before stepping outside, Chase turned, his eyes finding mine across the room. He lifted his chin slightly in question. I nodded, giving permission, and the ghost of a genuine smile crossed his face.

"Go," I whispered, though he couldn't hear me. "Be kids for once."

As they disappeared through the door, Levi actually laughed at something Theo said -- a clear, bright sound I'd almost forgotten existed. The sound pierced my heart, drawing tears I quickly blinked away.

Ridley squeezed my arm gently. "They're going to be okay, honey. We'll all make sure of it."

The noise of the party pressed in on me like a physical weight, each laugh and conversation adding to the pressure behind my eyes. I slipped out the door onto the clubhouse porch, the cooler night air a welcome relief as I drew in a deep breath. Stars punctured the dark canvas above. I leaned against the wooden railing, letting the distant rumble of motorcycles and the chirp of crickets wash over me, a gentler soundtrack than the one I'd left inside.

The door creaked open behind me. I tensed instinctively, then forced myself to relax as Venom's imposing figure emerged from the light. He came to stand beside me at the railing, not so close as to invade my space, but near enough for conversation. With practiced ease, he pulled a pack of cigarettes from his cut, tapping one out before offering the pack to me.

"No, thanks," I said. "I quit when I got pregnant with Chase."

Venom nodded, tucking the pack away after lighting his own. "Smart woman." He took a deep drag, exhaling smoke that curled away on the light breeze. "Ridley made me quit in the house years ago. Said she wouldn't raise our kids in a cloud of smoke."

I smiled at that, imagining the petite blonde laying down the law to this intimidating man. "She seems like someone who gets her way."

"You have no idea." He chuckled, the sound rumbling deep in his chest.

We stood in companionable silence for a few moments, watching moths dance around the string lights. The distant thump of bass from inside provided a steady heartbeat beneath the night sounds.

"How you adjusting?" Venom finally asked, studying the cherry of his cigarette. "To all this. To Hammer."

I considered my answer carefully. "It's… different. From what I'm used to."

"Different good or different bad?"

"Good," I said without hesitation. "The boys seem… lighter here. Less afraid." I hesitated, then added, "But I still worry. About Piston finding us. About what happens then."

Venom took another drag, his expression thoughtful beneath his silver-streaked beard. "You know what makes this club different from outfits like the Devil's Minions?"

I shook my head.

"Loyalty," he said simply. "Not just to the patch or the lifestyle, but to each other. To our families." He gestured with his cigarette toward the compound. "Every man who wears this cut would die for his brothers. But more importantly, they'd kill for their families."

The blunt declaration should have disturbed me. Instead, I found it oddly comforting. "Piston has a lot of connections. In law enforcement, in other clubs."

"So do we," Venom countered. "Difference is, our connections are built on respect, not fear or blackmail." He turned to face me directly. "The minute Hammer claimed you, you became Dixie Reapers' family. Your boys too. That means something here."

I believed him, yet doubt still niggled at the back of my mind. "Hammer and I… our arrangement… it's complicated."

Venom's mouth quirked upward beneath his beard. "Aren't they all?"

"I just mean…" I struggled to explain without revealing too much. "I don't want anyone fighting battles for me if this… if we…" Yes, I wanted them to protect us, but I hadn't really considered what that might mean. These people could get hurt or even die.

"Listen," Venom interrupted gently. "Few decades back, one of our Prospects fell for a woman with baggage. Ex-husband, mean son of a bitch who thought divorce papers were just suggestions. He tracked her down, showed up at her workplace."

I tensed, the scenario too familiar.

"Know what happened?" Venom continued. "Before he could even get to her, he was met by three Reapers who happened to be 'passing by.' They explained, very clearly, that the woman was under club protection now." Venom's eyes darkened. "When he didn't take the hint, they arranged a more permanent solution."

The implication hung in the air between us. I thought about how horrified I should feel at what he was suggesting. Instead, I felt only a cold satisfaction.

"Did she know?" I asked quietly. "The woman?"

"Some things are better not knowing the details of," Venom replied. "But she understood that her problem had been handled. She's not with the Prospect anymore, and he's not part of this club either. They broke up, and several months later, he took off."

I nodded, absorbing the weight of his story and what it meant for my own situation. "Thank you," I said simply.

"No need for thanks. Just wanted you to understand how things work here." He flicked his cigarette butt into an empty beer bottle with practiced precision. "We protect our own, Amelia. You and your boys will always have a place here."

A lump formed in my throat at the casual certainty in his voice. "Speaking of Hammer, I haven't seen him tonight."

Venom's smile was knowing. "Club business. He should be back soon." He studied me for a moment. "You know, I've known that ornery bastard for thirty-plus years. Never seen him tied up in knots over a woman before."

"Tied up in knots? He's barely been home all week."

"Exactly." Venom smiled. "Man doesn't run from things he doesn't care about." He leaned closer, lowering his voice. "You scare the hell out of him, Amelia Williams. And that's a good thing. Man his age needs shaking up."

Before I could respond, the boys came running up the porch steps. Both started talking simultaneously, their words tumbling over each other in a rush I hadn't heard from them in years. "Mom, you gotta see the garage --"

"Theo showed us this Panhead that's like sixty years old --"

"Atlas says he can teach me some advanced coding --"

I held up my hands, laughing at their enthusiasm. "Slow down. One at a time!"

Venom smiled, nodding to me as he quietly excused himself. Chase barely paused to acknowledge his departure before launching back into his story about engine parts I couldn't begin to understand. Levi kept interrupting with his own discoveries about the compound's security system, his eyes bright behind his glasses.

"Can we come back tomorrow?" Levi asked, a note of pleading in his voice I'd never heard before. "Atlas said he could show me how to access the camera feeds from my laptop. For security practice," he added quickly, seeing my expression.

"And Theo's dad said he'd let me help with an oil change on his Harley," Chase added, trying to sound casual though his excitement shone through.

I pulled them both into a hug, overcome with emotion at the simple normalcy of their request. Until now, I'd hugged them sparingly, knowing they had an aversion to being touched. But right now, they were just boys wanting to hang out with friends, pursue interests, learn new skills. Everything I'd wished for them but never thought possible while living under Piston's shadow.

"Yes," I said, my voice thick with unshed tears. "Yes, of course you can." As they hugged me back -- even Chase -- I felt something settle deep in my chest. Not just hope, but something more substantial. A sense of foundation. Of roots beginning to take hold in this unexpected soil.

For the first time since we'd fled Florida, I allowed myself to believe that we might truly belong somewhere after all. Not just as refugees seeking temporary shelter, but as family. I'd dressed up tonight to play a part, not realizing all I had to really do was embrace my role as Hammer's old lady. And that realization was both terrifying and exhilarating in equal measure.

Chapter Fourteen

Hammer

I tightened the carburetor bolt with practiced precision, my weathered hands moving through motions I could perform blindfolded after more than forty years of working on bikes. The Softail's engine had been giving Tank fits for weeks, but the problem was obvious to me -- timing was off, fuel mixture too rich. Simple fixes for simple problems. If only the rest of my life could be diagnosed and repaired so easily. The thought of Amelia waiting at home -- my home that was somehow now our home -- made my chest tighten in a way no amount of mechanical knowledge could fix.

The garage hummed with the comfortable soundtrack of my life -- metal tools clinking against steel parts, the hiss of the air compressor kicking on, classic rock playing from the ancient radio I refused to replace despite Aura's complaints about its poor reception. Oil stains marked the concrete floor like a roadmap of past repairs, each dark splatter a memory of some brother's broken-down ride. The familiar smell of gasoline, metal, and the sweet tang of WD-40 filled my nostrils with every breath.

Pegboards lined the walls, tools hanging in their designated spots. I'd enforced that system with iron discipline -- any Prospect who put a wrench back in the wrong place quickly learned the error of his ways. Order in the garage meant safety. Meant control. Something I felt slipping through my fingers with every passing day of this unexpected marriage.

I glanced at the clock -- just past four. Amelia would be finishing her shift at the diner soon. The boys would be home from school. As much as I'd wanted to put them on lockdown, Amelia had argued that they needed things to remain as normal as possible. And now, they'd be waiting, this ready-made family that had dropped into my life overnight thanks to a hacker kid's idea of helping. I still wanted to throttle Atlas for that stunt with the marriage certificate, but I couldn't deny the results. The boys were settling in. Amelia was safer. And I...

I was confused as hell.

She'd tried to seduce me the other night -- hell, she'd been trying for quite a few nights -- wearing those shorts that showed off her legs. She deserved better than some worn-out old biker with trouble even getting it up half the time.

I wiped my forehead with the back of my hand, leaving a streak of grease I didn't bother cleaning. My reflection caught in the chrome of the engine -- silver hair, weathered face lined with too many years of hard living. Christ, I looked every one of my sixty-one years today.

"You look like you're trying to solve world hunger instead of fixing that carburetor," a voice commented from behind me.

I didn't turn around, recognizing Dice's distinctive drawl. The kid was Spider's son from the Hades Abyss MC, patched over to us after he fell for Flicker's sister.

"Just thinking," I grunted, reaching for the intake manifold.

"Dangerous habit," Dice replied, moving around to lean against the workbench. His dark hair was pulled back in a ponytail, his beard neatly trimmed unlike my wild silver mess. "Sarge was looking for you earlier. Something about parts for the Road King."

"Already ordered them," I muttered, focusing on

the engine in front of me. "Should be here tomorrow."

Dice didn't leave like I'd hoped. Instead, he folded his arms across his chest, studying me with an intensity that made my skin itch. "So," he said finally. "How's married life treating you?"

My hands stilled for just a moment before resuming their work. "Fine."

"Fine?" Dice chuckled. "Man, you go from confirmed bachelor to instant family with a hot wife and two teenagers, and all you've got is 'fine'?"

"What do you want me to say?" I growled, tightening a bolt harder than necessary.

"I don't know. Maybe that you're happy? Terrified? Ready to run for the hills?" He shrugged. "Anything other than looking like someone shot your dog while you're supposed to be fixing an easy carburetor job."

I straightened up, my back protesting after being hunched over the engine for hours. "It's complicated."

"Life usually is," Dice agreed easily. "But Amelia seems good for you. Aura's over the moon about having her around. And those boys --"

"Those boys need a father who isn't pushing retirement age," I interrupted, the words escaping before I could stop them.

Dice's eyebrows shot up. "That what's eating you? Your age?"

I grabbed a rag and wiped my hands, buying time. Dice wasn't going to let this go -- the younger generation never knew when to mind their own fucking business. "She's young, beautiful," I said finally, my voice gruff. "One day she's gonna wake up and realize what it's like being married to an old man."

"You're not that old," Dice countered.

"I'm sixty-one. She's thirty-six."

"So?"

"So?" I repeated incredulously. "So I was riding with this club before she was born."

Dice considered this, then shrugged. "My dad and his wife have twenty plus years between them. They couldn't be happier."

"That's different."

"How?"

I turned away, focusing on organizing my tools rather than meeting his eyes. "She didn't choose this. She needed protection. For her and the boys."

Understanding dawned on Dice's face. "Ah. You think she's just using you."

"Wouldn't you?" I challenged. "In her position?"

Dice leaned against the workbench, his expression thoughtful. "Here's what I think. I think a woman who's survived what she has doesn't waste time with bullshit. She wouldn't be playing house with you if she didn't want to be there."

I snorted. "She doesn't have much choice."

"Bullshit," Dice said flatly. "Woman like that always has choices. She could've picked someone younger. Could've kept running. Hell, she could've stayed in the duplex instead of moving into your place. I bet she'd have found a way to convince Savior, at least until Piston and the Devil's Minions are handled."

His words hit a nerve I didn't want to acknowledge. Amelia had agreed to move in with minimal protest. In fact, she'd asked to be mine. Had made my house more of a home in three weeks than I had in years. Had cooked meals, learned my schedule, asked about my day like she genuinely cared about the answer.

"I've seen how she looks at you," Dice continued. "That's not a woman biding her time until something better comes along."

"What do you know about it?" I muttered, though the heat had left my voice.

"I know good women don't come along every day, especially in our world." Dice straightened up. "Don't waste this chance at happiness just because you're scared, old man."

"I'm not scared," I protested, the lie bitter on my tongue.

Dice just laughed. "Sure, and I'm the fucking Pope." He slapped my shoulder as he walked past. "Take it from someone who wasted his chance once. You'll regret the happiness you talked yourself out of more than any pain that might come from taking the risk."

I watched him leave, his words echoing in my head. Was I really so transparent that a kid half my age could read me like a manual? The thought was almost as unsettling as the truth he'd laid bare.

I turned back to the Softail, but my focus was shot. All I could think about was Amelia -- the way she'd felt in my arms during that brief kiss in the kitchen, the hurt in her eyes when I'd pulled away, the quiet dignity with which she accepted my distance while making it clear she wanted more.

Maybe Dice was right. Maybe I was sabotaging the first good thing to happen to me in decades because I was scared of eventually losing it. The thought sat heavy in my chest as I mechanically finished the carburetor adjustment, my hands working on autopilot while my mind wrestled with possibilities I'd refused to consider until now.

* * *

I set my tools back in their proper places, Dice's words still bouncing around my skull like a stray bullet. The kid had balls, I'd give him that. Not many brothers would call me out so directly. I glanced at the ancient calendar hanging by the office door -- more for decoration than function since cell phones had made it obsolete. A flyer was tacked next to it, bright colors advertising the county fair starting this weekend. Ferris wheels, carnival games, cotton candy. Normal family shit that I hadn't thought about -- ever. The kind of thing Amelia and her boys had probably missed out on, living under Piston's control. The kind of thing I could give them now, if I got my head out of my ass.

I stared at the flyer, something tugging at my chest. When was the last time I'd done anything just for fun? When had Amelia's boys last had a normal day out without looking over their shoulders? The fair would be crowded, public -- my security instincts immediately started cataloging potential threats. But with proper planning, with brothers watching our backs...

My fingers hesitated over my phone. What if she laughed at the idea? What if she saw it as obligation rather than genuine interest? What if the boys thought it was lame?

"Fuck it," I muttered to the empty garage. I was overthinking this like some teenage boy asking for a first date. I hit Amelia's number before I could talk myself out of it.

She answered on the third ring, her voice slightly breathless. "Hammer? Everything okay?"

Of course that was her first question. In our world, unexpected calls usually meant trouble. "Everything's fine," I said, my voice automatically softening in a way it only did with her and Aura. "Just finishing up at the garage."

"Oh. Good." She sounded relieved but confused.

I rarely called just to chat.

I cleared my throat. "Thought maybe you and the kids might want to go to that county fair this weekend," I said, trying to sound casual, like I suggested family outings every day. "Starts Friday. Runs through Sunday."

The silence on the other end stretched just long enough for my stomach to tighten with regret. Then came her response -- a warmth in her voice I wasn't expecting.

"A fair? The boys would love that. And so would I." She paused. "Are you sure, though? It would be pretty public."

Smart woman. Already thinking about security, just like I'd been. "I'll handle that part," I assured her. "Thought it might be good for the boys. And you. Something normal."

"Normal sounds wonderful," she said softly. In the background, I heard dishes clattering. She must be at the diner still. "What day were you thinking?"

"Saturday? I can get Aura to come too."

"She'll be thrilled." The smile in Amelia's voice made something warm unfurl in my chest. "Chase has been talking about her new motorcycle project all week."

"Got it from a junkyard," I confirmed. "More rust than metal, but she sees potential."

"Like father, like daughter."

The simple observation caught me off guard. Was that how Amelia saw me? Someone who found potential in broken things? The thought made me uncomfortable in a way I couldn't define.

"I should get back to work," she said after a moment. "But, Hammer? Thank you. This means a lot."

"Just a fair," I muttered, suddenly self-conscious.

"It's more than that," she replied. "I'll see you at home."

Home. The word hung in the air even after I ended the call. My house had become home because of her. Because of those boys. Because of the family we were awkwardly forming out of necessity and circumstance.

I shook off the sentiment and switched to security mode. A public outing meant exposure. Exposure meant risk. And with Piston still out there somewhere, I wasn't taking chances. I scrolled through my contacts and placed another call.

"Viking," came the graveled response.

"Need your eyes Saturday," I said without preamble. "County fair. Taking the family."

To Viking's credit, he didn't comment on "the family" part. "Time frame?"

"Midday to evening. Four others plus me."

"Piston situation?"

"No concrete intel but not taking chances."

"Copy that. Want me to bring Freya? Make it look casual?"

Smart. Viking's friend Freya could blend in, watch areas I couldn't. "Good idea. Bring the boy too if you want." Freya's son was a little younger than Levi, but he would help them blend into the crowd.

"Will do. Who else you calling in?"

"Prophet, Sticks, Warden."

"Solid choices. I'll coordinate with Prophet on surveillance points."

After hanging up, I called Sticks and Warden, then Prophet.

"Already talked to Viking," Prophet said after I laid out the plan. "I'll ask Wire to tap into the fair's security cameras. Got a guy who owes me working their system."

"Need eye-level surveillance too," I told him. "Blind spots."

"On it. Going as a family man these days, huh?" The observation held no judgment, just mild curiosity.

I grunted noncommittally and ended the call. Then I looked at my phone, scrolling to a photo Aura had sent me last week -- her arm thrown around Amelia's shoulders, Chase looking uncomfortable but not angry for once, Levi with a small smile. My family. Not by blood or choice, but by fate and necessity. And now, increasingly, by my own desire. I'd already had kids. One by blood, one adopted. So, why was it only now I was starting to truly feel like a father?

I stared at their faces, my weathered thumb hovering over the screen. What Dice had said echoed in my head: *"Don't waste this chance at happiness just because you're scared, old man."* Maybe he was right. Maybe I'd been holding back because I was afraid of how much I was beginning to care.

I tucked the phone away and grabbed my keys. Time to go home. Not to my house, but to them.

* * *

I pulled into the driveway, killing the engine of my Harley but sitting there for a moment, gathering myself. Light spilled from the kitchen windows, casting golden rectangles onto the gravel. Through the glass, I could see movement -- Amelia at the stove, Aura laughing as she stacked plates on the counter, the boys bent over books spread across the kitchen table. The scene hit me like a sucker punch to the gut. My house hadn't looked like this -- hadn't felt like this -- ever before. It was the kind of normal I'd convinced myself I didn't want, didn't need. The kind of normal that now scared me more than any prospect of violence ever could.

I forced myself off the bike, my knees protesting after a long day at the garage in town. The scent of garlic and tomatoes greeted me before I even opened the door -- Amelia's spaghetti. She'd figured out it was my favorite after just one time of making it. Made it every Wednesday now, like clockwork.

Inside, the house was warm and alive in a way my solitary existence had never achieved. When I'd adopted Aura, things had changed, but this was on another level. It wasn't just the two of us anymore. We'd added three people to our family. Aura's jacket thrown over a chair, Levi's laptop humming on the side table, Chase's boots lined up neatly by the door. Little signs of lives intersecting with mine. The radio played something soft in the background, barely audible beneath the sounds of cooking and conversation.

Amelia noticed me first, looking up from the stove with a smile that hit me square in the chest. "You're home," she said, like my arrival was something worth noting. Something that mattered.

I grunted, shrugging out of my cut and hanging it by the door. The patch -- my identity for four decades -- seemed different somehow. No longer just a symbol of the brotherhood, but of what these people expected from me. Protection. Stability. Things I wasn't sure I knew how to provide beyond physical safety.

"Dinner's almost ready," Amelia continued. "Aura helped with the garlic bread."

"Helped is generous." Aura laughed. "I watched while giving unhelpful commentary."

The boys glanced up from their homework. Chase's nod was brief but not hostile -- progress, considering where we'd started. Levi actually smiled slightly, pushing his glasses up his nose with one finger.

I cleared my throat, suddenly aware they were all looking at me, waiting for something. Words. Conversation. Normal family shit that I'd never been good at.

"About Saturday," I said, my voice rougher than I'd intended. "Thought we could go to that county fair that's in town."

The reaction was immediate -- Aura squealed like I'd offered her a new Harley, practically bouncing across the kitchen to throw her arms around me. "Seriously? The one with the Ferris wheel?" she asked, looking up at me with the same excited expression she'd had when I'd taught her to ride.

I placed an arm awkwardly around her shoulders. "That's the one."

"Dad, that's awesome!" She turned to Amelia. "They have the best funnel cakes. And last year they had this guy who carved wooden sculptures with a chainsaw."

Amelia's smile widened. "It sounds wonderful." She glanced at her sons. "What do you boys think?"

Chase and Levi exchanged one of those looks that communicated volumes between them. Chase, always the spokesman, straightened his shoulders. "Sounds cool," he said, trying to sound casual though I caught the hint of excitement he couldn't quite suppress. "Will there be rides other than the Ferris wheel?"

"Yes, and games," I confirmed. "Shooting gallery, ring toss. All that carnival crap."

"I'm terrible at those games," Levi admitted quietly.

"Me too," said Aura, nudging him with her elbow. "But it's still fun to try."

I caught Amelia watching me, something soft in her expression that made me uncomfortable yet pleased. Like I'd done something impressive instead of just suggesting a day at the fair. Like this small gesture actually mattered.

Dinner passed with more conversation than usual, the plans for Saturday dominating the discussion. Aura detailed her favorite fair attractions with her usual enthusiasm. I hadn't even realized she'd been so often. Apparently, she and Sam had gone a few times. Chase asked practical questions about the schedule. Levi wondered about the livestock exhibits. Throughout it all, Amelia kept glancing at me with that same warm expression, like she could see right through my gruff exterior to whatever was happening beneath it. Something I wasn't ready to name.

After the kids had cleared the table, Aura dragged Chase and Levi to the garage to show them progress on her motorcycle restoration project. I stepped out onto the back porch, needing a moment alone with my thoughts and a cigarette. The night air was cool against my face, the familiar scent of tobacco calming my nerves as I lit up.

I heard the door open behind me but didn't turn. The light footsteps told me it was Amelia before she appeared at my side, wrapping a cardigan around herself against the evening chill.

"I already thanked you on the phone," she said, leaning against the railing next to me, "but I wanted to say it again. This means a lot to them. To all of us."

I shrugged, uncomfortable with her gratitude. "Just a fair," I muttered around my cigarette.

"It's more than that and you know it." She

turned to face me, her eyes reflecting the porch light. "Chase hasn't looked forward to anything like this in years. Not since before…" She trailed off, but I knew what she meant. Before Piston had beaten the childhood out of him.

"Kids deserve normal," I said simply.

"They do." She hesitated, then added, "We've asked so much of you already. Taking us in, protecting us. You didn't have to do this too."

"Wanted to," I admitted, the closest I could come to expressing what was happening inside me.

Amelia touched my arm gently, her fingers warm through my shirtsleeve. "Thank you," she said again, her voice soft. "For giving us a chance at normal."

Our eyes met, and something passed between us -- something deeper than the physical attraction we'd been dancing around for weeks. Understanding, maybe. Or recognition of what we might become to each other, given time and trust.

I briefly covered her hand with mine, feeling the delicate bones beneath the skin, marveling at the strength contained in such a gentle touch. Then I pulled away, suddenly needing space from the intensity of the moment.

"Should check the perimeter," I muttered, dropping my cigarette and crushing it under my boot. "Make sure everything's secure."

Her smile told me she saw through the excuse, but she didn't call me on it. "Don't be too long. It's getting cold."

I nodded and descended the porch steps, walking the property line as I did every night. The security floodlights cast my shadow long across the grass as I moved methodically from one checkpoint to another, checking locks, testing the gate, scanning for anything out of place. The routine grounded me, gave me time to process the feelings I'd been fighting for weeks.

Dice had been right. I was afraid -- not of Piston or the Devil's Minions or any external threat. I was afraid of how much I was starting to care for Amelia and her boys. Afraid of the pain that would come if I fully opened myself to them and then lost them. Afraid of not being enough.

But standing there in the darkness, looking back at my house -- at the light and life within it -- I knew I was already lost. Already invested. Already caring more than I'd intended to. And maybe it was time to stop fighting it. Time to stop wasting whatever chance at happiness had unexpectedly landed in my life.

I turned back toward the house, toward them. Toward home.

Chapter Fifteen

Amelia

I locked the register with fingers that moved on autopilot, my body feeling the weight of an eight-hour shift that had stretched to ten when Marla, another waitress, called in sick. The diner's fluorescent lights buzzed overhead, harsh against my tired eyes as I counted out my tips -- decent tonight, enough to buy Chase those new sneakers he needed but wouldn't ask for. Beyond the windows, darkness had settled completely over the parking lot, the diner's neon sign casting alternating flashes of pink and blue across the cracked asphalt. I rubbed at the small of my back, dreaming of the hot shower waiting for me at home. At Hammer's home. Our home, I corrected myself, still not quite used to the thought.

"Night, Phil," I called to our evening shift cook, who grunted his goodbye from the kitchen where he was finishing cleanup.

I gathered my purse and jacket, tucking the tips inside my wallet before heading toward the back door. My car sat alone in the employee section, the only vehicle left besides Phil's ancient pickup. The manager had left hours ago, trusting me to close up as I'd done dozens of times since starting here.

The night air hit me with a welcome coolness after hours in the stuffy diner. I inhaled deeply, letting the tension in my shoulders ease slightly as I fumbled for my keys. My thoughts drifted to home, to the boys, to Hammer. Saturday's fair plans had lit something in all of them that warmed me through. Even Chase had seemed genuinely excited, though he tried to hide it behind his usual stoic facade.

My keys jingled as I shifted them to grab the car

remote. The parking lot lights flickered, one of them buzzing before going dark completely. I made a mental note to tell Phil tomorrow -- the lot was too dark already without losing another light. For the first time, I was cursing myself for being so independent. Hammer had told me I didn't need to work here anymore, and several people at the compound had tried to talk me out of keeping my shifts. Right now, I was wishing I'd listened, or that maybe Hammer had been a little less understanding and forced me to remain home.

The hairs on the back of my neck prickled.

I froze, my fingers tightening around my keys until the metal bit into my palm. Something shifted in the shadows behind me -- not the wind, not an animal. A presence. Heavy. Deliberate. Watching.

I spun around, heart hammering against my ribs, and that's when I saw him. The bulk of his frame separated from the darkness like a nightmare materializing. Broad shoulders. Close-cropped hair. The familiar swagger in his step that had once made my stomach flutter with attraction, now made it clench with dread.

Piston.

"Hey, baby," he drawled, stepping fully into the weak pool of light cast by the flickering neon sign. "Miss me?"

My throat closed up, breath shallow and quick in my chest. I backpedaled until my spine pressed against my car door, trapping me.

"What are you doing here?" My voice came out steadier than I felt, a small victory.

He moved closer, every step measured, predatory. The smell hit me before he did -- whiskey, cigarettes, and that cologne he always wore, the one that used to cling to my clothes after he'd been near me. His eyes, cold and calculating despite the whiskey on his breath, raked over me.

"That's not much of a greeting after I drove all this way." His lips curved into something that wasn't quite a smile. "But then, you never did have proper respect."

I gripped my keys tighter, pressing the sharp edge of one between my knuckles the way Aura had shown me. A small defense. Probably useless, but it steadied me.

"What do you want?" I asked, though I knew. Of course I knew.

"Where are my boys?" He spat the words, all pretense of casual conversation vanishing. His hand shot out, fingers closing around my upper arm with bruising force. "Where are you hiding them?"

The pain radiated up my arm, but I refused to wince. "They're not your boys," I said. "They never were. You never wanted them except as punching bags and leverage."

His grip tightened, fingers digging deeper. I could feel the cold metal of his rings against my skin, pressing little circles of ice where bruises would form tomorrow.

"Mouthy bitch," he growled, yanking me closer until his face was inches from mine. "You think you can just take my sons? My blood?" His other hand came up to grip my chin, forcing my face up. "Tell me where they are, Amelia. Now."

I stared into the eyes I'd once thought I loved, seeing nothing but emptiness and rage reflected back. My hands trembled, and my heart pounded so hard I was sure he could hear it, but I held his gaze.

"They're safe," I said. "They're happy. That's all

you need to know."

Something dangerous flashed across his face. "You think you're so fucking smart, don't you? Running to another club, spreading your legs for protection?" His fingers dug deeper into my chin. "Who is he? Which one of these backwater bikers are you fucking?"

I said nothing, which only infuriated him more. His hand slid from my chin to my throat, not squeezing yet, but the threat was clear.

"It doesn't matter," he continued, voice dropping to a whisper that frightened me more than his shouting ever had. "I'll find them. And when I do, I'll make sure they understand what happens to boys who betray their father."

My fear crystallized into something harder, sharper. "You'll never touch them again," I said, each word deliberate despite the tremor in my voice. "They're not yours anymore."

His face contorted, ugly with rage. "Everything I own has my mark on it, baby. Including you. Including them." The hand at my throat tightened fractionally. "The only way you escape me is if you're dead. Is that what you want?"

The threat hung in the air between us, heavy and real in a way that made my skin go cold. I'd known he would come eventually. Had prepared myself mentally for this moment. But standing here, with his hands on me again, the reality was so much worse than my imagination.

"Why now?" I asked, playing for time, hoping Phil might come out, though I knew he always left through the front. "You never cared about them before. Chase spent years trying to gain your attention, your approval. You barely noticed him."

"They're mine," he snarled, as if that explained everything. "My property. My bloodline. You think I'll let some other man raise my sons?" His breath, hot and whiskey-sour, washed over my face. "Is that who you're with now? Some father figure for them? Some replacement for me?"

The image of Hammer -- strong, steady, gentle with the boys despite his gruff exterior -- flashed through my mind. The absolute opposite of the man before me.

"They deserve better than you," I said, the words escaping before I could stop them.

His fingers spasmed against my throat, and for a moment, I thought he might actually strangle me right here in the parking lot. Instead, he leaned closer, his voice dropping to that terrifying whisper again.

"I'm going to find them, Amelia. I'm going to take them back. And before I do, I'm going to make you watch while I dismantle every piece of this new life you think you've built." The metal of his rings bit deeper into my skin. "Starting with whatever old man you've tricked into protecting you."

My breath caught. He knew about Hammer. Maybe not specifically, but he knew there was someone. Fear flooded through me, no longer just for myself or my boys, but for Hammer too.

"Leave us alone," I said, hating the pleading note that crept into my voice. "Just let us go."

Piston's laugh was cold and hollow. "You know that's not how this works, baby. You're mine until you're dead." His eyes, flat and shark-like, bore into mine. "And maybe I won't let you go even then."

Piston shoved me hard against the car, my back hitting the cold metal with enough force to knock the air from my lungs. His face loomed over mine, features twisted with a rage I knew too well -- the same expression that had preceded broken bones and black eyes in our past life together. I braced myself, muscles tensing, my body remembering exactly how to curl inward to protect vital organs. But something had changed in the weeks since I'd fled Florida. The fear was still there, primitive and overwhelming, but alongside it burned something new -- a certainty that I deserved better than this man's rage, that my boys deserved their freedom, that the life we were building with Hammer was worth fighting for.

"They don't want you," I said, my voice stronger now despite the pain radiating across my back. "They're happy now. Happier than they ever were with you."

His eyes narrowed to slits, nostrils flaring with each heavy breath. "Happy? With some washed-up old biker?"

I said nothing, but something in my expression must have confirmed his suspicions. His hand shot out, gripping my jaw with bruising force, fingers digging into my cheeks.

"You stupid bitch," he hissed. "You think you can just replace me? That my boys will call some other man 'Dad'?"

"They never called you that," I said, the words muffled by his grip but clear enough to hit their mark. At least, not to his face they hadn't. "Not once. Not even when they were little."

The truth of it seemed to slice through him. I saw the flicker of recognition in his eyes before rage consumed it. His free hand closed into a fist, drawing back as his weight pinned me against the car door.

"I'm going to remind you of your place," he growled. "Then we're going to get my boys, and you're going to wish you'd never --"

The sound cut through the night air like thunder -- a motorcycle engine, deep and powerful, growling in the distance but rapidly approaching. Relief crashed through me so intensely my knees nearly buckled. I knew that engine, knew its distinctive rumble that always announced Hammer's arrival at home.

Piston's head snapped toward the sound, his grip on me loosening just enough that I could wrench my face free. The motorcycle rounded the corner of the building, headlight slicing through the darkness, illuminating us in its path before the bike came to an abrupt stop.

Hammer.

He dismounted in one fluid motion that belied his age, his imposing figure silhouetted against the streetlight behind him. In the artificial glow of the diner sign, his silver hair and beard seemed to glow with an otherworldly aura.

"Let her go." His voice carried across the parking lot, low and even, yet somehow more threatening than if he'd shouted.

Piston's grip tightened on my arm, his body tensing like a predator scenting competition. "This is a private conversation," he called back. "Between me and my wife."

"I was never your wife," I corrected, earning another painful squeeze.

Hammer moved toward us, each step measured and deliberate. There was nothing rushed in his approach, nothing that betrayed panic or uncertainty. Just the steady advance of a man who knew exactly what he was capable of. I'd seen him gentle with Aura, patient with my boys, careful with me -- but this was different. This was the Hammer who had survived decades in a one-percenter club, who had done prison time, who commanded respect with his mere presence.

"Take your hands off my wife," Hammer stated, stopping a few yards away, his voice calm but lined with steel.

My heart stuttered at the word -- wife. Not old lady. Not woman. Wife. Claimed openly, definitively, without qualification.

"Your wife?" Piston's voice dripped with mockery. He looked down at me, then back at Hammer. "This is what you settled for? Some silver-haired grandpa who probably can't even get it up without those little blue pills?" His grip loosened on my arm as his attention shifted fully to Hammer. "Tell me, old timer, does she fake it for you like she did for me?"

Something dangerous flashed in Hammer's eyes -- a cold fury so controlled it was somehow more frightening than Piston's volatile rage. He took a single step forward.

"You don't talk about her like that," he said quietly.

Piston's smirk widened. "Hit a nerve? I'm just looking out for her satisfaction, man. She likes it rough, likes to be put in her place. You got the strength left for that? Or are you too busy taking your heart medication --"

Hammer moved so quickly I barely registered the shift. One moment he was standing still, the next his fist connected with Piston's jaw with a sickening *crack* that echoed across the empty parking lot. Piston staggered backward, releasing me completely as he struggled to keep his balance.

I pressed myself against the car, breath coming in shallow pants, unable to look away from the scene unfolding before me. Hammer positioned himself between Piston and me, his broad back creating a wall of protection.

"You nearly broke my fucking jaw!" Piston spat, blood dribbling down his chin.

"Not close enough," Hammer replied calmly. "But I'm considering it."

Piston steadied himself, touching his jaw gingerly before his eyes narrowed with hatred. "You have no idea who you're dealing with, old man. I've got an entire club behind me."

"And I've got mine," Hammer said, not bothering to raise his voice. "Difference is, I don't need them to handle you."

Piston's eyes darted from Hammer to me, then back again. Something calculating entered his expression. "She tell you about our boys? About how they've got my blood, my name?"

I wasn't about to correct him on the name part. I'd never given my children his name since we weren't married, and he hadn't bothered to show up when they were born. But bringing that up would only anger him more.

"They have her heart," Hammer countered. "Her strength. Nothing worthwhile from you."

The words struck me like physical blows -- not painful, but powerful enough to take my breath away. I'd never heard Hammer speak like this, never witnessed this fierce protection wrapped in such simple truth.

"You think you can just step in and play daddy?" Piston sneered, though I noticed he kept his distance now. "Those are my sons. Mine."

"Sons you beat," Hammer said, his voice dropping lower. "Sons you terrified. Sons who flinch when a door slams or a voice raises." He took another step toward Piston. "Not anymore."

Piston's eyes flicked to me. "This your plan, Amelia? Replace me with this old bastard? You think he can protect you? Protect my boys?"

Before I could answer, Hammer moved again -- another of those lightning-fast movements that belied his age. His fist connected with Piston's stomach, doubling him over. As Piston gasped for breath, Hammer gripped the back of his neck, forcing him to look up.

"Those boys aren't yours," he growled. "Not anymore. They're mine now. Under my protection. Under my roof."

Something cold and desperate flashed across Piston's face -- the look of a man realizing he might be outmatched. He straightened, shoving Hammer's hand away, his body tensing for a fight.

"We'll see about that," he snarled.

And then he lunged at Hammer, all restraint abandoned.

Piston charged like a bull, all rage and no technique, the way he'd always fought -- the way he'd always hit me. Brutal, full of fury, meant to overwhelm with sheer force. Hammer, though, didn't move. He stood his ground, waited until Piston was just within reach, then pivoted slightly, using Piston's own momentum to send him crashing into my car. The metal dented with a sickening *crunch*. I should have worried about the damage, about how I'd explain it, about the cost of repairs I couldn't afford. Instead, I felt nothing but a cold satisfaction seeing the man who'd terrorized me for years sprawled against the vehicle, momentarily stunned by his own violence turned against him.

Piston recovered quickly, spinning around with a roar. This time he swung with more precision, a right hook aimed at Hammer's jaw. Hammer blocked it with his forearm, the impact making a dull *thud* that echoed in the empty parking lot. His counter was swift -- a sharp jab to Piston's ribs followed by an uppercut that snapped Piston's head back.

Blood sprayed from Piston's nose, dark droplets splattering across the asphalt. I pressed myself against the side of the car, unable to look away, my heart hammering against my ribs. I'd seen Piston fight before -- had been on the receiving end of his violence more times than I could count -- but I'd never seen him matched like this. Never seen someone who could absorb his rage and return it with such controlled precision.

"Stay down," Hammer warned as Piston stumbled backward, blood streaming from his nose and split lip. "You get one chance to walk away."

But Piston had never known when to stop. It was what made him so dangerous -- that inability to back down, to admit defeat. He spat a mouthful of blood onto the pavement and lunged again.

This time, Hammer met him head-on. Their bodies collided with a sound like a car crash, both men grunting with the impact. Piston landed a glancing blow to Hammer's temple, but Hammer absorbed it, delivering three rapid punches to Piston's midsection that left him gasping. When Piston doubled over, Hammer brought his knee up into his face.

More blood. More of that sickening crack of bone against bone.

I should have been horrified by the violence. Should have been screaming for them to stop, calling for help, doing something other than standing frozen, watching as these two men tore at each other -- one from my past, one from my present, fighting over a future that hung in the balance.

But I couldn't move. Couldn't speak. Could only watch as Hammer systematically dismantled the man who had haunted my nightmares for years.

Piston went down again, harder this time, his body making a wet *smack* against the pavement. Blood pooled beneath his head, black in the dim light of the parking lot. For a moment, I thought it might be over -- that he'd finally stay down, finally accept defeat.

Then he rolled onto his side, pushing himself up on one elbow, his face a mask of blood and hatred. "You think you've won?" he wheezed, spitting out what looked like a tooth. "This is nothing. I've got brothers who'll --"

Hammer silenced him with a kick to the ribs that flipped Piston onto his back. Not full force -- I could tell Hammer was holding back -- but enough to drive the air from Piston's lungs.

"Stay down," Hammer repeated, his voice eerily calm despite the violence of his actions. "Last warning."

Blood bubbled between Piston's lips as he laughed -- a wet, choking sound that raised the hairs on my arms. "You can't protect them forever, old man. Those are my boys. My blood."

Hammer's expression hardened, the lines of his face deepening in the harsh glow of the neon sign. He reached down, grabbing a fistful of Piston's shirt, and hauled him partially off the ground.

"Like I said, those boys are mine now," he said, each word precise and measured despite the exertion of the fight. "You come near my family again, and you won't walk away. I'm giving you one chance to leave this place and never come back. Not for you, but for them."

Family. The word echoed in my chest, spreading warmth despite the chill of the night and the violence I'd just witnessed. Hammer hadn't just said my boys or Amelia's sons. He'd said my family. Claimed us all.

Piston's bloodied lips twisted in a grotesque approximation of a smile. "She's not worth the trouble," he sneered, eyes flickering to me. "Never was. But those are my sons, and no piece of paper, no old man playing hero changes that."

Hammer's response was immediate, his grip on Piston's shirt tightening until the fabric began to tear. "They're not your sons anymore," he said, his voice dropping to a dangerous growl that made my skin prickle. "They're mine."

He released Piston then, letting him fall back to the pavement with a *thud*.

Piston lay there, chest heaving, blood still seeping from various cuts on his face. For the first time since I'd known him, he looked genuinely afraid -- not of pain or physical damage, but of something deeper. The loss of control. The realization that his threats no longer held power.

In the distance, I heard the distinctive rumble of motorcycles -- multiple engines growing louder by the second. Hammer didn't turn to look, but a grim satisfaction flickered across his face.

"Hear that?" he asked, still standing over Piston. "Those are my brothers. Any minute now, this parking lot's going to be full of Dixie Reapers who'd be happy to continue this conversation if you're still here."

Piston's eyes darted toward the sound, then back to Hammer. With what looked like monumental effort, he rolled onto his side and pushed himself to his knees, then to his feet. He swayed dangerously, one arm wrapped around his ribs where Hammer's kick had landed.

"This isn't over," he spat, blood dribbling down his chin. "Not by a long shot."

"It is for tonight," Hammer replied, his stance relaxed but ready.

Piston's gaze shifted to me, and I instinctively pressed harder against the car door. "You better hope he never lets his guard down, Amelia," he said, voice thick with blood and malice. "Because when he does -- and he will -- I'll be waiting. For all of you."

Without waiting for a response, he staggered backward, putting distance between himself and Hammer. From the shadows beyond the parking lot, a figure emerged -- one of Piston's club brothers, I realized with a jolt of fear. The man helped Piston limp toward a car parked on the street, hidden from where I'd been standing earlier.

The distinctive headlights of several motorcycles cut through the darkness at the entrance to the parking lot. Venom led the procession, his massive frame recognizable even at a distance. Behind him came at least four other Reapers, their bikes moving in perfect formation.

Piston and his brother were already in their car, pulling away from the curb with a squeal of tires before the Reapers fully entered the lot.

Hammer turned to me then, the fierce protector of moments ago transforming back into the man I'd come to rely on over these past weeks. He approached slowly, giving me time to process, to breathe, to find my footing in the aftermath of violence.

"Are you hurt?" he asked, his voice gentler than I'd ever heard it. Blood -- Piston's blood -- smeared his knuckles, and a bruise was already forming at his temple where one of Piston's punches had landed.

I shook my head, though in truth I wasn't sure. My body felt numb, disconnected, like I was floating slightly above the scene rather than participating in it.

Hammer moved closer, positioning himself between me and the direction Piston had disappeared, his body a shield even now. His hand reached up, hesitating just short of touching my face where Piston's fingers had dug into my jaw.

"I should've killed him," he said quietly, the words not meant to frighten but offered as a simple truth.

"No," I whispered, finding my voice at last. "No more violence. Not for me."

His eyes, dark and intense in the dim light, searched mine. "And that's why I didn't, but... He won't stop, Amelia. A man like that doesn't back down. Doesn't let go."

"I know." I swallowed hard. "But I don't want his blood on your hands."

Hammer's expression softened, the fierce protector giving way to something more vulnerable. "Already got his blood on my hands," he said, lifting his battered knuckles with a ghost of a smile. "Question is, are you okay with that? With what happened here?"

I thought about Piston's threats, about the violence I'd witnessed, about Hammer claiming my boys -- claiming all of us -- as his family. About the fierce protectiveness that had driven this man to defend us without hesitation.

"Yes," I said, my voice stronger now. "I'm okay with that."

Hammer lifted his bloodied hand, cupping my

cheek with impossible gentleness.

"Let's go home," he said simply.

Home. To the house where my boys slept safely. Where Hammer's gruff kindness had slowly healed wounds we hadn't even recognized were still bleeding. Where, somehow, in the midst of danger and false starts and awkward beginnings, we had begun to build something real.

I nodded, leaning into his touch despite the blood, despite the violence, despite everything. "Home," I agreed.

Chapter Sixteen

Hammer

My knuckles throbbed as I pushed through the clubhouse door, the smell of whiskey, cigarettes, and brotherhood hitting me like a physical force. I flexed my fingers, feeling the skin pull tight over split flesh, Piston's blood still crusted in the creases. The satisfying ache reminded me of the solid connection my fist had made with his face. Not enough. Not nearly enough for threatening what was mine. The usual evening noise dropped to a low murmur as I stepped inside, brothers turning to watch my entrance, their eyes noting the blood on my hands, the bruise forming on my arm where I'd blocked his hit.

I'd sent Amelia home with Venom and Ridley, despite her protests. She'd wanted to stay with me, to face this together, but I needed her safe with the boys. Needed to know they were protected while I handled club business. The memory of Piston's hands on her burned in my gut like battery acid.

Viking approached first, handing me a glass of whiskey without asking. "Left that asshole bleeding pretty good," he said, voice low and approving. "Should've let us finish him."

"Next time," I growled, throwing back the whiskey in one burning swallow. "Amelia isn't ready. Not that she wants him alive, but she doesn't want us to kill him."

The clubhouse was unusually full for a weeknight, brothers gathered in tight clusters. Four had been at the diner when shit went down -- Prophet, Warden, Dice, and Venom -- called in by Wire as soon as Piston's bike had been spotted in town. They'd arrived just as the fight was ending and had apparently seen a Devil's Minions Prospect helping Piston into a car. I'd been more focused on my wife.

"He won't go far," Sticks remarked, leaning against the bar next to me. "Not with his face rearranged like that. You did a number on him, brother."

"Should've done more," I muttered, slamming my empty glass down harder than intended.

I scanned the room, counting brothers present. Almost everyone accounted for, save those on runs or guard duty. Word traveled fast in a club like ours. A brother in trouble, an old lady threatened -- it pulled everyone in like gravity.

"Church in five," Savior announced from across the room, his voice carrying effortlessly over the low rumble of conversation.

Brothers began moving toward the chapel doors, some clapping my shoulder as they passed, others nodding in silent solidarity. I remained at the bar, draining a second whiskey, needing the liquid fire to calm the rage still coursing through my system.

"You good?" Saint asked, pausing beside me.

I grunted an affirmative, though we both knew it was bullshit. I wouldn't be good until Piston was dealt with permanently. Until my family was safe.

My family. The words still felt strange rolling through my mind. Not long ago I'd been a confirmed bachelor with an adult son and an adopted daughter. Now I had a wife and two teenage boys. A ready-made family dropped into my life thanks to a hacker kid's meddling. And somehow, somewhere along the line, I'd started thinking of them as mine. The realization sat heavy in my chest, both comforting and terrifying.

The chapel fell silent as we filed in, boots thudding against the worn hardwood, leather cuts creaking as brothers took their seats around the scarred wooden table. Decades of cigarette burns, knife marks, and spilled whiskey decorated its surface, each imperfection a piece of club history.

I took my place, feeling the weight of eyes on me. Not judging -- never that -- but assessing, calculating. Measuring how far I'd go to protect what was mine. How far they'd need to go with me.

Savior called the meeting to order with a single rap of his knuckles against the table. No gavel needed -- just the simple authority of a respected President.

"Most of you know we've got a situation," Savior began, his gaze steady on the gathered faces. "Hammer's old lady was approached tonight. Threatened." He nodded in my direction. "Tell them what happened, brother."

I leaned forward, elbows on the table, feeling the familiar scratch of wood against my forearms. The words came out harsh, clipped, each one tasting like bile as I recounted finding Piston with his hands on Amelia. How he'd promised to take the boys back.

"Talking about her like she was property. Like the boys were his to claim when he's never done a Goddamn thing for them except terrorize them."

Murmurs of anger rippled around the table. There were lines even we didn't cross. Threatening women and children topped that list.

"He put his hands on her?" Tempest asked, his voice dangerously soft.

I nodded, feeling my jaw clench so tight my teeth might crack. "Had her pinned against her car. Would've done worse if I hadn't shown up. Thank God, Wire had spotted that asshole near the diner and called me."

"Did she tell you what he wanted?" Saint asked,

his voice calmer but no less intense.

"The boys," I answered flatly. "Claims they're his blood, his property. Said he'd dismantle everything she'd built here, starting with me."

Low curses circled the table. Brothers shifted in their seats, the air in the chapel growing thick with tension and unspoken violence.

"He knows you're married?" Savior confirmed.

"He knew she's with someone in the club. Didn't seem to know about the marriage certificate specifically." I leaned back, crossing my arms over my chest. "Doesn't matter. I told him, made it clear those boys are mine now. My family. Under my protection."

The words hung in the air, a formal declaration that carried weight in our world. I hadn't planned to say it -- hadn't even admitted it fully to myself until tonight -- but seeing Piston's hands on Amelia, hearing his threats against her and the boys, had crystallized something inside me. They were mine. Not just on paper, not just as an arrangement, but mine to protect. Mine to care for.

"Those boys," I continued, my voice dropping lower, "have been through hell with that man. Chase still stands between his brother and the door, every Goddamn time someone enters a room. Levi flinches at sudden movements. They've been carrying scars from that bastard their whole lives." I looked around the table, meeting each brother's gaze. "I won't let him near them again. I claimed them tonight, to his face. Told him they weren't his sons anymore. They're mine."

Prophet nodded slowly, his expression grim. "Devil's Minions won't take that lying down. This isn't just about an ex-wife anymore. It's about respect. About saving face."

"Fuck their respect," I snapped. "They want a war, I'll give them a war. And for the record, she made sure to tell him she was never his wife."

Savior raised his hand, a subtle gesture that immediately quieted the room. "We do this smart," he said, his voice level but carrying an undercurrent of steel. "We do this right. The Devil's Minions aren't just some random assholes. They've got reach. Got connections. But so do we." He looked around the table. "I want options. I want strategies. How do we handle this?"

We'd tossed some ideas around before, but when it had only been a Prospect in town, the club hadn't given the issue the attention it really needed. But now that Piston was here, things were different.

The floor opened, brothers exchanging glances, the seasoned members calculating potential moves like a chess game. The younger ones leaning forward, eyes bright with the prospect of conflict. All of them -- every last brother at this table -- ready to stand against anyone who threatened one of our own.

My rage simmered, hot and ready beneath my skin, but I forced myself to listen. To think beyond the blood I wanted to spill. Amelia and the boys needed protection, not just vengeance. They needed a permanent solution, not just temporary satisfaction.

And as I looked around at my brothers, at men I'd ridden with for decades, I knew we'd find that solution. Together. Because that's what family did.

Saint stood first, his voice cutting through the charged atmosphere. Unlike Tempest, who wore his emotions like his patches -- loud and proud -- Saint had always been more of a strategist, a thinker, the one who saw three moves ahead while the rest of us were still reaching for our weapons. "We need to think long-term here. The Devil's Boneyard already has beef with the Minions. We join forces, we can push them out for good."

I clenched my jaw, fighting the immediate urge to dismiss his words. The diplomat's approach felt too slow, too bloodless for the rage burning in my chest. Every time I blinked, I saw Piston's hands on Amelia, saw the fear in her eyes that she tried so hard to hide. Those boys -- my boys now -- deserved immediate protection, not political maneuvering.

Saint continued, oblivious to my internal struggle. "I'm not saying we don't respond. I'm saying we respond smart. Coordinated. The Boneyard's been looking for an excuse to push the Minions out of their territory. They're the ones who helped Amelia escape in the first place."

"And look how well that worked," I muttered, flexing my bruised knuckles. "Piston still found her."

"Because we've been playing defense," Saint countered, his gaze steady on mine. "I'm talking about offense. Strategic offense. We reach out to allied clubs -- Boneyard, Savage Knights, Southern Devils -- create a united front. Make it so the Minions have nowhere to run, nowhere to hide. No fueling stations, no safe houses, no friendly bars or dealers."

The logic made sense, and I hated it. Hated that my need for immediate blood was being countered with reason and strategy. But forty years in this life had taught me that Saint's approach was solid. Patient. Effective in the long run.

"How long?" I asked, the question coming out like gravel. "How long before Amelia and the boys are safe?"

Saint's expression softened marginally. "Sooner than going in half-cocked and starting a war we might not win cleanly. The Minions have reach in three states, if not more. They've got cops on payroll. Judges. We hit them directly, we risk blowback."

Before I could respond, Tempest slammed his fist onto the table, the impact sending an empty whiskey glass toppling. Our Sergeant-at-Arms had never been known for subtlety or patience. His face was flushed with anger, eyes burning as he leaned forward.

"Fuck diplomacy," he growled, his voice vibrating with barely contained fury. "They threatened one of our old ladies. We hit them now, hit them hard." He looked around the table, challenging anyone to disagree. "You think making nice with other clubs is gonna stop Piston? You think he gives a shit about territory lines or diplomatic pressure? He put his hands on Hammer's woman. He threatened to kill her."

Murmurs of agreement rippled around the table. Younger patches leaned forward, hungry for action, for blood. The older ones exchanged weighted glances, measuring options, calculating risks. The division was visible even without words -- the hotheads eager to mount up and ride versus the strategists wanting a planned approach.

"I'm not saying we do nothing," Saint clarified, his patience a testament to years of these debates. "I'm saying we make sure when we strike, it's final. No half measures. No loose ends. Taking out Piston isn't going to solve the issue of the Devil's Minions. If anything, it will only provoke them."

"While we're planning," Tempest countered, "Piston's out there licking his wounds, getting ready to make another move. You think he'll wait for us to form a strategic alliance? Fuck that. We send a message. Tonight. His clubhouse, his businesses. Anything we can locate, or other clubs can get their hands on. Burn them to the ground."

The part of me that was just a man, just a husband protecting his wife, roared in agreement with Tempest. I wanted to feel the satisfying crunch of Piston's bones under my fists again. Wanted to finish what I'd started in that parking lot.

But the other part of me -- the part that had spent time in prison, the part that now had two more boys looking to me for safety -- knew Saint's approach had merit. Fighting Piston one-on-one was one thing. Taking on his entire club without backup was another. The boys needed me alive and free more than they needed Piston dead quickly.

"Both approaches have good points and bad ones," Prophet offered, breaking his usual silence. "We can move on multiple fronts. Diplomatic channels take time to establish. While Saint works those angles, we make sure Piston understands the immediate consequences of threatening one of ours."

Warden nodded, his massive frame shifting as he leaned forward. "A show of force doesn't mean all-out war. Just enough to make them think twice before trying anything else."

The debate intensified, brothers talking over each other now, the chapel filled with the low rumble of aggressive suggestions, strategic concerns, and practical considerations. I sat silent, absorbing their words, weighing options. This wasn't just about my pride or my rage anymore. This was about Amelia's safety. About Chase and Levi growing up without looking over their shoulders.

"Hammer," Savior said, drawing my attention. "Your call. Your family that's been threatened."

The chapel fell silent, all eyes turning to me. The

weight of their expectations, their brotherhood, pressed against my shoulders. They would follow whatever direction I chose. Would back my play, whether it was Saint's measured approach or Tempest's immediate retaliation.

I drew a deep breath, forcing the red haze of rage to clear enough for rational thought. "Both," I said finally. "We do both. Saint starts reaching out to allied clubs tonight. Sets the diplomatic wheels in motion." I turned to Tempest. "And we send a message. Not the clubhouse -- too obvious, too expected. His businesses. His income. Hit him where it hurts while making it clear why we're doing it."

A slow smile spread across Tempest's face, eager and predatory. "Now you're talking."

"I'd already started digging," Wire said. "I can handle crippling him financially. As for physical attacks, those will be harder. Everything he has in his name is in Florida, and I don't think you want to leave long enough to handle that yourself."

I grunted and knew he was right. Didn't mean I had to like it.

"The response has to be proportional," Saint cautioned. "We make a point without pushing them into a corner where they have nothing to lose."

"He threatened to kill my wife," I said, the words coming out like bullets. "He promised to take my boys. There's nothing proportional about what I want to do to him."

"And we'll do it," Savior assured me, his voice calm but carrying absolute conviction. "But we'll do it right. We'll do it so it ends with him, not with a war that puts everyone at risk. Sure, we've gone up against some heavy players in the past, but the Devil's Minions aren't like the others. They have too many chapters and their reach is beyond what we can handle."

The tension in the room shifted subtly, brothers nodding in agreement, the divide between immediate action and strategic planning beginning to blur. It wasn't either/or. It was both. A show of force now, coupled with a longer strategy to eliminate the threat permanently.

"So we're agreed?" Savior asked, looking around the table.

The responses came in quick succession, brothers voicing support, some pounding the table in emphasis, others offering quiet but firm agreement. The path forward was taking shape, a compromise between blood and diplomacy, between immediate satisfaction and lasting security.

As the details of the plan began to emerge, I felt some of the savage tension in my chest ease slightly. The image of Piston's hands on Amelia still burned behind my eyes.

Tempest caught my eye across the table, a silent question in his gaze. *Are you with us? Are you satisfied with this?*

I nodded once, definitive. Piston would pay. Maybe not tonight, maybe not all at once, but he would pay. And when it was over, he would never threaten my family again.

Savior rose from his seat. He looked each of us in the eye, taking our measure, before laying out a plan that would change more than just Piston's future.

"We're not just running them out of Alabama," he declared, his voice cutting through the last murmurs of disagreement. "We're going to systematically push them north, state by state, until they have nowhere left to call home. Not down here."

The chapel fell silent, brothers leaning forward as

Savior continued, his calloused finger tracing a route across the map tacked to the wall beside our table. Something we'd added after the last few battles we'd faced.

"We coordinate with the Devil's Boneyard to squeeze them from the south. The Savage Knights and Southern Devils to block them from the west. We leave them only one direction to run -- north -- where they'll hit the Crimson Skulls' territory." A grim smile touched Savior's lips. "And the Skulls have been looking for an excuse to thin the Minions' ranks for years."

It was elegant in its brutality -- a strategic noose that would tighten slowly, deliberately, forcing Piston and his club into increasingly hostile territory. Not the immediate bloodbath Tempest had wanted, but not the diplomatic dance Saint had suggested either. Something more effective than either extreme.

"We start tonight," Savior continued. "Tempest, reach out to our contacts in Florida. Set up a team to hit their distribution warehouse. No casualties if it can be helped but tell them to make sure nothing's left standing. Also, get that list of Piston's properties from Wire. Make sure those are lit up. Saint, reach out to every club we have a connection with down here, as well as out west. Oklahoma, California, Texas, Nevada... I want as wide a reach as we can get."

Brothers around the table began nodding, fists pounding wood in approval. The division that had threatened to fracture our response melted away, replaced by unified purpose. This was why Savior had become President after Torch stepped down -- his ability to take competing approaches and forge them into something stronger than their parts.

"What about Piston specifically?" I asked,

needing to know how the man who had threatened my family would be handled.

Savior's eyes met mine, understanding the personal nature of my question. "He'll be isolated. Cut off from club resources. And then, when he's vulnerable, when he has nowhere to turn…" He left the sentence unfinished, but the implication was clear.

A slow, vicious satisfaction uncurled in my chest, replacing some of the burning rage. This was better than an immediate hit -- more thorough, more complete.

"And my family?" I pushed. "While this is happening?"

"Protected at all times," Savior assured me. "Rotating security details at your place, escorts for Amelia to and from work, surveillance on the boys' school. No one gets near them without going through us first. But after what they've been through, I also don't want to put them on lockdown. We just make sure they're covered every time they leave the compound."

The last of my objections dissolved. This wasn't just about vengeance anymore -- it was about ensuring Amelia and the boys could build a life without fear. A permanent solution rather than a temporary satisfaction.

"I'm calling Church adjourned," Savior announced. "Prophet, Warden, coordinate security rotations for Hammer's family. Tempest, in addition to setting up a team in Florida, make sure we have eyes on Piston at all times. Saint, my office -- we'll start making calls."

The chapel erupted into controlled chaos, brothers rising from their seats, breaking into smaller groups, assignments being handed out, burner phones appearing. I remained seated, watching as my brothers mobilized to protect what was mine, a strange tightness forming in my throat. Many times I'd been part of this chaos, willing to lay down my life for someone else's family. It felt different when we were protecting my wife and kids.

Forty plus years in this life, and still the loyalty, the absolute brotherhood, had the power to humble me. These men would risk their freedom, their lives, for my family -- not just because they were my blood, but because I had claimed them. Because I had brought them under the protection of the patch. In our world, that meant something sacred, something unbreakable.

"Hammer," Savior called from the doorway where he stood with Saint. "Need anything specific from the Boneyard?"

I considered the question, thinking of all Amelia had been through, of the fear that still lingered in her eyes. "Information," I said finally. "Everything they have on Piston's operations, his weaknesses. And..." I hesitated, then added, "Ask if they know about Amelia's father. She mentioned he was with another club. Might be worth reaching out. From what I gathered, she never knew him. Mom might have lied to her too, so could be a wild goose chase."

Savior nodded, understanding my logic without needing elaboration. More allies meant more protection. And if Amelia's father was in the life, he had a right to know his daughter and grandsons were in danger -- and a right to stand with us against that threat.

The chapel emptied quickly, brothers moving with purpose toward their assignments. I rose finally, crossing to the map on the wall where Savior had traced the planned extermination of the Devil's

Minions. My weathered finger traced the same path, imagining Piston running like a rat in a maze, each exit blocked, each hiding place exposed. The thought brought a grim satisfaction that settled like whiskey in my blood, warm and potent.

Behind me, chairs scraped as Prospects entered to clean the chapel; ashtrays emptied, whiskey glasses collected, the evidence of our meeting erased with practiced efficiency. I barely noticed them, my focus entirely on the map, on the plan, on the future it represented for my unlikely family.

Piston would pay for threatening to take what was mine. He would never get his hands on her because I would burn his entire world to the ground. Because the Dixie Reapers protected their own. Because I had claimed her and those boys as mine, and nothing -- not Piston, not his club, not hell itself -- would take them from me.

That wasn't just a husband's promise or a biker's threat. It was a vow written in my soul, as permanent as the ink on my skin, as binding as the patch on my back. And God help anyone who tested it.

Chapter Seventeen

Amelia

I paced from window to window, checking locks I'd already verified three times in the last hour. The compound had transformed since we'd returned home, brothers appearing from all corners with weapons visible at their hips, stern-faced men posting up at entrances and patrolling the perimeter. Our small house that had begun to feel like home now felt like the center of a storm, everything outside our walls a potential threat. My fingers trembled slightly as I tugged on another window latch, needing the physical reassurance that it was secured, that nothing could slip through to harm my boys.

"Mom, you checked that one already," Chase said from across the room, his voice tense as he continued his own patrol, moving between the front door and the hallway leading to Levi's room. His shoulders were bunched tight beneath his T-shirt, fists clenching and unclenching at his sides.

"I know," I admitted, not stopping as I moved to the next window. "Just being thorough."

What I didn't say was that the image of Piston's bloodied face was seared into my mind, along with his promise that this wasn't over. I'd seen that look in his eyes too many times -- the cold calculation beneath the rage that meant he was already planning his revenge.

Levi sat in the corner of the living room, as far from the windows as possible while still maintaining sight lines to both exterior doors. His laptop was open, but his fingers weren't flying across the keyboard like usual. Instead, they tapped a nervous rhythm against the edge, his eyes darting between the screen and his brother's pacing figure.

"Can you see anything on the cameras?" Chase asked him, pausing mid-stride.

Levi adjusted his glasses, which had slipped down his nose. "Four Reapers at the main gate. Two walking the east fence line. Another three by the clubhouse." His voice was quiet but steady as he reported what he saw on the security feed Atlas had helped him access. "No unusual activity."

I moved to peek around the edge of the curtain, careful not to disturb the fabric enough that someone watching could spot my movement. The compound looked like it was preparing for war. And maybe they were.

The sound of motorcycles approaching made my heart leap into my throat. I pressed my face closer to the glass, straining to see through the darkness until I recognized Hammer's distinctive silhouette leading three other riders. Relief washed through me.

Chase had heard the engines too. He moved to the front window, positioning himself between the door and where Levi sat. "It's them," he confirmed, his body language betraying none of the relief I felt.

The front door opened, and Hammer entered, followed by Viking and two Prospects whose names I couldn't remember. The scent of gasoline and smoke clung to Hammer's clothes, and there was a darkness in his eyes that hadn't been there when he left. Not rage, exactly, but something colder, more focused.

"Perimeter's secure," Viking reported, his massive frame filling the doorway as Hammer moved toward me.

Hammer nodded, his gaze sweeping over me and the boys, cataloging our positions, our tension, before turning back to his brother. "Double the patrols on the east fence. It's the weakest point."

"Already done," Viking confirmed. "Savior and Tempest are coordinating with the Boneyard. They're moving tonight as planned."

Hammer dismissed the men with a nod, waiting until the door closed behind them before crossing to where I stood. His hand touched my lower back briefly, the gesture oddly intimate in its casualness, as if we'd been together for years.

"You're back early," I said, searching his face for clues about what had happened.

Before I could ask more, Chase approached, his stance still coiled tight as a spring. "What's going on?" he demanded. "Are we under attack?"

Hammer turned to face him, not offended by the tone that bordered on disrespect. "Precautions," he explained. "Standard procedure when there's a threat."

"This doesn't look standard," Chase challenged, gesturing toward the window and the activity outside. "This looks like a fortress."

Levi had abandoned his laptop, moving to stand closer but still half-hidden behind his brother. His thin shoulders were hunched inward, making him appear even smaller than his five-foot-eight frame.

Hammer's expression softened slightly as he looked at them, these boys who'd been thrown into his life by circumstance and were now his to protect. "That's exactly what it is," he agreed. "And that's why you're safe here."

He moved to the center of the room, commanding attention without raising his voice. "Silent alarms on every entrance. Brothers patrolling 24/7. Nobody gets in without us knowing. Three layers of security before anyone reaches this house. And they'd have to get through me to reach any of you."

Chase's jaw worked, his eyes hard and skeptical. "What happens if Piston shows up? What if he brings his whole club?"

I tensed at the question, at the name spoken aloud in our space. But Hammer didn't flinch, didn't hesitate. He looked my son directly in the eye.

"Then he deals with me and thirty other Reapers who won't let him near you." The certainty in his voice carried the weight of decades spent keeping his word, of promises made and kept in blood if necessary. "He comes here, he doesn't leave again."

Chase and Levi exchanged a look -- one I recognized immediately: cautious hope tempered by too much experience with broken promises, with protection that failed when they needed it most.

"We've heard that before," Chase said, not accusingly, just stating a fact. "People say they'll protect us, then they don't. Or can't."

Honestly, that had only happened once. A neighbor had noticed the bruises and hadn't bought my excuses. Piston had made sure the man would never stick his nose in anyone else's business ever again.

Something shifted in Hammer's expression -- not anger, but a deeper resolve. He stepped closer to Chase, not touching him, but eliminating the safe distance my son tried to maintain from all adults, especially men.

"I'm not people," Hammer said, his voice dropping lower. "I'm a Dixie Reaper." His eyes held Chase's, forcing my son to either meet his gaze or back down. "More importantly, I'm your stepfather now. That means something to me, even if it doesn't to you yet."

The silence that followed felt charged, like the air

before lightning strikes. I held my breath, watching my eldest son -- so hurt, so wary -- measure this man who'd claimed us with nothing but a fake marriage certificate and his word. Chase had seemed to like Hammer well enough, until I'd offered myself to the man. I wondered if Chase blamed himself for my decision. We hadn't discussed it. I'd known it wouldn't do me any good. If he'd wanted to talk about it, he'd have let me know.

"What if he comes with more men than you have?" Levi asked suddenly, his voice small but clear in the tension-filled room. "What if he has a plan? He always has a plan."

Hammer turned to my youngest, his expression gentling further. "Then we have a better one," he assured him. "And more allies than he knows about. We're reaching out to your grandfather."

My heart stuttered. Sure, I'd mentioned my dad was part of a club. I didn't remember ever saying his name. How had he known? Wait. Atlas and his family... had they figured it out?

"Wrath? You're contacting Wrath?" I asked.

It was a name I'd heard several times as I'd grown up, wondering about my father. If my mother had been telling the truth, he was part of a motorcycle club in Nevada called the Savage Knights. I'd never tried to track him down. She'd said he hadn't wanted a family, so I'd tried to respect that.

Hammer nodded once. "Saint's making the call tonight. The Savage Knights will want to know their President has a daughter and grandsons being threatened."

The implications of that stunned me into silence. My father -- the man who'd never known I existed, who led another MC across the country -- was about to learn not only that he had a daughter, but that she was in danger. The potential for that response felt both overwhelming and strangely comforting. Assuming he gave a shit.

Chase's face had gone carefully blank, but I could see the calculations happening behind his eyes. Levi looked torn between hope and deeper fear, as if adding more players to this dangerous game might tip it in either direction.

"You should get some rest," Hammer said, coming to stand beside me. "All of you. It's been a long day and tomorrow won't be easier."

I knew he was right, but the thought of closing my eyes, of letting my guard down even for a moment, sent a fresh wave of anxiety through me. "I don't think I can sleep," I admitted quietly.

"You should try," he insisted, his hand finding the small of my back again. "I'll be right here. Nothing gets past me."

Looking into his weathered face, at the silver beard that had tickled my skin during our brief, stolen kiss, I found myself believing him despite years of learned distrust. Hammer was nothing like Piston -- nothing like any man I'd known before. When he made a promise, I was beginning to understand it wasn't just words.

It was a vow written in iron and blood.

The sound of tires on gravel had Chase at the window before I could even move, his body tense as he peered through a narrow gap in the curtains. I held my breath, hand already reaching for Levi who'd gone perfectly still in his corner. The subtle shift in Chase's shoulders -- a loosening, a recognition -- came before his words. "It's Aura," he reported, voice carefully neutral though I caught the hint of relief. "She's got bags. Looks like supplies."

"The girl never could follow a simple order to stay put," Hammer muttered, though I noted the fondness underlying his gruff tone. He moved to the front door, checking through the peephole before disengaging the three deadbolts we'd installed just yesterday. For whatever reason, she'd wanted to give us a little space and had gotten permission to use the duplex for a few days. But I had to wonder if that was her way of slowly moving out on her own and leaving the nest, so to speak.

Aura burst in like a breath of fresh air, her arms laden with grocery bags. Her dark hair was pulled into a messy bun, her tattooed arms exposed by her tank top despite the evening chill. "Food for the troops," she announced, kicking the door closed behind her. "And backup chargers, flashlights, first aid kit -- you know, siege essentials."

The tension in the room eased fractionally at her arrival. Even Chase's perpetual scowl softened as she thrust a bag into his arms. "Make yourself useful, big guy. These are heavy."

Levi approached cautiously, his need to help warring with his instinct to stay hidden. Aura solved his dilemma by gently placing a smaller bag in his hands. "This one's got the tech stuff. Figured you'd want first crack at organizing it."

"Thanks," he mumbled, but took the bag, the ghost of a smile touching his lips as he peeked inside and lifted out what looked like portable battery packs.

I watched this interaction with a mixture of gratitude and fascination. Aura had a way with my boys that I couldn't quite explain -- a casualness that bypassed their defenses, an understanding that didn't demand their trust but somehow earned it anyway. In the short time since we'd moved in, she'd become something between a sister and daughter to me, and something entirely her own to my sons.

"Perimeter check in fifteen," Hammer told me, his hand briefly touching my lower back as he passed. "Need to coordinate with the night shift."

I nodded, unconsciously leaning into his touch. "I'll help Aura unpack."

He hesitated, glancing at her with a look that carried entire conversations. "Keep them occupied," he said, the words casual but loaded with meaning.

"Always do, old man," she replied with an easy grin that softened the gravity of our situation. "Now go do your thing. We're fine here."

Aura herded us all toward the kitchen, distributing bags and assigning tasks with the efficiency of someone used to managing chaos. "Levi, can you sort the batteries? Chase, start unpacking the groceries. Amelia, I think it would be best if we had the leftover chili for dinner tonight."

We fell into the work, the simple rhythm of domestic tasks creating a bubble of normalcy in the midst of our fortress-like surroundings. After nearly twenty minutes of this strange domesticity, Hammer appeared in the doorway.

I hesitated, looking at my boys. Chase was methodically arranging canned goods in the pantry, his back deliberately turned to the room, while Levi sat cross-legged on the floor, sorting through electronic equipment with Aura.

Chase turned and met my gaze briefly, something new in his expression -- not quite trust, but perhaps the seedling of it. Levi seemed more relaxed than he had been all day.

"It's getting late," I said, noting the shadows

under my youngest's eyes. "You two should try to get some sleep."

Surprisingly, neither argued -- another sign of their exhaustion. Chase moved first, his movement triggering Levi's automatic response to follow. But before they left the kitchen, Chase paused beside Aura.

"Thanks," he said simply, the word carrying more weight than its single syllable should allow.

Aura reached up, adjusting the collar of his shirt with casual affection. "Anytime, kiddo. That's what family does."

The word hung in the air between us all -- family. Not by blood, not by choice initially, but forged in necessity and slowly, tentatively, becoming something real. As I watched my boys retreat to their room, I caught Hammer's gaze across the kitchen. Even though he'd spent our days together running from any intimacy, we'd somehow still managed to merge our families together into a cohesive unit. Now if I could just get him on board for the husband side of this relationship.

* * *

Rain pattered against the windows, the gentle rhythm at odds with the harsh reality of armed men patrolling outside. I sat at the kitchen table across from Hammer, maps of the compound spread between us, his calloused finger tracing potential escape routes while I committed them to memory. The boys had finally fallen asleep in their bedrooms, Aura had gone to the duplex for the night, and for the first time since the confrontation with Piston, Hammer and I found ourselves truly alone.

"If anything happens, you go out this service exit," Hammer was saying, his weathered finger tapping a point on the map. "There's always someone posted here, but they'll know to let you through. From there, you take this path to the garage in town."

I leaned closer, my hair falling forward as I studied the route he indicated. The proximity brought his scent to me -- motor oil, leather, and something distinctly male that I'd come to associate with safety. Our shoulders brushed, the contact sending a current of awareness through me despite the seriousness of our conversation.

"What about the boys?" I asked, voice low though there was no need to whisper. "Chase would never leave me, and Levi --"

"They'll be with you," he assured me, his finger sliding to another position on the map. "Viking knows to get them if I can't. He'll bring them to this meeting point." His hand shifted, accidentally covering mine where it rested on the table. Neither of us moved to break the contact.

"You've thought of everything," I murmured, not moving my hand from beneath his.

He grunted softly. "That's the job." After a pause, he added more quietly, "That's my promise to you."

The simple declaration hung in the air between us, weighted with meanings neither of us had fully acknowledged yet. My gaze lifted from the maps to his face, studying the lines that years had carved around his eyes. He'd removed his cut hours ago, wearing just a worn black T-shirt that revealed the strength still present in his arms despite his age.

Rain drummed harder against the windows, the sound creating a cocoon of isolation around us. Outside, men patrolled with guns, planning violence against those who'd threatened us. Inside, this small bubble of quiet felt almost sacred -- a moment of stillness in the chaos our lives had become.

"I'm afraid," I admitted, the words slipping out before I could stop them. "Not for me. For them. Chase is so angry all the time, waiting for the next threat. And Levi -- he tries to make himself invisible, like if no one notices him, no one can hurt him."

Hammer's hand tightened over mine. "They're survivors. Like their mother."

"I'm no survivor," I argued softly. "I stayed with him for years. Let him hurt them, hurt me. A survivor would have --"

"Would have what?" Hammer interrupted, his gaze holding mine. "Left with nothing? No money, no protection, no plan? With two kids depending on you?" He shook his head. "You did leave. When you could. That's what matters."

His understanding -- so different from the judgment I'd been carrying against myself for years -- made my throat tighten. "What if it wasn't soon enough? What if they're too damaged to ever feel safe?"

"They're not damaged," he said firmly. "They're adapting. Learning who to trust. How to live without constant threat." His free hand reached across the table, hesitating before brushing a strand of hair from my face. "It takes time."

The gentle touch, so at odds with his gruff exterior, broke something open inside me. "I can't lose them," I whispered, my greatest fear finally given voice. "If Piston takes them --"

"He won't," Hammer stated, the certainty in his voice absolute. "I swear it, Amelia. He will never touch those boys again. Never touch you again."

His hand still cupped my cheek, warm and calloused against my skin. All the tension that had been building since our brief kitchen kiss -- the distance he'd maintained, the careful space between us in bed -- seemed to crystallize in this moment of vulnerability.

I didn't know which of us moved first. Maybe both. One moment we were near enough to touch, yet not, and the next his lips were on mine, his beard tickling my skin as his mouth claimed me with surprising gentleness.

The kiss was nothing like our first hesitant contact in the kitchen. This was deliberate, hungry, his hand sliding from my cheek to the back of my neck, holding me to him as if afraid I might pull away. I gripped his shirt, the worn cotton bunching in my fingers as I kissed him back with all the fear and need and gratitude I couldn't put into words.

"Amelia," he murmured against my lips, my name a question and a prayer.

"Yes," I answered, though he hadn't actually asked. "Please."

The table between us became an unbearable obstacle. Hammer stood, his chair scraping against the floor as he pulled me to my feet and back into his arms. His body was solid against mine, stronger than his age would suggest, his hands spanning my waist as he backed me against the kitchen counter.

Our kiss deepened, his tongue sliding against mine, drawing a sound from me I hadn't made in years -- a hungry whimper that seemed to fuel his own desire. His hands didn't wander, didn't grab or take, but held me with a careful restraint that made me want to break his control.

"The boys," I gasped against his mouth, remembering where we were.

"Sleeping," he reminded me between kisses.

That simple assurance was all I needed. I let my hands explore him, tracing the solid muscle of his chest beneath his shirt, feeling the beat of his heart against my palm. His breath hitched when my fingers brushed across his stomach, dipping toward his belt.

"Bedroom," he growled, the word vibrating against my throat where his mouth had moved to taste my skin.

"Too far," I answered, tugging him toward the living room instead. "Couch."

He didn't argue, his hands steady on my hips as we moved together, unwilling to break contact even to walk across the house. When my legs hit the couch, he paused, pulling back just enough to search my face in the dim light.

"You sure about this?" he asked, his voice rough with desire but his eyes serious. "About me?"

"I've never been more sure of anything," I told him honestly.

Something vulnerable flickered across his face. "I'm not a young man," he said, the admission clearly costing him. "It's been a while. Might not be what you're --"

I silenced him with a kiss, pouring everything I felt into it -- desire, yes, but also trust, gratitude, and something deeper that neither of us was ready to name. "I don't want a young man," I whispered against his lips. "I want you. Just you."

The last of his hesitation dissolved at my words. His hands found the hem of my shirt, sliding beneath to touch bare skin with a reverence that made me tremble. I tugged at his shirt in return, needing to feel him, all of him, against me. When he lowered me to the couch, his body covering mine, I felt protected rather than trapped, desired rather than owned. The difference was monumental.

"Tell me what you need," he murmured against my neck, his beard creating delicious friction against my sensitive skin.

"Just this," I answered, guiding his hand where I wanted it. "Just you."

Hammer explored my body, pressing against my skin with a possessive force that ignited fires within me. His fingers traced the outline of my breasts, teasing my nipples until they hardened into tight peaks. Then he swiftly pulled my shirt over my head, and unclasped my bra, as if he couldn't wait another moment to see more of me.

His lips were soft and his breath hot as they whispered against my sensitive skin before enveloping one erect nipple with his warm mouth. His teeth scraped gently against it, sending shivers down my spine.

I arched my back in response, moaning softly as he continued to worship my body. My fingers dug into his hair, urging him closer even as I felt myself growing wetter for him. When he finally switched to the other nipple, drawing it between his teeth and tugging gently, I thought I might explode.

"Please," I gasped out, my voice husky with desire. "Take me."

He stood and quickly removed his clothes. I watched him hungrily as I struggled to remove my own jeans and panties. He covered my body with his, his eyes burning with a fierce intent that made my heart race. Without another word, he positioned himself at the entrance of my pussy and pushed inside with one powerful thrust. I cried out at the thickness of him filling me completely, feeling both stretched and fulfilled in ways I never knew possible.

"You're so tight," he groaned, pumping into me slowly but surely. "So fucking hot."

I couldn't form coherent thoughts anymore, lost in the sensation of being claimed by him. My body rocked against his, meeting each of his thrusts with feverish eagerness. When he reached down to play with my clit, I came undone with a muffled scream, as I slapped my hand over my mouth to silence the noise. The force of it surprised both of us, my muscles clenching around him as waves of pleasure washed over me.

"Oh God," I moaned, barely able to catch my breath. "Don't stop." And he didn't. He continued to pound into me, our hips slapping together in rhythm as he relentlessly brought us both closer to the edge once more. His rough hands roamed my body. The taste of him was on my tongue, and I wanted more -- more of this incredible connection, more of his dominance that left me aching and yearning for more.

"Look at me," he growled, pulling out almost entirely before pushing back in with renewed force. "Admit it -- you belong to me."

The words were ugly in some ways, yet they held an irresistible power that made me shiver with need. "Yes," I whispered back, meeting his gaze unflinchingly. "I belong to you."

He grunted, and after a few more strokes, I felt the heat of his release inside me. He closed his eyes and tipped his head back, pure bliss etched on his features. When he pulled out, he quickly lifted me into his arms and carried me to our bedroom, where he shut and locked the door.

"I thought you said I'd be disappointed, that you probably wouldn't be able to get it up," I said, teasing him a little.

He looked down at me. "I didn't lie. I think I was just more turned-on than I realized."

I smiled up at him softly. "Hammer, if it gets any better than that, the pleasure may kill me. It was perfect. Better than anything I've experienced before."

He eased me onto the bed and followed me down, tugging me against him. I traced idle patterns across his chest, feeling the steady beat of his heart beneath my fingertips. His arm held me close, protective even in this moment of vulnerability.

"I felt more with you just now than I ever did with him in all those years," I confessed, the words slipping out in the safe darkness between us.

Hammer's arm tightened around me, his lips pressing against my forehead. "You deserve more."

I lifted my head to look at him. "So do you. More than a wife who came with a ready-made crisis and teenage boys."

His mouth curved in a rare smile, one hand coming up to brush hair from my face with surprising tenderness. "Turns out that's exactly what I needed. Just didn't know it."

The simple honesty in his voice broke me open further. I laid my head back on his chest, listening to his heartbeat, feeling the rise and fall of his breathing. Outside, the rain continued, washing the world clean, while inside our fortress, something new and fragile had begun to bloom.

The marriage certificate might have been fake, created by a hacker kid's meddling, but what we'd just shared was undeniably real. And for the first time since fleeing Florida, I allowed myself to imagine a future where this -- this man, this family, this life -- wasn't just a temporary shelter from a storm, but a home I could actually keep.

Chapter Eighteen

Hammer

I stood in the center of the clubhouse, the familiar smell of leather, whiskey, and gun oil filling my lungs as I watched my brothers prepare for war. Not the flashy, media-friendly kind, but our kind -- brutal, efficient, and final. The last time I'd gone hunting like this had been years ago, before my knees started giving me shit in cold weather. But some things a man couldn't delegate. When someone threatened your family, you handled it yourself.

Savior unrolled a map across the scarred wooden table, weighing down the corners with spent shell casings he'd turned into mini paperweights. Brothers gathered around, their faces grim in the harsh overhead lighting. The usual rowdy banter was absent, replaced by a focused silence that only came when blood was inevitable.

"Intel puts the Minions here," Savior said, tapping a spot just outside the town limits. "They've set up some kind of barricade on the old service road. Tempest's scout counted at least twenty of them, all armed, with Piston front and center."

Saint leaned forward, studying the terrain. "They've chosen their ground well. Limited approach options, good sight lines."

"They're expecting us," Savior confirmed, his finger tracing potential routes. "Which means we give them exactly what they expect -- and then hit them where they're not looking." He outlined the plan with the precision of a man who'd spent years leading men into combat situations, pointing out approach vectors, fallback positions, and rally points.

The strategy was solid -- brothers would

approach in a standard formation, drawing attention to the main road while a secondary team circled behind using the dry creek bed that ran parallel to the service road. Simple, effective, with minimal risk to our side.

My focus zeroed in on one detail above all others: Piston would be there.

Ghost shifted beside me, his lanky frame rigid with tension. "Hammer should stay back," he said suddenly, drawing all eyes in the room. "Handle security at the compound."

I turned to face my son, seeing concern etched in lines that reminded me too much of my own face at his age. The worry in his eyes might have touched me if it weren't so Goddamn insulting.

"That's not happening," I replied, my voice low but firm.

Ghost didn't back down. "You've got a family to protect. Amelia and the boys need you here, not out there playing hero."

Several brothers exchanged glances, clearly uncomfortable with the public challenge. In any other situation, a patch questioning another patch's place in a run would earn a swift correction, but this was different. This was my son worried about his old man. This was family.

I stepped closer to him, dropping my voice so only he could hear. "I am protecting my family. By cutting off the threat at its source."

"There are twenty brothers who can handle Piston," Ghost argued, still loud enough for nearby patches to hear. "Let us deal with him."

"No." The word came out final, brooking no further argument. I turned back to the table, addressing the room. "I'll be riding point with Savior. This son of a bitch threatened my wife, threatened my boys. He's mine."

Ghost's jaw clenched, but he didn't argue further. Smart of him. Some lessons a son had to learn the hard way, and one of those was knowing when to shut up when his father had made a decision.

Savior continued outlining positions and responsibilities as if the interruption hadn't happened, though I caught the slight nod of approval he sent my way. Whatever Ghost thought, my President understood. There were some debts a man had to collect personally.

"Thunder, you and Ghost take security at the compound," I said when Savior finished. "No one gets within a hundred yards of my family. *Our* family."

Thunder nodded once, accepting the assignment without question. He probably preferred to stay behind and watch over my granddaughter and great-grandson anyway. Ghost's eyes flashed with frustration but he gave a terse nod. He might not like it, but he'd do his job. Family or not, he was a Reaper first.

I moved to the back of the clubhouse, where I'd dropped my bag earlier. I unzipped it, revealing the tools of my trade lined up with military precision. My fingers grazed each item, checking, confirming, a ritual as old as my time with the club.

First, my Glock, its weight familiar and comforting as I checked the magazine and slid it into my waistband. The brass knuckles came next, slipping into my right front pocket, the metal cold against my thigh even through the denim. My KA-BAR knife went into my boot sheath, the blade razor-sharp and oiled.

The preparations felt both ancient and new. Ancient because my body remembered these movements from a thousand similar situations over decades with the club. New because this time, the stakes were different. It wasn't just about club business or brotherhood. This was about the look in Amelia's eyes when I'd told her I was going after Piston directly. About the way Chase had watched me from the doorway, his face carefully blank but his knuckles white where he gripped the frame. About Levi's silence, more devastating than any protest could have been.

I closed the bag, feeling the weight of choices I'd never expected to make at my age. Staying behind would keep me physically close to them, but letting Piston live another day meant leaving a knife hanging over their heads. Better to face the threat head-on, eliminate it completely, even if it meant risking everything.

Behind me, brothers checked weapons, donned cuts, exchanged the quiet words and ritual handshakes that preceded every run where blood was likely. The familiar choreography of men preparing for violence settled over me like an old coat, worn but reliable.

"Five minutes," Savior called out, his voice carrying over the low murmur of conversation.

I stepped outside, the evening air cool against my face as I surveyed the compound. Brothers moved with purpose between buildings, securing entrances, checking sight lines. I spotted Ghost speaking with Warden, probably coordinating security positions. Good. Whatever his feelings about my decision, he wouldn't let it interfere with protecting Amelia and the boys.

The thought of them sent a tightness through my chest that had nothing to do with age. I'd never been the sentimental type, had spent more years than not convinced I was better off alone. Yet somehow, in the space of a few turbulent weeks, these people had become essential to me. Had become mine in a way nothing ever had before.

Brothers began filing out of the clubhouse, heading for their bikes parked in formation at the gate. Engines roared to life, one after another, the sound echoing off the surrounding buildings like a war cry. I made my way to my own Harley, running my hand over the familiar handlebars before swinging my leg over.

Savior pulled up beside me, his face half-hidden by the gathering dusk. "You good?"

I nodded once. "I'm good."

"Remember the objective," he said, not quite a warning but close. "We push them out. Make a statement. This isn't about personal vendettas."

We both knew it was a lie even as he said it. For the club, yes, this was strategic. For me, it was entirely personal. I didn't bother responding. Some things didn't need saying between men who'd ridden together as long as we had.

Savior gave the signal, and twenty bikes rolled forward in precise formation, headlights cutting through the growing darkness. As we passed through the compound gates, I caught a glimpse of Ghost standing watch, his gaze following my back until I turned the corner.

My last thought before focusing entirely on the road ahead was of Amelia's face when I'd kissed her goodbye. Not tearful or pleading, but fierce. Understanding. She hadn't asked me to stay, hadn't tried to change my mind. She'd simply pressed her lips to mine and whispered, "Make him pay." In that moment, I'd known with bone-deep certainty that I'd found exactly the woman I needed -- strong enough to understand that some threats could only be answered one way.

And I intended to keep my promise to her.

* * *

We rolled toward the barricade like a black tide, our engines a synchronized growl that echoed off the abandoned buildings at the town's edge. The last rays of sunlight caught on chrome and steel, painting everything in blood-orange hues that seemed fitting for what was coming. I rode three bikes behind Savior and Saint, my position giving me a clear view of the makeshift barrier the Minions had constructed -- vehicles parked at angles, debris piled between them, men with rifles visible behind the improvised fortress. My focus narrowed to a single figure standing front and center: Piston, his face still showing the damage I'd inflicted days ago.

Savior raised his fist, and as one, we slowed, then stopped, our formation an arrowhead pointed directly at the Devil's Minions' barricade. The rumble of engines died away gradually, leaving an unnatural silence broken only by the pinging of cooling metal. I heard a flutter of wings and looked to my right, spotting three turkey vultures. Fitting audience for what was about to happen.

Dust kicked up by our arrival hung in the air, mixing with exhaust fumes and the acrid scent of fear. You could smell it on them even from this distance -- sweat and tension and the desperate bravado of men who knew they were outmatched but too proud to back down. Twenty Minions, give or take. Roughly our number, but numbers didn't tell the whole story. The difference was in the eyes, in the stance, in the invisible weight that separated men who fought for territory from men who fought for family.

Most of the Minions carried handguns or shotguns. A few had rifles. At least one had what looked like an AK slung across his back, which was concerning. The rest of us remained on our bikes, engines off but keys in the ignition, ready to move at a moment's notice.

My hand rested casually near my waistband, fingers just inches from my Glock. Warden had positioned himself to my left, Prophet to my right. Both men sat unnaturally still, the kind of stillness that came before explosive violence.

Savior stood with his hands visible at his sides, making no move toward the weapons we all knew he carried. His voice carried across the no-man's-land between our groups, calm and measured, yet loud enough to reach the back row of Minions.

"You're in the wrong town," he called to Piston. "Take your men and head back to Florida. This doesn't have to get ugly."

Piston stepped forward, limping slightly -- another souvenir from our previous encounter. Even from this distance, I could see the mottled bruising around his left eye and the split in his lip that hadn't fully healed. Good. Every twinge of pain was a reminder of what happened when he put his hands on what was mine.

"Fuck you," Piston shouted back, his voice carrying a strained edge that hadn't been there before I rearranged his face. "You Reapers attacked our clubhouse. Burned three of our businesses to the ground. You think we'd just let that slide?"

Interesting. Either he was lying to rally his men, or someone had figured out we'd orchestrated the hit, even if we weren't present. Looked like we were getting the credit. Either way, it worked in our favor.

"Don't know what you're talking about," Savior replied evenly. "But I know you came to our town, put hands on a Reaper's wife. That's why we're here. To make sure you understand the consequences."

Piston spat on the ground, the gesture visible even at this distance. "That bitch was never his wife. Those boys are my blood. I'm taking what's mine, and I'm not leaving without them."

My fingers twitched toward my gun. Beside me, I heard Warden's sharp intake of breath, felt the ripple of tension run through our formation. Brothers who'd been relatively relaxed moments before now sat straighter, hands moving subtly toward weapons.

"Only thing you're taking is a message back to your chapter," Savior continued, his voice hardening slightly. "The woman and boys are under Dixie Reapers' protection now. You come near them again, we'll wipe the Devil's Minions off the map. Every chapter, every clubhouse, every man who wears your colors."

A murmur ran through the Minions' ranks. Several exchanged glances, clearly weighing whether this beef was worth the price Savior was threatening. Piston noticed too, turning to glare at his men before facing us again.

"Big talk from an old man and his retirement community," Piston sneered, raising his voice for his brothers' benefit as much as ours. "You attacked us first. Burned down our businesses. Don't think we don't know it was you."

"We didn't hit your clubhouse," Saint interjected, his tone reasonable, almost conciliatory. "But we have friends who might have. Friends who feel the same way we do about men who beat women and children."

Another ripple ran through the Minions' ranks,

more pronounced this time. From my position, I could see faces turning toward Piston, expressions questioning, suspicious. The accusation had hit home, revealing a crack in their unity. Savior noticed too, pressing the advantage.

"You've got thirty seconds to turn around and start riding back to Florida," he said, his voice carrying the absolute authority of a man who meant every word. "After that, we stop asking nice."

"Twenty-eight. Twenty-nine. Thirty." Piston mocked, then raised his arm in a sharp gesture. "Fuck you and your countdown."

The crack of a rifle shot shattered the evening air. A puff of dust erupted at Savior's feet -- a warning shot, deliberate miss. All bets were off.

Everything happened at once. Brothers reached for weapons. Engines roared to life. The barricade erupted in muzzle flashes as the Minions opened fire. I gunned my Harley's engine, swerving left as bullets whizzed past, following the pre-arranged plan to flank their position.

The world compressed into a series of snapshots, burned into my retinas by adrenaline and decades of similar situations. Savior and Saint diving behind a concrete barrier. Warden returning fire from behind his bike. Prophet coordinating the left flank's movement with hand signals. The air filled with the smell of cordite and the deafening percussion of gunfire.

I kept low over my handlebars, weaving between abandoned cars as I circled toward my assigned position. Through the chaos, a flash of movement caught my eye -- Piston, breaking away from the main group, ducking between two buildings with two of his men. Running, the coward.

My blood roared in my ears, drowning out

everything but the sight of his retreating back. This was it -- the chance to end his threat permanently. Without conscious thought, I veered sharply, breaking from our formation to follow.

"Hammer! Hold position!" Saint's voice carried over the gunfire, sharp with command.

I ignored it, throttling harder as I watched Piston disappear between the rusted hulks of abandoned trailers. The fight behind me faded to background noise, irrelevant compared to the singular focus of my pursuit. Behind me, boots pounded on pavement -- brothers trying to follow, to back me up -- but I didn't slow, didn't wait.

Piston was mine.

The narrow gap between buildings swallowed me, darkness replacing the bloody sunset as I cut my engine, coasting the last twenty yards in near silence. Ahead, footsteps echoed against corrugated metal -- three sets, moving fast. I dismounted, drawing my Glock as I followed, the weight of the brass knuckles in my pocket a promise of what would happen when I caught up.

The rational part of my brain knew I should wait for backup, knew this could be a trap. But rationality had no place in this moment. This was primal. This was the culmination of everything that had been building since I found his hands on Amelia. He'd threatened my family. Now he would answer for it.

I moved deeper into the shadows, tracking my prey through the labyrinth of abandoned structures. Just me, my weapons, and a debt to collect.

I tracked Piston through the maze of abandoned buildings, my boots silent on the dirt path between rusted trailers and collapsed storage sheds. The gunfire from the main confrontation had faded to distant pops and cracks, like faraway fireworks. Here, in this forgotten corner of town, the only sounds were my own measured breathing and the occasional scuff of footsteps ahead -- Piston and his two shadows, thinking they were being quiet, having no idea how loud fear made a man. I'd been hunting men since before these punks could piss standing up. I knew how to follow, when to move, when to freeze.

The path opened into a small clearing between four derelict warehouses, moonlight spilling through broken skylights to create patches of silver against rust-stained concrete. Gravel crunched under my boots, the sound seeming unnaturally loud in the stillness. The footsteps ahead had stopped. I paused, every sense heightened, my hand drifting to the brass knuckles in my pocket.

A rat scurried across my path, disappearing into the shadows. Somewhere above, metal groaned as wind pushed against weakened structures. I scanned the area -- too many hiding places, too many blind spots. Decades of similar situations had taught me to recognize a killing ground when I saw one.

They were waiting. Watching.

I slid the brass knuckles onto my right hand, feeling the familiar weight settle against my knuckles. My left hand kept the Glock ready, though I hoped I wouldn't need it. Some debts were better paid up close and personal.

"Come on out, Piston," I called, my voice echoing against corrugated metal walls. "Just you and me. Let's finish what we started."

Silence answered me, heavy and expectant. Then a chuckle -- low, mean -- from somewhere to my left.

"Old man," Piston's voice floated from the darkness, "you should've stayed home with my whore."

The slur against Amelia sent a fresh wave of rage through me, but I tamped it down. Anger made men sloppy. I needed cold precision now. "Big talk from a man hiding in the shadows," I replied, moving slowly toward the sound of his voice. "Guess those bruises I gave you last time taught you something after all."

Movement flickered in my peripheral vision -- a shadow detaching from darkness, rushing toward me. Not Piston -- one of his goons, thinking to take me from behind while the boss distracted me. Fucking amateur!

I pivoted smoothly, decades of bar fights and club beefs making the movement as natural as breathing. The brass knuckles connected with his jaw in a satisfying crunch of bone and cartilage. His momentum carried him past me, his feet tangling as his brain tried to process the sudden pain. He went down hard, face-first into the gravel.

Before I could press the advantage, Piston emerged from behind a stack of pallets, a tire iron gripped in his fist. Moonlight gleamed off the metal as he swung it in a vicious arc toward my head.

I blocked with my left forearm, pain exploding from wrist to elbow as the iron connected. Better my arm than my skull. I countered with a sharp jab to his ribs, brass knuckles sinking into flesh where I'd broken ribs in our last encounter. His breath left him in a pained *whoosh*, but he didn't go down.

We circled each other, two predators locked in a dance as old as time. Blood trickled down my arm where the tire iron had split skin, but I barely noticed. My focus had narrowed to Piston's movements, cataloging weaknesses -- the slight favoring of his left side, the way he winced when he breathed too deeply.

"I'm going to enjoy watching you die," Piston spat, blood flecking his lips from some internal damage I'd done. "Then I'll take back what's mine."

I lifted my hand to land another blow, but I'd fucked up. Forgotten about the other man. Something slammed into the back of my head and black dots swam across my vision. I grunted and swayed but refused to fall. Piston took advantage, landing a few blows. The lackey behind me must have motioned something to him, because he gave me one last glare, then Piston took off.

Before I could follow, another blow took me to my knees. I wondered if I was about to meet my end, then I heard them. My brothers. The man behind me went down, I heard him hit the ground right after the sound of two gunshots. Then my world began to fade.

Chapter Nineteen

Amelia

My hands trembled as I dabbed alcohol on the gash running down Hammer's forearm, willing myself to stay steady despite the knot of fear still lodged in my throat. He'd returned just an hour ago, bloodied but alive, limping through our front door with that same stoic expression he always wore. Only the tightness around his eyes betrayed the pain he felt, and the way he'd immediately sought me out, his gaze locking with mine across the room, told me more than words ever could about what had happened out there in the darkness.

"Hold still," I murmured, pressing the gauze harder against the wound. "This one's deep. Might need stitches."

"It's fine," he grunted, though he couldn't quite hide the wince when I cleaned a particularly nasty part of the gash. "Had worse."

The bedroom was quiet around us, dim light from the bedside lamp casting our shadows against the wall. I'd sent the boys to their room as soon as Hammer arrived, not wanting them to see the extent of his injuries. Chase had protested, of course, but one look from Hammer had silenced him. Even battered and bleeding, Hammer commanded respect without raising his voice.

"That tire iron could have taken your head off," I said, carefully applying butterfly strips to hold the wound closed. "Savior told me what happened. How you went after Piston alone, then got outnumbered."

Hammer's jaw tightened beneath his silver beard. "Had to be done."

I moved from his arm to his face, gently cleaning

a cut above his eye. Our proximity felt charged, intimate in a way that went beyond the physical. His breath warmed my skin as I leaned closer, the familiar scent of him surrounded me despite the medicinal smell of alcohol and antiseptic. My fingers lingered longer than necessary against his weathered skin.

"You could have been killed," I whispered, not trusting my voice to remain steady at full volume.

His eyes met mine, dark and unreadable. "Worth the risk. He won't threaten you or the boys again."

The simple declaration sent a shiver through me. Not from fear, but from the certainty that this man -- this unexpected protector who'd come into our lives -- meant every word. He'd gone after Piston not for revenge, not for his pride, but for us. For me.

"Let me see your ribs," I said, setting aside the bloody gauze.

Hammer hesitated before stiffly removing his shirt, revealing a torso marked by decades of scars and tattoos, now blooming with fresh bruises. I gasped softly at the mottled purple-black spreading across his left side.

"Jesus, Hammer."

"Just bruised," he insisted, though his sharp intake of breath when I gently pressed my fingers against his side suggested otherwise.

"Maybe broken," I countered, reaching for the bandages. "You should see a doctor."

"Had broken ribs before. These are just cracked, maybe. They'll heal."

I began wrapping the bandage around his torso, each circuit bringing me close enough to feel the heat radiating from his skin. My arms encircled him as I passed the bandage from one hand to the other, creating an embrace that was both medical and something more. He sat perfectly still, only his accelerated breathing betraying his awareness of our position.

"I was so afraid," I admitted, securing the bandage with metal clips. "When they told me you'd broken formation to go after Piston alone… I thought I might never see you again."

"How the fuck…" His brow furrowed.

"I asked. No, more like pleaded. I needed to know something. Anything. I was about to lose my mind I was so scared." My hands stilled against his chest, feeling the steady thud of his heart beneath my palm. The fear that had gripped me while he was gone surged back, making my next words tumble out before I could stop them. "I can't lose you, Hammer. I'm falling in love with you."

His body went rigid beneath my touch. Slowly, deliberately, he took my wrists and moved my hands away from his chest. The rejection was gentle but unmistakable.

"Amelia," he said, his voice rougher than usual. "Don't."

I stepped back, my heart pounding painfully against my ribs. "Don't what? Don't feel what I feel?"

He stood, wincing slightly as the movement pulled at his injured side. "I'm too old for this. Too old for" -- he gestured between us --"whatever this is becoming."

"That's bullshit," I said, heat rising to my face.

"It's reality." He ran a hand through his silver hair, frustration evident in the gesture. "Look at me, Amelia. I'm sixty-one years old. Got twenty-five years on you. You deserve better than some worn-out old biker who needs pills half the time to --" He cut himself off, jaw clenching.

"To what?" I pressed, stepping closer again. "To make love to me? Because I seem to remember you doing just fine without any pills the other night."

His eyes darkened. "That was --"

"That was real," I insisted. "What we have is real. Your age doesn't matter to me."

"It should." His voice dropped lower, threaded with something that might have been regret. "I can't give you what a younger man could. Can't give you more children, can't promise you decades. Hell, my knees creak when it rains."

This man who'd faced down an entire motorcycle club without flinching was afraid -- not of violence or death, but of inadequacy. Of not being enough for me.

I stepped back, hurt blooming in my chest despite my understanding of his fears. For a moment, we stood in silence, the space between us charged with unspoken things. Then, watching him turn away, something hardened within me. A resolve I'd thought beaten out of me by years with Piston suddenly crystallized into certainty.

I moved toward him again, determination guiding each step. This time, when I placed my hands on his chest, I didn't let him push me away.

"Listen to me, Hammer," I said, my voice low but firm. "I've been with younger men. I was with Piston for years, and all his youth and strength brought me was pain and fear. I don't want young. I don't want promises you can't keep. I want you. Just you. Nothing you say will change how I feel."

Before he could respond, I pressed my lips to his, pouring everything I couldn't articulate into the kiss. For one heart-stopping moment, he remained passive, unresponsive. Then, with a groan that seemed torn from somewhere deep inside him, his arms came around me, one hand fisting in my hair as he took control of the kiss.

The gentleness from before was gone, replaced by raw hunger that matched my own. I pressed myself against him, mindful of his injuries but unwilling to allow any space between us. His beard tickled my skin as his mouth moved from my lips to my neck, his teeth grazing the sensitive spot below my ear that he'd discovered during our first night together.

"This is a mistake," he murmured against my skin, even as his hands slid beneath my shirt, calloused palms rough against my back.

"Then it's my mistake to make," I whispered, arching into his touch. "I want you, Hammer. All of you. The gray hair, the creaky knees, every scar, every year."

Something broke in him then -- the last barrier of restraint giving way to need. He lifted me with surprising strength despite his injuries, carrying me the few steps to our bed before laying me down with unexpected gentleness.

"If we do this," he said, his voice hoarse as he looked down at me, "you become mine. For real."

I reached up, cupping the strong jaw that had become so dear to me. "I'm already yours. Have been since you claimed us as your family."

The admission seemed to satisfy something in him. His eyes, normally guarded and unreadable, softened with an emotion I'd never seen there before. Then he was kissing me again, his body covering mine, and we were speaking a different language altogether -- one of touch and taste and breathless sighs.

His hesitation melted away beneath my hands as I showed him with every caress exactly how much I desired him. Age, scars, the gray in his beard -- none of it mattered. What mattered was the way he moved against me, the way his touch made me feel both protected and desired, the way he whispered my name against my skin like a prayer.

Our kisses grew deeper and hotter as he nibbled his way down my neck, sending shivers down my spine. His rough hands trailed along my sides, causing me to arch into him with anticipation.

"I want you," he said softly against my ear. All I could do was nod in agreement, wanting him every bit as much.

Seeing he'd made it back alive was one thing, but I needed to feel it too, remind myself he was alive and well, right here with me. We quickly stripped out of our clothes and his weight settled over me. No foreplay tonight. Just raw, aching need.

"Please," I whispered, spreading my legs wider, inviting him in.

His eyes, dark with desire, held mine as he positioned himself. In one powerful thrust, he buried himself inside me, both of us gasping at the sensation. The slight sting of his entry quickly gave way to pleasure as he began to move, setting a rhythm that spoke of possession and need.

"Mine," he growled against my throat, his silver beard tickling my sensitive skin. "Say it."

"Yours," I whispered, wrapping my legs around his waist to draw him deeper. "I'm yours, Hammer."

"Jeff. Use my real name when it's just us," he demanded.

Tears stung my eyes. I knew what it meant that he wanted me to use his name and not his road name. "Jeff."

Despite his injuries, he moved with surprising

strength, each thrust deliberate and claiming. I ran my hands down his back, careful of his bruises but needing to touch him, to feel the solid warmth of him above me. Alive. Here. Mine.

Our lovemaking was different this time -- more intense, more desperate. The shadow of what could have happened hung over us, making each touch more meaningful, each kiss more urgent. I felt myself climbing toward release, the tension building low in my belly as Hammer shifted his angle, hitting that perfect spot inside me.

"Let go," he commanded, his voice rough with exertion and desire. "Let me see you come apart."

His words pushed me over the edge. I shattered beneath him, waves of pleasure rolling over me as I clung to his shoulders. He followed moments later with a deep groan, his body tensing above mine before collapsing carefully to avoid crushing me.

We lay tangled together, breathing hard, sweat cooling on our skin. His weight was a welcome anchor, grounding me in the reality that he had returned, that we were still here, still together.

"I meant what I said," I murmured against his chest once our breathing had steadied. "I'm falling in love with you."

He was quiet for so long I thought he might have fallen asleep. Then his arms tightened around me.

"Never thought I'd have this," he admitted, his voice low and rough. "Never wanted it. Too much risk. Too much to lose."

I lifted my head to look at him, finding his eyes open and surprisingly vulnerable. "And now?"

A slight smile curved his lips. "Now I'd burn the world down to keep it."

It wasn't quite a declaration of love, but from

Hammer, it was enough. More than enough.

Tangled in sheets damp with sweat, his arm heavy across my waist, I pressed my lips to his shoulder where an old bullet wound had left its mark. "Still think you're too old for this?" I teased gently.

His chuckle rumbled through his chest, vibrating against my skin. "Might kill me." He pulled me closer despite his words. "But what a way to go."

* * *

The night air held a lingering chill as I wrapped Hammer's oversized flannel around my shoulders and settled onto the porch steps. The compound had fallen eerily quiet in the aftermath of the battle, with only distant sounds of activity from the clubhouse breaking the silence. Most of the brothers had gathered there to debrief and celebrate their victory, leaving our little house in a pocket of calm that felt almost surreal after the chaos of the past few days. I took a deep breath, letting the tension drain from my body as I watched the security lights cast long shadows across the yard.

Hammer had fallen asleep after our lovemaking, his body finally surrendering to exhaustion and injury. I'd covered him with a blanket, pressing a kiss to his forehead before slipping out to clear my head. So much had changed in such a short time -- my feelings for Hammer, his for me, and whatever uncertain future lay ahead of us.

The screen door creaked behind me, and I turned to see Chase hesitating in the doorway. His tall frame seemed smaller somehow, his shoulders hunched forward in a way that reminded me painfully of when he was little, those moments before he'd ask for something he was afraid might be denied.

"Can't sleep?" I asked, patting the space beside me.

He shook his head, shuffling forward to sit on the step, careful to leave a few inches between us -- not quite the sullen distance he'd maintained when we'd first arrived, but not the easy closeness we'd shared before Piston had stolen that from us too.

"Too quiet," he muttered, rubbing his palms against his jeans. "Kept thinking I heard something."

I understood immediately. After years of living with Piston, silence often felt more threatening than noise. Quiet meant something was coming, something was wrong.

"Hammer will sleep for hours," I said, offering what I knew was his real concern. "The pain, not to mention the adrenaline wearing off, knocked him out. But he's okay. Nothing life-threatening."

Chase nodded, his fingers playing with a loose thread on the hem of his shirt. It was a childhood habit I hadn't seen in years, this nervous fidgeting that signaled he had something important to say but didn't know how to begin.

"He went after Piston alone," Chase said finally, his voice barely above a whisper. "For us."

"Yes," I agreed simply.

"Dad --" Chase stopped, cleared his throat. "Piston never would have done that. He would have sent someone else. If he bothered at all."

The slip didn't escape my notice, but I didn't comment on it. Instead, I watched my son's profile in the dim porch light, seeing the man he was becoming despite everything he'd endured. The resemblance to Piston was there in the shape of his jaw, the color of his eyes, but nothing of that man's cruelty had taken root in my boy.

"Hammer's nothing like him," I said softly.

Chase picked at the thread more vigorously,

unraveling the hem of his shirt further. "I know that now." He took a deep breath, the kind that preceded a confession. "Mom, I... I wish Hammer was my real dad. Levi feels the same way."

The words hung in the night air between us, fragile and weightless yet somehow the heaviest thing in the world. My heart squeezed painfully in my chest, both aching and soaring at once. I wrapped my arm around Chase's shoulders, pulling him close, half-expecting him to resist as he often did lately, too proud and too hurt to accept comfort. Since we'd moved in with Hammer, I'd noticed both boys didn't tense up as much when I touched them. It was progress and gave me hope they were healing.

Instead, he leaned into me, reminding me of the little boy who used to crawl into my lap after Piston's rages. Back when he still believed I could protect him.

"Oh, Chase," I said, my voice thick with emotion. "Hammer already thinks of you and Levi as his kids. He told Piston as much, right to his face. Said you weren't Piston's sons anymore -- you were his."

Chase looked up sharply. "He said that?"

"He did." I smoothed his hair back, a gesture he usually avoided but now allowed. "He claimed you both as his family. He's acted like your father in all the ways that matter."

"By protecting us," Chase murmured.

"Not just protecting," I corrected gently. "By respecting you. By giving you space when you needed it and boundaries when you pushed too hard. By teaching you things about engines when you showed interest. By treating you like someone who matters, not just an extension of himself."

Chase was quiet for a long moment, absorbing this. "He doesn't even like us that much," he said, but there was a question in his voice rather than certainty.

I laughed softly. "Hammer doesn't show affection the way most people do. But have you noticed how he checks your schoolwork over his morning coffee? How he made sure your bedroom had a lock after he heard what Piston used to do? How he never raises his voice, even when you're being a complete pain in the ass?"

The ghost of a smile touched Chase's lips at that last part. "I have been kind of a jerk to him."

"You've been protecting yourself and Levi, just like you always do," I told him. "And Hammer understands that better than anyone."

We sat in comfortable silence for a few minutes, listening to the night sounds around us -- crickets, the distant rumble of motorcycles, the soft creaking of the house settling. So different from the tense silences that had filled our old life.

"Will we stay with him?" Chase finally asked, his voice small. "Even now that Piston..." He trailed off, unwilling to finish the thought.

I turned to face him fully, wanting him to see the truth in my eyes. "I've found something with Hammer I never expected to find after everything with Piston. A chance at real love. A real family. Not to mention, we're married. This is our home now."

"You love him?" Chase asked, surprise evident in his voice.

"I do," I admitted, the words easier the second time I'd spoken them aloud. "And I think he loves me too, in his own gruff way."

Chase seemed to consider this, his brow furrowed in thought. "He treats you different. Not like Piston did."

"Very different," I agreed. "Hammer sees me.

The real me. And he sees you boys too -- not as possessions, but as people with your own thoughts and feelings."

"That's what a real dad is supposed to do, isn't it?" Chase asked, and the naked hope in his voice nearly broke me.

I pulled him closer, pressing a kiss to the top of his head like I used to when he was small. "Yes," I whispered. "That's exactly what a real dad does."

Chase nodded against my shoulder, seeming to find some resolution in our conversation. When he finally pulled away, his expression was lighter than I'd seen it in years, as if some invisible burden had shifted.

"I should check on Levi," he said, rising to his feet. "He was worrying about Hammer too."

"Tell him Hammer's fine," I said. "And, Chase? Thank you for telling me how you feel. It means a lot."

He ducked his head, suddenly shy. "Yeah, well. Don't tell Hammer yet, okay? I want to... I need to tell him myself. When I'm ready."

I nodded, understanding completely. "It'll be your choice. When and if you ever do."

As I watched him disappear back into the house, I felt a sense of peace settle over me. The path ahead might not be easy -- nothing worth having ever was -- but I felt like we were moving toward something instead of just running away.

I returned to our bedroom after my talk with Chase, settling into the chair by the window to watch Hammer sleep. His face looked softer in repose, the hard lines of vigilance smoothed away by exhaustion and painkillers. An hour had passed in this quiet vigil, my mind replaying Chase's words again and again. That my son could want Hammer as a father, despite his initial distrust of all men, especially bikers, felt like a small miracle. A healing I hadn't dared hope for when we'd fled Florida with hardly anything and terror nipping at our heels.

Hammer stirred, grimacing as consciousness brought pain back into focus. His eyes found mine immediately, a silent question in them.

"The boys are fine," I assured him, answering before he could ask.

He nodded, pushing himself up against the headboard with a poorly concealed wince. I moved to help him, but his raised hand stopped me. Always so stubborn about showing weakness, even now.

"How long was I out?" he asked, voice rough with sleep.

"About two hours," I replied, glancing at the bedside clock. "Most of the brothers are still at the clubhouse. It's quiet."

Before he could respond, a sharp knock sounded at the front door. Hammer was on his feet in an instant, reaching for the gun he'd placed on the nightstand, despite his injuries. I followed him into the hallway, heart racing despite the relative safety of the compound. Old habits died hard.

Hammer checked through the peephole, muscles visibly relaxing when he saw who stood outside. He disengaged the locks with practiced efficiency, opening the door to reveal Atlas, his slender frame silhouetted against the security lights. The young hacker held a manila folder in one hand, his expression uncharacteristically serious.

"It's late," Hammer said by way of greeting, stepping back to let Atlas enter.

Atlas slipped inside, nodding briefly to me before turning back to Hammer. "Need to talk to you," he said, his gaze flicking toward the boys' rooms.

"Both of you. It's important."

Something in his tone made me uneasy. "Is there trouble? Are the Minions --"

"Nothing like that," Atlas assured me quickly. "This is... personal."

Hammer's eyebrows drew together, his body language shifting from alert to suspicious. "What kind of personal?"

Atlas clutched the folder tighter. "I was near the house when you were talking with Chase," he said to me. "Not eavesdropping on purpose. Just happened to be close enough to hear."

My stomach dropped. Chase's vulnerable confession was never meant for other ears. "That was a private conversation," I said, keeping my voice low.

"I know," Atlas acknowledged, looking genuinely contrite. "And I wouldn't normally... but this was different." He glanced at Hammer. "I heard what he said. About wishing you were his real dad."

Hammer went perfectly still, only his eyes moving as they shifted from Atlas to me. "What's he talking about, Amelia?"

Before I could answer, the boys emerged from their room, drawn by the late-night voices. Chase froze when he saw Atlas, his face paling as he read the situation instantly.

"You were listening?" he demanded, fists clenching at his sides.

"Not intentionally," Atlas replied, holding up a placating hand. "But yeah, I heard. And it got me thinking."

He turned back to Hammer, extending the folder. "You know what I can do with computers. How I... fixed things to help you and Amelia before."

Hammer's expression darkened, memories of the

marriage certificate clearly surfacing. "What did you do now?"

Atlas opened the folder, revealing official-looking documents. "I registered you as Chase and Levi's adoptive father in the system. Changed their last name to Williams." He spoke matter-of-factly, as if he hadn't just dropped a bombshell in our living room. "Everything's legal. Well, legal enough. No one will question it."

The silence that followed was absolute. Chase and Levi stood frozen, wide-eyed, looking between Hammer and Atlas with expressions caught between hope and terror. I held my breath, watching Hammer's face as he processed what Atlas had done.

His thick eyebrows drew together in a scowl that would have intimidated most men into immediate retreat. "You had no right," he growled, taking a menacing step toward Atlas.

To his credit, Atlas didn't back away. "Probably not," he conceded with a small shrug. "But sometimes families need a push. You claimed them as yours to Piston's face. Now it's official."

"Official?" Hammer's voice dropped dangerously low. "You fucking with government records is official?"

"As official as anything in our world gets," Atlas replied calmly. He held Hammer's gaze, unflinching despite the older man's obvious anger. "I thought it would help. Make you all a real family."

Something shifted in Hammer's eyes then -- a softening so subtle most would have missed it. His gaze moved from Atlas to the boys who still stood frozen in the hallway. The tense silence stretched, broken only by the distant sound of a motorcycle engine somewhere in the compound.

"Dad?" Levi's voice was barely audible, the word experimental on his lips.

The single syllable seemed to pierce something in Hammer. His shoulders lowered slightly, the rigid anger in his stance melting away. Without a word, he crossed to where the boys stood, his movements careful, deliberate, as if approaching wild animals that might bolt.

"Come here," he said, his gruff voice gentler than I'd ever heard it.

Chase and Levi exchanged a hesitant glance before stepping forward. What happened next took my breath away. Hammer, who rarely initiated physical contact beyond a shoulder clasp or head nod, pulled both boys into his arms, enfolding them in an embrace that seemed to shield them from the entire world.

"I'm proud to be your dad," he said, the words rough with emotion. "Been trying to be that for you since day one, papers or no papers."

Levi's arms went around Hammer immediately, his thin frame melting against the older man's chest. Chase stood stiff for one heartbeat, two, before his resistance crumbled. His arms lifted, wrapping around both Hammer and Levi, his face pressed against Hammer's shoulder to hide whatever emotion had overwhelmed him.

My vision blurred with tears as I watched them, this unlikely family forged in crisis and cemented by choice. Hammer, who'd claimed to be too old for love just hours ago, now held my sons with the fierce protectiveness of a man who'd found something worth more than his own life.

"This doesn't change anything," he told them, his voice low and certain. "You were already mine. Have been since your mother brought you into my life. These papers just make it harder for anyone to take you away."

Chase lifted his head, meeting Hammer's gaze directly. "You mean that? Even though I've been such an ass?"

A rare smile crossed Hammer's face. "Especially because you've been an ass. Got my temper, apparently."

A choked laugh escaped Chase, the sound so unexpected it made us all smile. Levi, always quieter, simply pressed closer to Hammer, his thin fingers clutching the older man's shirt as if afraid he might disappear if he let go.

I wiped at my tears, overwhelmed by the scene before me. From across the room, Atlas caught my eye, his expression unusually soft. I mouthed "thank you" to him, unable to voice my gratitude aloud without completely breaking down.

He nodded once, satisfaction clear in his slight smile. Without another word, he slipped toward the door, his task completed. As he left, I heard him mutter, "That's twice now," under his breath, and I couldn't help but smile through my tears. Twice he'd used his skills to forge our family -- first binding Hammer and me together, now connecting him to my sons.

As the door closed behind Atlas, Hammer looked over the boys' heads, his eyes finding mine. The emotion in his gaze -- unchecked, unguarded for perhaps the first time since I'd known him -- said everything words couldn't. We had become something neither of us had sought or expected: a real family, bound not by blood or obligation, but by choice and love and shared battles. "Williams," Chase said suddenly, testing the name. "Chase Williams. Doesn't sound half bad."

Hammer released them slowly, keeping one hand on each boy's shoulder. "It's a good name," he said simply. "Carried it my whole life. It'll serve you well."

As I watched them standing together -- Hammer flanked by my sons, all three wearing matching expressions of cautious joy -- I felt the last pieces of our fractured lives finally slide into place. We had survived Piston. Had built something stronger from the broken pieces he'd left behind. We were Williams now. All of us. And nothing would tear us apart again.

Chapter Twenty

Hammer

The phone buzzed against the nightstand, dragging me from a dreamless sleep with its insistent vibration. The dim light of early morning filtered through the curtains, casting shadows across Amelia's sleeping form beside me. I reached for the phone with my bruised hand, wincing as my split knuckles protested the movement. Savior's name lit up the screen. My President wouldn't call at this hour unless it was important. Unless it was about Piston.

I slid from the bed carefully, not wanting to wake Amelia. She'd finally fallen asleep just a few hours ago, the tension of the past days etched in the lines around her eyes even in rest. She deserved whatever peace sleep could give her.

"Yeah," I answered, my voice rough with sleep as I stepped into the hallway, pulling the bedroom door shut behind me.

"It's done," Savior said without preamble. "Piston's dead."

Four simple words. Just four words to end the nightmare that had followed Amelia and her boys across state lines. Three words that should have filled me with nothing but relief.

"How?" I asked, my bruised knuckles tightening around the phone.

"Crimson Skulls caught him trying to rally reinforcements at a truck stop just inside their territory," Savior explained, his voice matter of fact. "Seems our plan worked better than expected. The Boneyard pushed from the south, we held the middle, and the Savage Knights blocked the west. Minions had nowhere to go but north."

"And the Skulls were waiting," I finished for him.

"Exactly. Their President called an hour ago. Said Piston made the mistake of mouthing off about Amelia and the boys. About you." Savior paused, and I could almost see the grim satisfaction on his face. "Skulls' President took personal offense to how Piston talked about family. Said he didn't suffer fools who didn't understand the value of blood."

I leaned against the wall, processing the information. It was over. The threat Piston posed to my family -- and they were my family now, no matter what papers said -- was eliminated. Yet instead of pure relief, I felt a tangle of emotions I hadn't expected. Satisfaction, yes. But also a hollow disappointment that I hadn't been the one to end him myself. That I hadn't gotten to look in his eyes as he realized he'd never threaten what was mine again.

"You still there?" Savior's voice cut through my thoughts.

"Yeah," I replied. "Just taking it in."

"Figured you might have wanted to handle him yourself," Savior said, reading my mind the way only a brother could. "But it's cleaner this way. No blowback on us. No risk to Amelia or the boys."

He was right, of course. Piston's death at the hands of another club, in another territory, during what could be explained as a turf dispute -- it was strategically perfect. My personal satisfaction wasn't worth risking my family's safety.

"What about the rest of the Minions?" I asked, practical concerns taking over.

"Scattered. Some headed back to Florida with their tails between their legs. Others holed up in Georgia. Their national President is already sending signals about a truce. Seems they've decided Piston's vendetta died with him."

"Good," I said, the tension in my shoulders easing slightly. "Thanks for the call."

"Figured you'd want to know right away. Give Amelia and the boys the good news." There was a pause, then Savior added, "It's really over, brother. You can breathe now."

I ended the call, standing motionless in the hallway for a long moment. The house was quiet except for the soft sounds of movement from the kitchen -- dishes clinking, murmured voices. Had to be the boys, or Aura. I just didn't know why they would be awake at this hour.

I made my way to the kitchen, pausing in the doorway to take in the scene. Aura stood at the stove, her back to me as she flipped pancakes. Chase sat at the table, hunched over a textbook Looked like he'd forgotten to do his homework, or was cramming for a test. Levi was arranging bacon on a plate, his methodical movements reminding me of how Wire organized his tech gear before a job.

It was such a normal moment. Domestic. Ordinary. Everything Piston had threatened to destroy.

Aura tensed then looked my way. Her smile faltered when she saw my expression. "Dad, what is it?"

Chase's head snapped up, immediately alert to the shift in tone. Levi froze mid-motion, bacon forgotten as his eyes darted between Aura and me.

I stepped fully into the kitchen, feeling the weight of all three gazes. "It's over," I said, keeping my voice steady, measured. "Piston's dead."

Chase drew in a sharp breath, his knuckles whitening around his spoon. Levi's eyes widened to perfect circles, his slight frame seeming to shrink further into itself.

"Well, that's good news. Right?" She glanced at the boys, probably trying to determine how they felt about the news. "When did it happen?"

"Early this morning," I replied. "Crimson Skulls territory. Our plan worked -- we forced the Minions north, and the Skulls were waiting."

"You weren't there?" The question came from Chase, surprising me. His expression was unreadable, somewhere between relief and disappointment.

"No," I admitted. "It happened up north, and it was fast. The clubs worked together. Pushed the Minions exactly where we wanted them. Savior confirmed it. The Minions are scattered. Their national President is already signaling for peace. Piston's vendetta died with him."

Levi's voice was small, uncertain. "Does that mean we're safe now?"

"Yes," I told him with absolute certainty. "It means you're safe."

"But what if some of his friends --" Chase began, ever the protector, always searching for the next threat.

"There's no 'what if'," I interrupted, moving to stand beside him. I placed my hand on his shoulder, feeling the tension in his muscles. "Nobody's coming after you again. Not ever."

The finality in my tone seemed to reach him. Something shifted in his expression, a guard lowering fractionally. "You promise?"

In that moment, he wasn't the tough teenager who'd been shouldering responsibility beyond his years. He was just a kid asking for reassurance from his father -- from me. The weight of that trust settled in my chest, heavy but welcome.

"I promise," I said, squeezing his shoulder. "You, your brother, your mom -- you're Williams now. Under my protection. Under the club's protection. That means something in our world."

I could clearly see the relief on Chase's face. "We can stop running."

The magnitude of what that meant for them -- for all of us -- hung in the air. No more looking over shoulders. No more worst-case scenarios. No more nightmares about Piston returning to reclaim what he considered his property.

"We can just… live," Levi said quietly, wonder in his voice.

I nodded, taking in their faces, the one who had become the center of my world in such a short time. My family. My responsibility. Mine to protect, but now -- finally -- also mine to see flourish without the shadow of Piston's threat hanging over us.

"Yeah," I confirmed, the gruffness in my voice unable to hide the emotion behind it. "We can just live."

* * *

The kitchen fell into a strange quiet as we all adjusted to the news. I watched Amelia move mechanically to the stove, rescuing pancakes that had nearly burned after Aura had run off saying she needed a bathroom break. My wife walked in right after I'd delivered the news, and she'd reacted about the same as the boys.

Chase returned to his book without really seeing the pages. Or so I assumed, since I doubted it took him ten minutes to read one page. Levi methodically arranged and rearranged the bacon strips on the plate, finding comfort in the simple task. It was the quiet after a storm -- relief mixed with disbelief, our minds still struggling to accept that the threat was truly gone. My phone buzzed again in my pocket, and for a moment I considered ignoring it. But old habits die hard in this life. I pulled it out, expecting Savior with more details about Piston, and instead found a text from Wire that made my stomach drop.

WRATH WANTS TO MEET HIS DAUGHTER AND GRANDSONS. HE'S REQUESTING A CALL ASAP.

I stared at the screen, reading the message three times as its implications settled into my bones like a winter chill. Wrath. Amelia's father. For one, Wire had sent it in all caps. That was never a good sign. For another, I hadn't expected Wrath to make a decision so quickly. The President of the Savage Knights who'd never known he had a daughter -- until we'd reached out to him for help against Piston. I'd never met the man personally, but his reputation stretched across state lines. A powerful President, respected, feared. The kind of man who took care of his own.

I shoved the phone back into my pocket, not ready to share its contents. The threat of Piston might be gone, but now another possibility loomed -- one I hadn't fully considered when we'd contacted Wrath. What if Amelia and the boys preferred the protection of her biological father? What if they chose to leave Alabama behind for a fresh start in Nevada?

My chest tightened at the thought of the empty rooms they would leave behind. The silence in place of Levi's quiet questions about engines. The absence of Chase's reluctant half-smiles when I showed him something new on the bikes. The loss of Amelia's warmth beside me in our bed. My life before them seemed like a faded photograph now -- recognizable but lacking color and substance. And despite the fact

Reapers never divorced, I wouldn't lock her down and force her to remain. We'd just be married and living in different states.

I watched Amelia set a plate of pancakes on the table, her movements steadier now, some of the shock wearing off. She caught my eye, offering a small smile that didn't quite reach her eyes. Still processing. Still adjusting to a world without Piston's shadow hanging over her.

And now I had to give her news that might change everything again.

But I wouldn't hide it from her. That wasn't what real partners did. And besides, it wasn't my choice to make. It was hers.

"Boys," I said, my voice rougher than I intended. "Give your mom and me a minute."

Levi glanced up, alarm flashing across his face until Amelia reached out to squeeze his shoulder. "It's okay," she assured him. "Just grown-up talk."

Chase's eyes narrowed with the suspicion that never fully left him. "Is it about Piston? Is there something you're not telling us?"

"No," I answered honestly. "Piston's finished. This is something else." I met his gaze directly, acknowledging the protective instinct we shared. "I'll fill you in after I talk to your mom. Promise."

He studied my face for a moment before nodding once. "Come on, Levi. Let's eat outside."

I waited until the door closed behind them before turning to Amelia. She stood with her back against the counter, arms folded across her chest, her posture both defensive and expectant.

"What is it?" she asked, tension creeping back into her voice. "Your face went white when you checked your phone."

Instead of answering, I pulled the phone from my pocket and handed it to her, Wire's message still displayed on the screen. Her fingers trembled slightly as she took it, her eyes widening as she read.

"Wrath," she whispered.

I moved closer but didn't touch her, sensing she needed space to process. "Like I mentioned before, when Piston threatened you, we needed allies. The Savage Knights have territory not only in Nevada, but other states as well, including near the Crimson Skulls. Strategic position. Saint reached out to them, told Wrath the situation." I hesitated, then added, "Told him about you and the boys."

Her hand pressed against her mouth, eyes closing briefly. "After all these years. My whole life, I thought he didn't want me. That's what my mother always said. She claimed he hadn't wanted a family and hadn't told him about me."

"He may not have, but if he'd known about you, then maybe he would have come around," I suggested gently.

She nodded slowly. "What did he say exactly? When he found out about me?"

I shifted uncomfortably. "I wasn't on the call. Saint handled it. But as you saw, according to Wire's message, he wants to talk to you. Soon."

Amelia set the phone carefully on the counter as if it might explode. Her face had gone pale. "I don't know what to say to him. What do you say to a father who's been absent your entire life? 'Hi, nice to finally meet you after thirty-six years'?"

The hint of bitterness in her tone was understandable. Expected, even. But beneath it lurked something else -- curiosity, perhaps. Or longing. The natural human desire to know where you came from, who you came from.

"You don't have to call him," I told her, though the words felt hollow. "It's your choice."

Her eyes met mine, searching for something. "What do you think I should do?"

The question caught me off guard. I wasn't used to being asked for advice on family matters -- hadn't had much of a family to advise until recently. But I knew what she deserved.

"I think…" I started, choosing my words carefully. "I think everyone has a right to know where they came from. And everyone deserves the chance to decide for themselves who to keep in their life."

She nodded slowly, a slight smile tugging at her lips. "That's surprisingly wise for a man who solves most problems with his fists."

"And what makes you say that?"

She arched an eyebrow. "I doubt you got your name because of the tool. I assumed it was hammering on people with your fists."

I shrugged, returning her smile with a small one of my own. "Even old dogs learn new tricks."

She stepped closer, her hand finding mine, fingers intertwining. "You're worried," she observed, her gaze too perceptive for comfort. "About what this means. About him."

"Not about him," I corrected quietly. "About you. The boys. What you might want once you know him."

Understanding dawned in her eyes. "You think we'd leave? Go to Nevada?"

I didn't answer, but my silence was confirmation enough.

Her free hand came up to rest against my cheek, her touch gentle against my weathered skin.

"Hammer," she said firmly, "we're not going anywhere. The boys are settling in here. They have you. I have you." She shook her head slightly. "I'm not looking for a father figure. I'm a grown woman. What I want -- what I need -- is exactly what I have right here."

The tightness in my chest eased slightly at her words. I believed her -- mostly. But I also knew how powerful blood ties could be, how the pull of biological family might affect her once the reality of having a father entered her life.

"I'd like to call him," she said after a moment. "But I need a little privacy. To process. To figure out what to say."

I nodded, stepping back to give her space. "Of course."

She picked up the phone again, staring at Wire's message. "Can you check on the boys? Make sure they're okay?"

"Yeah," I agreed, moving toward the door. I paused with my hand on the handle. "Take your time. I'll be right outside if you need me."

Once outside, I found Chase and Levi at the small picnic table we'd set up on the back lawn. They were eating in silence, but both looked up as I approached.

"Mom's okay?" Chase asked immediately.

"She's fine," I assured him. "Just needs a few minutes alone."

From where I stood, I could see Amelia through the kitchen window. She paced back and forth, the phone pressed to her ear, her free hand gesturing as she spoke. I couldn't hear her words, but I could read her body language -- tense, then gradually relaxing. At one point, she laughed, the sound carrying faintly through the closed window. Something in my chest loosened at the sound.

I'd been afraid -- was still afraid, if I was being honest -- that her father would somehow take away what we'd built. That blood would prove stronger than what we had. But watching her through the window, seeing her face animated as she spoke to the man who'd helped create her, I realized something.

Family isn't always about blood. Sometimes it's about who stands beside you when the world goes to shit. Who holds you together when everything falls apart. Who accepts you, protects you, loves you without condition or expectation.

By those measures, Amelia, Chase, and Levi were my family. And I was theirs. Nothing -- not Piston, not distance, not even blood -- could change that now.

Epilogue

Amelia
One Week Later

The Las Vegas airport buzzed with activity as we collected our bags from the carousel, the harsh fluorescent lighting highlighting the exhaustion etched on all our faces after the cross-country flight. Hammer stayed close to my right side, his substantial frame a constant presence I'd come to rely on more than I cared to admit. My stomach churned with nerves, a lifetime of questions about to be answered in the next hour. Thirty-six years of wondering who my father was, and now we were in his city, about to meet the man who'd never known I existed until a week ago. Mom might have told me he was a biker who went by Wrath, but it wasn't like I'd had any proof she'd been telling the truth. Nor had I really known many details about him. She'd never wanted to talk about him.

"You okay?" Hammer asked, his voice low enough that only I could hear. His hand rested at the small of my back, steady and warm.

I nodded, not trusting my voice. The week since that first phone call with Wrath had passed in a blur of preparations -- arrangements with the diner for time off, the boys' school absences, Hammer coordinating with the club. Through it all, I'd oscillated between excitement and terror, unable to settle on how I actually felt about meeting my father.

"Got it," Chase announced, hefting the last of our bags from the carousel. My oldest son had insisted on handling the luggage, his shoulders squared with the responsibility he'd always taken too seriously for his age. Beside him, Levi fidgeted with his backpack straps, eyes darting nervously around the crowded terminal.

Aura appeared at my left, her arm linking through mine. "Vegas is wild," she commented, nodding toward a group of bachelorettes staggering past in matching pink sashes and tiaras. "Never been here before."

I was grateful for her attempt at normalcy, at distraction. That was Aura -- perceptive enough to know exactly what everyone needed. She'd become such an essential part of our strange little family that I couldn't imagine making this trip without her.

"Dad," she said suddenly, her voice dropping to match his earlier tone. "Three o'clock. Cuts."

I followed her gaze across the baggage claim area to where three men stood near the exit doors. Even without the leather vests emblazoned with the Savage Knights insignia, I would have recognized them as bikers. It was in their stance, the watchful way they surveyed the crowd, the invisible bubble of space other travelers unconsciously gave them.

Hammer shifted subtly, positioning himself slightly behind me where he'd have better access to his waistband if necessary. I knew he wasn't carrying -- we'd flown commercial -- but the instinct to protect was bone-deep for him.

"That's our welcoming committee," he said, his voice neutral though I could feel the tension radiating from him. "Stay together."

Chase moved closer to Levi, one hand on his younger brother's shoulder. The protective gesture made my heart ache -- he'd been doing that since he was tiny, standing between Levi and any potential threat.

The three men began walking toward us with measured steps, their eyes locked on our group. The tallest led the way, his face creased in a permanent scowl beneath a bandana tied around his head. The patch on his cut identified him as the Sergeant-at-Arms.

"Amelia," the tall one said as they reached us, my name sounding strange in his gravelly voice. His eyes flicked briefly to me before settling on Hammer with open assessment. "These the boys?"

I nodded, finding my voice. "Yes. Chase and Levi." I gestured to each of them in turn, then to Aura. "And this is Aura. Hammer's daughter."

The man nodded once, his gaze still fixed on Hammer. I could feel the silent evaluation happening -- sizing up the man who'd claimed me as his, measuring him against whatever standard these men used to judge others.

"Knuckles," he finally introduced himself, extending a hand to Hammer first. "Sergeant-at-Arms for the Knights. Wrath sent us to bring you to the clubhouse."

Hammer grasped the offered hand, neither man flinching at what I suspected was a test of strength disguised as a handshake. "Appreciate the escort," Hammer replied, his tone carefully neutral.

Knuckles' mouth twitched in something that might have been approval. "Got a van outside. Your luggage is coming with Diesel and Quake in the truck." He gestured to the two men flanking him, who nodded in acknowledgment.

The walk through the terminal felt like running a gauntlet, with Knuckles leading the way, the other Knights taking up positions behind us, and Hammer keeping me tucked against his side. Aura had fallen in step with the boys, her arm slung casually around Levi's shoulders while Chase walked on his other side.

Outside, the dry Vegas heat hit like a physical wall after the air-conditioned terminal. Knuckles led us to a black van with tinted windows parked in the loading zone. A man in a Knights cut sat behind the wheel, nodding once as Knuckles opened the side door for us.

"Boys and Aura in the middle," Hammer directed, helping me into the back row before joining me. The seating arrangement wasn't accidental -- he wanted the kids contained in the center, protected from both front and back if necessary.

As we pulled away from the curb, silence filled the van like a living thing. I stared out the tinted window at the Vegas skyline, the midday sun glinting off glass and steel. So different from the small Alabama town I'd called home since fleeing Florida.

"First time in Vegas?" Knuckles asked, breaking the silence as we merged onto the highway.

"For most of us," I replied, grateful for the attempt at conversation. "Hammer's been here before."

"Club business," Hammer added, not elaborating further.

Knuckles nodded as if this explained everything. "Wrath's been busy since your call. Had the clubhouse cleaned top to bottom. Old ladies bringing in food all week."

The idea of my father -- this stranger -- preparing for our arrival sent a fresh wave of nerves through me. What was he expecting? What was I expecting?

"That's the Strip," Knuckles commented, nodding toward the glittering hotels rising in the distance. "Tourists think that's Vegas, but the real city's out here." He gestured to the sprawling neighborhoods beyond the famous boulevard. "Knights territory covers most of the north and east sides."

The boys pressed closer to the windows, momentarily distracted from their nerves by the spectacle of Vegas. Even Chase's perpetual wariness seemed to ease as he pointed out the Stratosphere tower to Levi.

Aura caught my eye in the reflection of the window, giving me a reassuring smile. She'd been my rock through this entire process, from that first phone call with Wrath to the frantic packing last night.

We turned off the main road onto a quieter street lined with warehouses and industrial buildings. The van slowed as we approached a large compound surrounded by a high concrete wall topped with security cameras. The Savage Knights logo -- a grinning skull wearing a medieval helmet -- was painted on the gate that slowly swung open as we approached.

"Home, sweet home," Knuckles announced as we pulled into a parking lot filled with motorcycles arranged in neat rows. "Wrath's waiting inside."

Hammer's hand found mine, squeezing gently. "Ready?"

I wasn't. Not even close. But I nodded anyway, because some moments you're never ready for until you're already living them.

"As I'll ever be," I replied, my stomach twisting as the van came to a stop.

We got out and approached the building. As we entered, I took in the differences between this one and the one back home. The clubhouse interior smelled of leather, cigarette smoke, and floor polish -- the latter clearly a recent addition in preparation for our arrival. Brothers nodded respectfully as Knuckles led us through the main room, where pool tables and a long bar occupied most of the space. Eyes followed our progress, curious but not hostile, a subtle difference I'd learned to distinguish during my time around the Dixie Reapers. These men had been told we were family, and in their world, that meant something. Still, I felt Hammer's protective presence at my back as we approached a closed door at the far end of the room, my heart hammering against my ribs with each step.

"He's waiting in there," Knuckles said, stopping before the door. His face softened slightly as he looked at me. "Been pacing all morning. Never seen the boss this worked up."

That simple observation -- that my father was nervous too -- somehow steadied me. I glanced back at my family: Hammer, solid and watchful; Chase and Levi, both trying to appear braver than they felt; and Aura, offering an encouraging smile. Whatever happened next, I wasn't alone.

Knuckles knocked once, then opened the door without waiting for a response. "They're here," he announced, stepping aside to let us enter.

The room was smaller than I'd expected, with a worn leather couch against one wall and a desk positioned in the center rather than behind it. And there, rising from his seat as we entered, stood my father.

Wrath stood tall and broad-shouldered, his salt-and-pepper hair swept back from a face that bore the marks of a life lived hard. His beard was neatly trimmed, showing more silver than his hair, and his skin was tanned and lined from years in the sun. But it was his eyes that caught me -- brown eyes exactly like mine, widening slightly as they took me in. In them, I saw the same shock of recognition I felt seeing my own features reflected in his face.

"Amelia," he said, my name sounding heavy with decades of absence.

I couldn't speak. Words had abandoned me completely as I stood facing the missing piece of my life -- the man whose existence my mother had acknowledged only in bitter comments about bikers and irresponsibility. The man who had never even known I existed until the Dixie Reapers had reached out for help with Piston.

He moved first, crossing the space between us with surprising grace for such a large man. His arms opened, hesitant, and I stepped into his embrace automatically. The hug was stiff, awkward -- the embrace of strangers trying to be family. He smelled of leather and expensive cologne, his cut creaking as his arms tightened briefly around me before releasing me just as quickly.

"You look like her," he said gruffly, stepping back. "Your mother. But your eyes..." He trailed off, shaking his head slightly. "Guess there's no question who your old man is."

"I guess not," I agreed, finding my voice at last. The resemblance was uncanny now that I stood before him -- the shape of our jaws, the set of our eyes, even the way he held himself with one shoulder slightly lower than the other.

His gaze shifted beyond me, taking in the rest of our group with the assessing stare of a man used to evaluating potential threats. His eyes lingered on Hammer, narrowing slightly as he took in the silver beard, the weathered face, the Dixie Reapers cut.

"So you're the old man who married my daughter," Wrath said, crossing his arms over his broad chest. The words held an edge, a challenge beneath the surface politeness.

Hammer stepped forward, his face impassive. "I am."

The two men stared at each other, an entire conversation happening without words. I recognized the language of alpha males establishing boundaries -- had seen it often enough having been around more than one MC now. This was different, though. More personal. More charged.

"You realize you're older than me, right?" Wrath asked, the question deliberately provocative.

I tensed, but Hammer didn't rise to the bait. "Not by more than a few years," he acknowledged calmly. "Doesn't change anything."

"Doesn't it?" Wrath's voice hardened.

"Dad," I interrupted, the word feeling strange on my tongue. I hadn't planned to call him that yet, but it slipped out naturally in my urgency to diffuse the tension. "These are my sons. Your grandsons."

The diversion worked. Wrath's attention shifted to the boys, who stood slightly behind Hammer, watching the exchange with wary eyes.

"Chase and Levi," I continued, gesturing them forward. "Boys, this is… your grandfather."

Levi, surprisingly, moved first, stepping around his brother with cautious curiosity. "You look like mom around the eyes," he observed quietly.

Something in Wrath's expression softened at Levi's directness. "That so?" He extended a hand to my younger son. "Good to meet you, Levi."

Levi shook the offered hand, his small fingers disappearing in Wrath's massive grasp. "Your clubhouse is cool," he added, a tentative olive branch.

Chase moved forward then, his jaw set in that stubborn expression I recognized all too well. He extended his hand with determined formality. "Sir," he said simply.

Wrath's eyebrows rose slightly at the formal address, but he accepted Chase's handshake with equal seriousness. "No need for 'sir,' boy. Grandpa works. Or Wrath, if you prefer."

Chase nodded but didn't commit to either option, retreating to stand beside his brother. I could see the wheels turning behind his eyes, evaluating this new addition to our complicated family tree.

"And this is Aura," I added, drawing the focus to where she stood quietly observing the interactions. "Hammer's daughter."

Wrath nodded to her. "Knuckles mentioned you. Said you're looking to prospect. Didn't think the Dixie Reapers allowed women in their club, except as old ladies."

Aura's eyebrows shot up in surprise. "Word travels fast between clubs."

"When it's interesting news," Wrath agreed, a hint of approval in his tone.

His gaze hardened again as it returned to Hammer. "We need to talk, you and me. About intentions."

"No, we don't," I interjected, my voice firmer than before. Both men looked at me in surprise, clearly not expecting the interruption. "Hammer's intentions are clear from his actions. He took us in when we had nowhere else to go. Protected us when Piston came after us. Gave the boys his name." I stepped closer to Hammer, my hand finding his. "He loves us. And we love him."

Wrath studied my face, perhaps hearing the steel beneath my words. I'd spent too many years being silent when I should have spoken. I wouldn't make that mistake again -- not even with the father I'd just found.

"That true?" he asked Hammer, though his gaze stayed on me.

"Every word," Hammer confirmed.

Something shifted in Wrath's expression -- not quite acceptance, but a grudging respect. "Well," he said after a moment, "guess that's what matters, then."

The tension in the room eased by fractions. Not gone completely but reduced to a more manageable level. Wrath gestured toward the door. "Let's join the others. Food's ready in the main room. We can talk more out there."

As we followed him from the private room back into the clubhouse proper, Hammer leaned close to my ear. "Nice defense, wife," he murmured.

I squeezed his hand in response. "Nobody gets to question us. Not even my newly discovered father."

Hammer's eyes crinkled at the corners -- his version of a smile. "That's my girl."

The simple praise warmed me more than it should have. As we entered the main room where Knights and their old ladies waited with curious eyes, I held my head higher. I might be meeting my father for the first time, might be navigating waters I'd never expected to chart, but I knew exactly who I was and who I loved.

That certainty would carry me through whatever came next.

* * *

The clubhouse common area had been transformed into something resembling a family gathering, with tables of food lining one wall and Knights mingling with their old ladies. Children darted between the adults' legs, a surprising sight in what I'd expected to be an adults-only space. Everything felt both strange and familiar -- the rituals of MC life were similar enough to what I'd experienced with the Dixie Reapers to create a sense of *déjà vu*, yet distinctly different in ways I couldn't quite name. I stuck close to Hammer's side as Wrath introduced us to key members of his club, hyperaware of the curious glances thrown our way and the protective stance Hammer maintained beside me.

"That's Santa's old lady," Wrath explained, nodding toward a woman passing out plates. "She's been cooking since dawn. Says it's not every day she gets to feed the President's newfound family."

"That's very kind," I replied, overwhelmed by the effort that had clearly gone into welcoming us, despite the lingering tension between the men.

Wrath guided us to a table. Chase and Levi followed, their earlier wariness giving way to cautious curiosity as they took in the clubhouse environment. Aura had already drifted toward a group of younger Knights, her natural charisma drawing them in despite her outsider status.

"Eat," Wrath instructed, gesturing toward the food. "We'll talk after."

I felt Hammer's hand settle at the small of my back as we navigated the buffet line, a casual touch that communicated volumes. Mine. Safe. Here. That simple contact grounded me in the surreal experience of standing in my father's clubhouse, surrounded by his family of choice while accompanied by my own.

We settled at the table with full plates, an awkward family dinner with decades of absence between us. Wrath sat directly across from Hammer, their gazes meeting briefly over the spread of food. I caught him watching as Hammer passed Levi the salt without being asked, anticipating my son's preference before he could voice it. A small thing but telling.

"So," Wrath began, directing his attention to Levi. "Heard you're pretty good with computers. Got a few brothers here who could learn a thing or two."

My boy shrugged, but I could see the pleased flush on his cheeks at being singled out. "I'm okay. Not as good as Atlas back home, but I know some stuff."

"He's being modest," Hammer interjected, his gruff voice softened with pride. "Kid figured out how to boost our security system at the compound. Rigged up motion sensors where we had blind spots."

I watched as Levi's posture straightened at Hammer's praise, his chest puffing slightly as he added, "It wasn't that complex. Just repurposed some old equipment."

Wrath's eyes narrowed thoughtfully as he observed the exchange, something shifting in his expression as he noted the genuine pride in Hammer's voice, the way Levi leaned almost imperceptibly toward Hammer as he spoke.

"How'd you learn that?" Wrath asked Levi directly, his interest sincere.

"I learned a lot on my own while we lived in Florida, but Dad also got me some books," Levi replied, glancing briefly at the older man beside him. "And let me practice on the clubhouse systems."

"With supervision," Hammer added with a hint of a smile. "Kid's a natural. Just needed the right tools and someone to point him in the right direction."

Again, that thoughtful look crossed Wrath's face, his gaze moving between Hammer and my son as if reassessing something fundamental.

Chase remained quiet, and Hammer noticed. He glanced at our son before facing Wrath again. "Your grandson here has a natural feel for engines that most grown men would kill for. Show him something once, he's got it memorized."

"He's teaching me about bikes," Chase explained. "How the V-twin works and the difference in the various engines. I've learned how to do oil changes and tune-ups. Even worked on some cars."

"That right?" Wrath asked, genuine surprise coloring his tone.

"He understands the mechanics better than brothers twice his age," Hammer confirmed. "Got the touch."

Across the room, a burst of laughter drew our attention to where Aura sat surrounded by several younger Knights, gesturing animatedly as she told some story that had them hanging on every word.

"Your daughter's making friends," Wrath observed, nodding toward the group.

"She does that," Hammer replied, a mixture of pride and resignation in his voice. "Never met a stranger she couldn't charm or a fighter she couldn't stand toe-to-toe with."

"That how she ended up wanting to prospect? Fighting spirit?"

Hammer's expression sobered. "Partly. Mostly it's about belonging. About making her own place in the world that tried to break her."

Something passed between the men then -- an understanding that transcended their earlier tension. Men who'd seen the darkest corners of the world and still found reasons to protect what they loved.

"Excuse me," I said, suddenly needing a moment to collect myself. "Restroom?"

"Down that hall, second door on the left," Wrath directed, his eyes following me as I stood.

I felt Hammer's questioning gaze but gave him a

reassuring smile. "I'm fine. Just need a minute."

The restroom was empty, thankfully. I leaned against the sink, studying my reflection in the mirror. My father's eyes looked back at me, the resemblance uncanny now that I'd seen him in person. How had my mother never mentioned it? How had she kept this secret for so many years? I'd known I didn't exactly look like her, but I guess it hadn't ever occurred to me I'd resemble my father.

I splashed water on my face, taking deep breaths before heading back out. As I approached our table, I slowed, noticing that Hammer and Wrath were now sitting together, slightly apart from the boys who had been drawn into conversation with some of the younger Knights. The two men leaned toward each other, their expressions intense. I lingered just out of earshot, not wanting to interrupt what appeared to be an important exchange.

Wrath's face was serious, his posture rigid as he said something that made Hammer straighten. I caught the tail end of my father's question as I drew closer.

"-- intentions with my daughter and grandsons?" His voice was low but clear, the challenge unmistakable.

Hammer didn't flinch, didn't hesitate. "My intentions are to love them for however many years I've got left," he replied, his voice carrying the same certainty it had when he'd promised to protect us from Piston. "To give those boys a father who sees them as people, not possessions. To give Amelia the respect and partnership she deserves." He leaned closer to Wrath. "To make up for the years she didn't have a father in her life."

The barb landed, but instead of anger, I saw something like grudging respect cross Wrath's face.

"And if I don't approve?"

"Then you'd be a fool," Hammer said bluntly. "But it wouldn't change anything. They're mine now. My family. My responsibility." His voice softened slightly. "But they have room for you too, if you're smart enough to take what's being offered."

I stepped forward then, unwilling to eavesdrop any longer. Both men looked up as I approached, something passing between them that felt like a truce.

"Everything okay?" I asked, slipping back into my seat beside Hammer.

Wrath leaned back, his posture noticeably more relaxed than it had been all day. "Just getting to know my son-in-law," he said, the term no longer laced with skepticism.

The afternoon mellowed into evening, the initial stiffness gradually giving way to something that, if not quite comfortable, was at least less strained. I watched in amazement as Wrath showed the boys his prized collection of vintage motorcycle parts, Chase asking technical questions that clearly impressed his grandfather. Levi eventually gravitated toward the club's tech setup, drawn into conversation with their intelligence officer who seemed genuinely interested in his insights.

Later, as we gathered near the bar, Wrath approached Hammer with an extended hand. "Welcome to the family," he said, loud enough for those nearby to hear, making the acceptance official.

Hammer accepted the handshake but snorted. "I was family first," he replied with unexpected humor. "So I'm the one accepting you." For a moment, tension crackled between them -- then Wrath's booming laugh broke the silence, echoed seconds later by Hammer's deeper chuckle. The sound of their shared laughter seemed to release the last of the day's strain, like a thunderstorm clearing heavy air.

I smiled, watching these two powerful men find common ground in their stubborn pride and shared commitment to family. Beside me, Chase nudged Levi, both boys wearing expressions of cautious hope as they observed this unexpected camaraderie between my dad and theirs.

Aura appeared at my side, slipping her arm through mine. "Found my people," she murmured, nodding toward the younger Knights who'd adopted her for the day. "They've got some interesting ideas about female Prospects. Might be useful back home."

Since I hadn't noticed any female Prospects, I wondered if they were just hoping to convince her to stick around. I'd noticed the way a few of them watched her.

"Making alliances already?" I teased.

"Always," she replied with a wink.

As I looked around at this unlikely gathering -- Hammer and Wrath now engaged in what appeared to be a detailed comparison of their respective clubs' territories, the boys cautiously integrating with their new extended family, Aura building bridges with typical charm -- I felt a profound shift inside me. The father I'd never known. The husband I'd never expected. The sons who were healing from their past. The stepdaughter who'd become sister and friend.

Family. Not perfect or conventional by any measure, but mine. Ours. For the first time in my life, I felt complete -- not because I'd found my father, though that filled a hole I'd carried for decades. But because I'd found myself among these people who chose each other, who protected each other, who built something stronger from the broken pieces life had dealt them.

As Hammer caught my gaze across the room, his subtle nod communicating volumes in the language we'd developed together, I knew with bone-deep certainty: This was home. These people were home. And nothing -- not distance, not complicated pasts, not uncertain futures -- could take that away from us now.

Harley Wylde

Harley Wylde is an accomplished author known for her captivating MC Romances. With an unwavering commitment to sensual storytelling, Wylde immerses her readers in an exciting world of fierce men and irresistible women. Her works exude passion, danger, and gritty realism, while still managing to end on a satisfying note each time.

When not crafting her tales, Wylde spends her time brainstorming new plotlines, indulging in a hot cup of Starbucks, or delving into a good book. She has a particular affinity for supernatural horror literature and movies. Visit Wylde's website to learn more about her works and upcoming events, and don't forget to sign up for her newsletter to receive exclusive discounts and other exciting perks.

Harley at Changeling: changelingpress.com/harley-wylde-a-196

Bad Boys Multiverse
Contemporary MC, Organized Crime, and Crossovers
A Bad Boy Romance
Dixie Reapers MC
Devil's Boneyard MC
Hades Abyss MC
Devil's Fury MC
Reckless Kings MC
Savage Raptors MC
Swift Angels MC
Owned by the Mob
Bryson Corners
Underland MC

Paranormal MC
Devoted Guardians MC
Balor's Saints MC

Print and Audio:
Dixie Reapers MC Print
Dixie Reapers MC Audio
Devil's Boneyard MC Audio
Hades Abyss MC Audio
Devil's Fury MC Audio

Changeling Press LLC

Contemporary Action Adventure, Sci-Fi, Steampunk, Dark Fantasy, Urban Fantasy, Paranormal, and BDSM Romance available in e-book, audio, and print format at ChangelingPress.com – MC Romance, Werewolves, Vampires, Dragons, Shapeshifters and Horror -- Tales from the edge of your imagination.

Where can I get Changeling Press Books?

Changeling Press e-books are available at ChangelingPress.com, Amazon, Apple Books, Barnes & Noble, Kobo, Smashwords, and other online retailers, including Everand Subscription and Kobo Subscription Services. Print books are available at Amazon, Barnes and Noble, and by ISBN special order through your local bookstores.

Changeling Press LLC

ChangelingPress.com